THE WHITE SERPENT

Colorblind Book Two

RC Hancock

An Uncommon Press

ISBN-13: 9781707924301

Cover design by: Tony Pham
Library of Congress Control Number: 2018675309
Printed in the United States of America

*to my five little piggies, may you always
come home for roast beef*

"Now the serpent was more crafty than any beast of the field."

GENESIS 3:1

CONTENTS

PRONUNCIATION GUIDE

Aro (A-rohng)

Arnaud (ah-NO)

Baptiste (bah-TEEST)

Gaspard (gas-POWL)

Camille (keh-ME-yuh)

Clarque (CLAR-keh)

Claude (CLOH-duh)

cuivre (QUEEV)

Delaney (doo-la-NAY)

DeGrave (doo-GRAHV)

Drea (DREY-ah)

Durand (JOO-rohng)

Eloi (eh-low-EE)

Feu Noir (FOO NWAH)

Gravois (gav-WAH)

Hameau Vert (AH-mo VER)

Jade (ZSHAHD)

Jean Pierre (ZSHOH pee-AIR)

Juenes (ZSHEN)

Lefebvre (loo-FEHV-ruh)

Letty (LEE-tee)

Livius (lih-vee-OHNG)

Loup (LOO)

Marin (MER-ohng)

Mélangé (mel-AHNJ)

Mére Blanche (MEHR BLAHNSH)

Molyneux (moh-lee-NUH)

monsieur (muh-SYOOR)

Philippe (fill-EEP)

Po (POO)

Poisson du Roi (pweh-SOH doo RWAH)

Pont en Pierre (pohn-pee-AIR)

Quinlin (keen-LEEN)

Rouge (ROOZSH)

Talbot (TAL-boh)

Taudis (toh-DEE)

Télesphore (tel-ees-FOR)

Toi (TWAH)

Tremper (TLAHM-pee)

Véronique (ver-oh-NEEK)

Victorieux (veek-toll-ee-YOO)

Ville Bleu (VEE BLUH)

Zacharie (zeh-sheh-REE)

A NOTE FROM THE AUTHOR:

Thanks for picking up this book! Chances are you've read book 1 of the Colorblind series (An Uncommon Blue.) Thanks for that too, btw.

If you've read the 5th Anniversary version of An Uncommon Blue (with a cover similiar to The White Serpent) just skip this page and get on with the story.

If you've read the original (published by Cedar Fort—with two hands on the cover), I suggest reading the 5th Anniversary edition before The White Serpent. It's about twice as long as the original and there are quite a few changes.

If you'd rather get right to The White Serpent, here is a list of things you should know.

Calixte is now Gaspard. Aaren is Aro. Marie is Orie. Drea and Marin have 'signed papers' meaning they're engaged to be married. Marin does not die in the second edition. Drea's sister is the High Priestess (and head of the Feu Noir.) She shows Bruno the underground tunnels they often use to circumvent the laws and shade barriers. There are many more changes, but those are the big ones. Apologies if I made any changes that disappoint you. My editors had a LOT to say about the rewrite. :)

CHAPTER ONE

NINE YEARS PAST

I was seven when I killed my father. He had taken me to the river to find shells.

"Let's see what you've got so far," Papi said.

I doubted he'd be able to see them properly while bouncing the baby on his hip, but I unfolded the piece of cloth. The red light of my palm shone through the fabric and made the shells glow pink. I thought Papi might frown at the chipped ones, but instead his eyes grew big.

"How did you find so many?"

I shrugged. No need to tell him I'd been collecting for months without his permission.

The baby reached for the cloth.

"No, baby!" I pulled the shells away from her fat fingers. Normal kids played with their fire for the first year, but not my sister. She only wanted stuff that belonged to me.

"Here's a good spot." Papi laid a pair of tattered shirts on the riverbank and sat on the smaller one.

I kept standing. "It's going to take forever to string the necklace."

Papi held up his fire. "We've still got fifteen good fingers between us."

I couldn't help glancing at the hand holding the baby. After four weeks, the dead fingers hadn't improved. Mama said they'd have to be taken off soon. I couldn't decide which would be worse, black skeleton fingers or none at all. The thought that he'd never be able to braid my hair again made me feel angry and sad at the same time.

"Does it hurt?" I asked when he caught me looking.

"We can string the shells in the morning before Mama wakes up."

"You better be home by then," I said with all the menace I could muster. "You'll ruin her birthday."

Papi raised his fire in a mock oath. "I'll be back before dawn, even if I have to call you to help me mine tin."

"Just get your light home," I said in a soft voice. I wanted nothing to do with the freezing caves. The idea of Papi getting lost again haunted my dreams.

He patted the shirt beside him.

I figured I'd made my point, so I sat and accepted a bean sandwich. Instead of eating, however, I set the food on my lap and began organizing the shells. I'd recently realized that the hungry feeling right before I ate was much more enjoyable than the hungry feeling after the food was gone, so I took my time.

"What profundities are they teaching you at École Rouge?" Papi asked.

I gave him my best bored stare. Papi always wanted to talk about school—like he was worried the teachers were all dumb.

"Well?"

"They taught us a poem to learn the continents. On Port, something, something…"

"At least you know the name of the planet," he said with a grin.

"It's a stupid song anyway. It leaves out Télesphore."

"Télesphore Island is too small to be a continent. We're part of Eyefall Continent."

I released an enormous sigh. "Can we not talk about boring stuff?"

Papi fed the baby a piece of his bread. She slobbered it down and kicked her legs for more.

"Okay, then. What would you like to talk about?"

"There are two boys in my class. One asked me to be his girlfriend and I said yes."

Papi choked on his sandwich.

"I know you said I have to wait until I'm sixteen, but if you saw how cute he is—"

Papi hit himself in the chest, jostling the baby and making her cry.

"Papi?"

With a cough, he dislodged the food and pointed at me.

"Sixteen is your mother's rule. Mine is twenty-one."

"Well, my rule is seven. He asked me last year, but I told him..."

I trailed off as I noticed a lady at the top of the bridge. She had a bright green fire and beautiful golden hair—not black like our family's. Even though the lady was fifty feet above us, I could hear her speaking.

"Is she talking to us?"

"She's calling her cat," Papi said. "See it on the lower ledge?"

My eyes traced the old stone bridge until I spotted the white ball of fur.

"Dumb kitty. Serves it right if it falls."

"What if it was your kitty?"

"My kitty would be smart. And I'd teach it to swim."

The lady reached over the railing only to have the cat move out of reach and sit down again. I smiled. It was playing with her. She scooted closer and reached out again, this time with a leg up on the railing.

Papi frowned. "If she's not careful she—"

The lady screamed and I went cold all over. I wanted to cry out, but all I could do was watch as she fell. For a moment, she looked like she was dancing in the air, then she hit the concrete at the base of one of the pillars and slid into the water.

Papi pushed the baby at me. "Do not move from this spot."

Before I could balance the baby enough to put the shells back in my pocket, he had jumped into the river.

"Papi!" I struggled to my feet and scanned the far bank. It was as empty as our side. I didn't know if that was a good thing or not. It meant no Greens would see Papi leaving the Red side, but it also meant there would be no help if he started to drown.

Was it already happening? There seemed way too much splashing going on out there. Yet somehow his head continued to break the surface and gradually, he moved toward the center of the river. When had he learned to swim? He wouldn't be able to fight the water very long. Maybe I should get help. Papi had told me to stay put, but what good was I doing here?

The baby started to fuss, and I realized I was squeezing her too hard.

The current pushed the lady to the surface. She looked like a pile of Mama's laundry floating down the river. Was she already dead? No, her green fire still glowed beneath the water. Papi must have seen her too, because his splashing grew wilder. He wasn't going to make it. The lady was moving too fast.

Then Papi disappeared under the water. I started counting. After I got to twenty-three the numbers morphed into a prayer. Don't let him drown. I'll do anything. Don't let him. Don't.

Papi's head reappeared. His light hand flew from the water and closed on the lady's long hair. He began flailing in the other direction, this time with one blackened limb.

I started counting again. For some reason I thought if I got to twenty-three again he'd have to be back on shore.

As I counted, Papi went under twice more. I kept mechanically repeating numbers. Each time he came back up. The lady must have been knocked out because she wasn't complaining about him dragging her by the hair.

Twenty-one, twenty-two. I waded into the cold water.

Papi shook his head. He meant for me to get back on the bank, but I ignored him. I wasn't going to drop the baby and he would need my help. I had to get to him before I reached twenty-three.

With a final splash, Papi stumbled in the mud and lifted the lady onto the bank.

Twenty-three. Was she dead? Her wet jacket sleeve covered her light hand.

I crouched and pushed the lady's hair out of her face.

Twenty-three. Twenty-three. Twenty-three. The Green wasn't dead. She was staring straight ahead and trembling, her wide eyes the only part of her face that looked human. I stumbled backward but couldn't tear my gaze from the raw, oozing face.

Her face. She'd landed on her face. The nose was flattened and cut open. A large flap of skin hung in her eyes, like her forehead had come loose. Her lips seemed to be missing completely.

Papi peeled the baby from my arms. "I'm going to get help."

A hole opened in the woman's ruined face. "No." She lifted her light arm. "Take it."

Take what? Her jacket? I took another step back, but Papi stepped closer.

"You need help," he said.

"Too late," the lady said. "Take my green... quickly."

Papi looked at her for a moment with worried eyes. Then he faced me.

"Neek, come hold this woman's hand."

"You mean react with her?" Had Papi hit his head on a rock, too? "We'll get in trouble!"

"Not if she gives us permission. And it will give you a pretty new fire." Papi carefully pulled the jacket off the lady's light hand. Her fire was beautiful.

My eyes burned with tears. I wanted to do what Papi asked. Even if I disobeyed him on a daily basis, I could tell this was important to him.

But it didn't make any sense. It went against everything he'd ever told me. Was he testing me? "Papi, you said red was the most beautiful shade in the world, you said I should love my fire."

The woman groaned and lowered her pale white arm. Papi's face changed. He almost looked angry.

"I don't expect you to understand, I just need you to trust me. It's going to be better for you if you change your shade. Your life will be easier."

Something was wrong. Papi never got angry. Did something happen to him in the water? How would taking some of this lady's green make my life easier? This had to be a test. And even if it wasn't, everyone I knew was Red. Why would I want to be a different shade than my family? I shook my head. That was the correct answer. I was sure of it.

Papi grabbed the baby's light hand and pressed it into the woman's. "Look how easy it is."

The baby screamed as he held her arm in place. Tears dripped from my chin. Why was Papi doing this? It felt like he was going crazy. There was a flash of light, and the woman groaned again. Her eyes closed and her face relaxed.

Papi lay the baby on her back in the dirt, and before I could move, he grabbed my arm.

"No!" I screamed. It was now clear this wasn't a test. He really wanted me to react with the dying Green. I needed to do what he said. But those thoughts were drown out by the panic raging through me. The idea of holding hands with that faceless creature made me want to jump into the river.

"It's for your own good, angel. We don't have much time."

He pulled me closer to the bloody woman. I no longer cared whether he was right or wrong. I no longer cared that I would disappoint him if I didn't obey. I could not touch that dead body. My screams grew louder and more desperate. Where was Mama? Mama wouldn't let him do this.

"Hey, river trash!"

Papi released me. I fell to the ground and crawled toward where the baby was eating fist-fulls of dirt.

Another shout came. I looked across the river where a group of teenage Greens made a line along the far bank. Had they heard my screams in Green Park?

"We're trying to have a barbecue over here." One of them said. "And all we hear is screaming river rats. You want us to call an officer to shut you up, or what?"

Papi's face went sky white. "I was disciplining my daughter," he shouted back. "I'm sorry if we disturbed you."

"What's wrong with the lady?"

"She fell from the bridge," Papi shouted. "I tried to save her..."

But the kids were already running up the bank toward the bridge. One pressed an emergency beacon and a siren wailed.

A two-hundred-pound weight replaced my panic. The knowledge of what I had caused seemed to press me deeper into the mud. I should have shut my mouth and trusted Papi. I hadn't tried hard enough to obey him and now it was too late. The lady's fire had faded. Without any light, the dome of her palm looked like an enormous blister. I shivered. Somehow I'd gotten wet. And Papi's shirt was spotted with blood. Even at seven years old, I understood how bad it looked.

"I'm sorry, Papi."

Papi didn't look angry or nervous anymore. He helped position the baby on my lap and kissed her wispy hair. Then he took me by the shoulders. "It was my fault. You were right. You're my perfect girl."

And then the Greens were there. They pulled Papi away. They saw the blond hair in his fingers. I tried to tell them what happened. Papi did too. Meanwhile the baby cried herself purple. But the boys didn't care about any of it. The police came and took Papi. I tried to follow them over the bridge, but a young officer with red cheeks pushed me back and called me a diseased little rodent.

I tried to think of something I could do or say to make the

men give Papi back. But the image of the lady's come-apart face filled my mind, making it impossible to think clearly.

The baby grew heavy. One of the old shirts blew into the river. Flesh flies gathered on the yellow-haired lady. Still I stood on the bank, hoping to see a familiar face—someone who could explain everything to the police.

A crowd of Greens and even a few Blues gathered on the bridge. They seemed scared to step onto the Taudis side of the river. Greens in white uniforms came to get the dead lady. One with orange hair looked at me with sad eyes. I wiped my face and hurried over to the woman. She was milk-skinned with very thin lips.

"Can you please tell me where they're taking my dad?"

The nurse knelt on the dirt. "Are you hurt, child?"

I shook my head.

"The eye is hot today, you should head indoors before your brother gets heat rash."

"Sister. And it doesn't matter. You need to take us to Papi."

Without warning the nurse touched my face with her fire. Warmth bloomed in my cheek and a low hum filled my ear. It was such an intimate gesture, that for a second I considered giving the lady a hug. But then she spoke.

"The punishment for murder is death."

"He's not a murderer! He tried to help."

"Your little brother is going to need you now more than ever."

"She's a girl!" I screamed. "And Papi's the only one who can get her to eat her oat mush. You have to tell them."

The nurse shook her head. "There's nothing anyone can do. I'm sorry."

I grabbed the lady's hair and yanked it, twisting her head into an awkward angle. "Give him back."

The lady slapped my hand away, stood, and joined the rest of the people in green uniforms. The body was already across the bridge in Hameau Vert. And of course the stupid cat was nowhere around.

I looked at the strands of orange hair in my hand. I hated the nurse lady. And I hated the yellow-haired woman for being stupid enough to fall off the bridge. But most of all I hated myself. Papi would die and it was my fault. I shouldn't have screamed. I shouldn't have been such a cockroach.

By the time the baby's fire changed to a deep orange, the crowds had gone and my eyelashes had dried. I felt strange. Maybe it was from the heat. Or hunger. I noticed part of my bean sandwich squashed into the mud.

We needed to go. Mama would wonder why we weren't back. But leaving the river without Papi would be giving up. I couldn't go home without him. If I stood there long enough, something would change. Someone would come and fix everything.

It was the sight of the baby's bright red skin that finally sent me up the embankment.

"Poor Jeannette," I whispered to the sleeping head on my shoulder. "I'm sorry you don't have a good sister." That's when I noticed a piece of fabric clutched in her meaty little fist. My carrying cloth. I scanned the ground. I had to find the shells. Philippe or La-la could help me string them. Then at least Mama's birthday wouldn't be ruined too. I walked along the sand, praying I'd find the shells in a neat little pile.

It was no use. They were gone.

All twenty-three of them.

CHAPTER TWO

GOLDEN EGGS

C aviar is judged on three factors.
1. Size
2. Taste
3. How the pearls pop against the roof of your mouth

This last one, I call the bubble-wrap effect. My royal theory is that a dark part of the brain enjoys a bit of destruction. Whether bursting air-filled packaging, cracking ice puddles— or popping fish eggs with the tongue—I find breakage under incessant pressure uniquely satisfying. That's basically how I got Véronique to be my girlfriend. I'm the incessant pressure and she's the uniquely satisfying.

"Tastes like seawater," Véronique said. "I don't like it."

I scooted closer to her on the wall, careful not to catch my shirt on the razor wire. "You didn't leave it on your fire long enough. The warmth liberates each pearl's fragrance." I took another scoop from the caviar tin. "One more try. Let it grow on you."

"Drinking from the ocean would be cheaper."

"This was free. I stole it from the royal pantry."

"Do you have to keep using that adjective? We get it. You're king. Everything you touch is royal."

I adopted an injured-hamster face, which was convincing enough that Véronique sighed and held out her palm for another few pearls.

"Actually..." I surveyed the brightening mountainside.

"Now that the eye is up I want to show you something else."
I tapped the caviar back into the tin and pulled out a smaller
container. "If Gaspard knew I took this he'd bust his light." I
opened the tin, scooped out a half spoonful, and set it gingerly
on Véronique's glowing, red palm.

She squinted at it. "I thought caviar was black."

I smiled. "Usually. Black or gray depending on the type of
fish. The lighter the better."

"That's four."

"Four what?"

"Factors. You said it was judged by three."

I knew what she was trying to do. Whenever things went
well she seemed ill-at-ease for some reason—almost like she
needed some sort of conflict to relax—but I was not going to
let her turn this into a debate. I pressed my light hand under
hers. Now she looked extremely uncomfortable.

Good.

"One in a thousand *Poisson du Roi* is born white. If it's female and lives long enough to become a mother, her eggs are
unique and incredibly expensive. What you have in your delicate hand is golden caviar."

Véronique raised an eyebrow. "Delicate?"

"Shapely?"

Véronique narrowed her eyes, but I caught the hint of a
smile. Then she brought her face to her fire and breathed in.

I'd visited her several times a week for the last month and
her features still hypnotized me. "Try it," I managed to get out.

Véronique clapped her hand to her mouth as if she were
eating nuts and began chewing. "Not bad. Tastes like butter."

Not the reaction I was going for, but at least she hadn't spit
it out again.

"So what's the special occasion?" Véronique asked.

That girl was too perceptive for my own good. I'd been
trying to soften her up before springing my agenda on her, but
apart from lying, there wasn't much I could do about it now.

"I have two questions for you."

"If it's about reacting with me, the answer is still no."

I closed my eyes. "Your red is not going to affect my color."

"You don't know that. And I'm not going to ruin your life just because you'd like me better as a Pink. What would I even do as a Pink?"

"Anything you want! They'd let you cross the river for one thing. Probably."

"Been there. Not doing that again."

"So the answer is no."

"The answer is don't ask me again or I'll tell Philippe to sic *Les Feu Noir* on you."

I chuckled. "The scary Black Fire Gang. Will they sneak into my pantry and…"

My smiled faded when I saw her expression. The second question was definitely going to have to wait.

After a few more bites we packed up, climbed onto a tree branch conveniently close to the wall, and started down the mountain. I grabbed her light hand with my dark. "If I fall I'm taking you with me." To my astonishment she didn't pull away. We were still holding hands when we stepped onto the pathway that lead to the community shelter.

"We made good time," Véronique said. She pulled her hand free to hold the hair off her neck. A single lock of black framed the side of her face.

She started toward the shelter, but I hung back, still partially concealed by trees. My skin was no longer bright pink from acid burns, and there were plenty of people at the shelter that would recognize me. The last thing I needed was Gaspard hearing I'd snuck into the worst part of Télesphore again.

I expected Véronique to leave without a goodbye as she normally did, but after a few more steps she glanced back. "You want to catch a few?"

Blank, yes. But it was impossible. If I didn't show up to breakfast, Gaspard would send someone to my room, then organize a city-wide manhunt. The former Commissare of Télesphore was not known for his moderation.

Then again... this was the first time she'd asked me to stay longer. The first sign she was more than simply putting up with me. And something about that strand of hair—still bisecting her cheekbone—turned me into a weak-willed serum sucker.

Okay, the hair had nothing to do with it, I could never say no to that girl. Besides, a little recreation may be just what she needed to get in a receptive frame of mind. I'd worry about Gaspard later.

Véronique retrieved her blunted homemade javelins from her hiding tree and we jogged downhill to an empty lot well out of sight of the shelter.

"Keep your gloves on," Véronique said. "I don't want to injure your 'royal' fire."

I hadn't removed the old leather gloves since I left my rooms. She just liked to needle me. "I'm not worried; your aim has been pretty off lately."

Her aim had been nothing of the sort. But my comment had the desired effect. She immediately launched a stick at me —only afterward calling, "Light shoulder."

I jumped out of the way to avoid being skewered. Her aim had been right on, but sadly, my catching arm was out of practice. Her subsequent throws were no less brutal. It took a few minutes, but I finally caught one aimed at my stomach. By that time, a small group of Reds had gathered to watch. So much for privacy. I didn't recognize anyone but was glad to have La-la's ratty clothes and one of Philippe's costume mustaches. With a little dirt rubbed onto my face I fit right in. Of course the disguise would be useless if I took my gloves off.

After a few more throws, I realized our little spot was getting crowded with Reds. I started to recognized a few people and tried to keep my face turned away from them.

The Taudis certainly took some getting used to. One lady was giving milk to twin babies and didn't seem to care who watched. And everyone was touching each other. Holding hands, braiding hair, impromptu shoulder massages. Most of the spectators were boys without shoes or shirts. One old man shuffled among the onlookers trying to sell fish he'd roasted on the spokes of a bicycle wheel. I grimaced. Rust wasn't poisonous was it? Despite the sanitary concerns, a woman produced a quarter-cuivre coin and exchanged it for one of the spokes.

The crowd continued to grow as we practiced. It was only a matter of time before one of them realized I was the King of Télesphore and everyone freaked out. Which was probably what Gaspard was doing at the moment.

But Véronique's mood was improving. Did she enjoy the attention? Maybe just a few more catches, then I could ask her my second question before high-tailing it back to the estate.

I raised my arms to signal I was ready for another, but Véronique shook her head and looked toward the shelter. A pair of police officers approached. One looked about my age. Probably recently classified. He held his Green fire at an awkward angle and waved it as if to ward off any riffraff that might get too close.

The other officer was Claude Terry, one of my least favorite people in Télesphore. He resembled a shaved mountain bear with a skinburn and had no qualms about striding rudely into the group of Red bystanders.

"Smells good," Claude said, his eyes hidden behind shadow glasses. "Catfish?"

The woman who'd purchased a fish-kabob casually dropped it in the underbrush and, along with the rest of the crowd, remembered she had pressing business elsewhere.

When the old man noticed he was all but alone with the officers he grunted and handed them a spoke. Claude tasted a piece of the white flesh. "Yup." He offered some to his partner, but the new recruit covered his mouth and began coughing.

The old man tried to step past Claude, but the officer extended the spoke to bar his way. "Cadet, what does the procedures manual say about freshwater fish?"

The boy perked up and pulled a tiny book out of a pouch

on his belt. After a minute of searching, he read, "The river and its banks—ten feet from the water on both sides—belong to the Dominateur. As such, all water, wildlife, and treasure found therein shall be surrendered to the Haut Commissaire. Poaching is expressly prohibited. Boating is permitted by non-Reds, but swimming is forbidden unless—"

Claude waved the boy quiet, then pointed at the old man. "Did a Dom give you permission to catch and sell these fish?"

The old man spat on the ground. "The fish belong to the White King now."

Claude raised his eyebrows and tossed his metal spoke to the ground. "Cadet, what's the penalty for poaching?"

"Six months in prison, I think. Or maybe that's for Reds crossing the river." He fumbled with his book, but Claude held up a hand to silence him.

"An officer's number-one tool is not his procedures manual. It's his brain. For example, I can see this river trash has all the muscle definition of a five-year-old girl. Catfish are strong. He didn't catch these. At least not by himself."

Véronique nodded toward the street. I shook my head. There was a time when I might have slipped away to avoid causing a stir, but lately I'd been all about stirring. And it had been a while since I'd seen Claude. It would be nice to catch up.

"Grandpops," I said, " are these clowns bothering you?"

Véronique's eyes went wide and she shook her head. What was she so worried about?

Claude regarded me with a smirk. The younger officer eyed the empty street as if contemplating making a break for it. Clearly, the years I spent beefing up for rugby were not wasted.

"I caught those fish in the river," I said. "And I'd do it again. Told the old man they were flounder."

Claude rested a hand on his tranq gun and peered at me over his dark lenses. "I've seen you before, haven't I?"

I hunched my shoulders. "Black if I know. You gonna take me in or what?"

Claude sniffed. "Well, Cadet Clarque, looks like you've got your first arrest."

That gave me an idea. "Bring my girlfriend, too. She caught more than I did." If I was already going to catch brimstone from Gaspard, at least I could use the time to talk to Véronique.

"Just when I was starting to like you," Véronique said under her breath.

The officers were picking through my bag. Don't know why they needed more poaching evidence since I'd just confessed. Véronique and I had been handcuffed to a wooden fence—one we easily could have uprooted.

"It's a social experiment," I said. "Don't you want to see how the justice system works?"

"I've seen it. Can we finish this up? I'm supposed to help Adisa clean the fanrooms."

Had this escapade been a bad idea? I had pictured us alone in a cell together with nothing to do but hold hands, but Véronique didn't seem to be in the hand-holding mood. Probably not the best time to discuss our future together.

"Help me get my glove off then."

"So dramatic," Véronique said. "Just tell them who you are and take off the stupid lip toupee. I'm sure they'll recognize you."

"Where's the fun in that? Besides, my hand is nearly free.

Can you just—"

Claude whistled. "Oh, they are in it now. That's another six months at least." He stuck his finger into one of the black caviar tins and scooped it into his mouth.

"What is it?" Clarque asked.

"Eggs from the King's Fish. Never seen the yellow stuff. Must be old." He sniffed it and dumped it back into the bag without putting the lid on. I made an involuntary squeal of indignation. Enough fiddling with my disguise. This was over now. No one messes with my golden caviar. "You were right, Monsieur Officer. You have seen me before."

"I just had an idea," Claude said to Clarque. "But it will require some procedure-bending. You in?"

Clarque nodded and glanced at the old man who was making a slow and laborious dash toward freedom. "He's getting away."

Claude took another fingerful of the black caviar. "We've got the real criminals right here. But if we take them to the pen we'll have to do a blackload of paperwork—and give up our snack."

"Excuse me," I said. "You might remember me. The last time we met I shot you with a tranquilizer dart."

"Where else would we send them?" Clarque asked.

"Since they like fish eggs so much, maybe they'd like to see how they're harvested. Just two days ago my cousin told me they're short staffed. Lost three to hypothermia last month."

"You mean the tin mines?" Clarque asked. "Don't they have to be classified into that?"

"The Dominateur won't care. It'll save them the hassle of finding replacements."

"Hello?" I shouted. "Let me make this clear for you. My name is—"

Véronique elbowed me. "I want to hear this."

Hear what? Claude making idle threats? But I fell silent. I guess I could keep playing along.

Véronique didn't hold my hand on the walk to the tin mines. She also resisted any attempts to start a conversation. Why was she so interested in seeing the mines? Had one of her friends been classified there?

Claude led us down the mountain, almost to the Royal Estate itself, but stopped in front of a large slab of metal. It looked like a rust-colored picnic blanket spread over the grass. Clarque kicked the door twice and after a few moments the ground beneath us began to creak and groan. The slab slowly rose into the air. A cage appeared—an elevator? Through the metal bars, a tall Green woman with black hair applied glitter eyeshadow. She stowed her makeup and clapped when she saw us.

"Lovely warm bodies!" The elevator rattled to a stop. The woman wrenched open the door, skipped to Claude, and planted a kiss on his ruddy cheek. "You're an angel, cousin. Mére Blanche is three weeks late spawning. I was about to get in with her myself. Tell me they're permanent?"

Claude nodded. "If they give you any trouble just assign them an extra shift. They've got more fingers than they know what to do with."

I glanced at Véronique, but she didn't seem as confused by this statement as I was. "Neek, you sure you want to—"

Véronique nodded.

This didn't seem like a romantic place for a relationship

discussion, but something in her expression told me not to interfere.

The black-haired woman brought Véronique into a hug. "So good of you to come. I'm Letty. What a pretty little... Anyways, wish you had a bit more meat on you." She looked me over. "This one's more like it. Although he'll distract the salters sure enough." She ruffled my hair.

"Letty," Claude said. "Is yellow caviar safe to eat?"

Letty's head snapped up. "Who told you... Anyways, you're not even suppose to know about... Don't you dare let anyone —"

"So it is safe?"

"Safe enough to eat, sure. But if anyone found out..."

"That's all I wanted to know," he said with a smile.

I gritted my teeth. The thought of Claude eating my golden caviar made me want to punch something. But until I figured out what Véronique wanted in the mines, I'd have to bite my tongue.

Letty ushered Véronique and me into the elevator and pulled a lever. The floor seemed to drop out from under us.

I may have screamed.

We didn't crash to the bottom, but there was an unpleasant spine-crunching stop. Letty picked an eyelash from her cheek and smiled. "I always forget to warn the recruits."

We stepped into cold darkness.

"The tin mines are lit only by human light as you can... Anyway, the mothers don't react well to smoke or electricity. Even the elevator is man-powered."

By the light of Véronique and Letty's fires I could make out two or three human shapes next to a complicated series of wheels and pulleys. Probably gloved to protect their fires. Did they stand there until someone needed to come up?

"What are we doing down here?" I whispered to Véronique.

"This way!" Letty said.

Véronique grabbed my elbow and guided me forward. "My

father worked here. I don't know why, but I felt like I needed to see it. I'm already starting to forget him."

"Did you know they had fish down here?"

Véronique shook her head. "Papi never said anything."

I picked up my pace so we were right behind Letty. "Excuse me, ma'am. We were wondering what the tin mines have to do with fish."

Letty sighed. "You're making me give my presentation out of order, but I suppose... Anyways, King Xavier discovered this place over a hundred years ago. The underwater ponds were fed by the river and already contained thousands of *Poisson Du Roi*."

The tunnel descended as we walked. If I wasn't mistaken we were headed toward Hameau Vert. Was this connected to the network of tunnels I'd used as a fugitive? Doubtful—if so, the passage under the Crystal Cathedral would be common knowledge—at least among the government officials. But hadn't the High Priestess said one of the tunnels led to the mines?

I tripped on a rock, but Véronique caught me before I faceplanted into the floor.

"So," I said, mostly to distract from my clumsiness, "Xavier finds a cavern full of fish and naturally he calls it the Tin Mines."

"If you take your gloves off," Letty said, "you might be able to see where you're... Anyways, he called it the tin mine because he didn't want folk to steal his caviar. But technically the caviar does go into tins, so it isn't that far... Anyways, Xavier discovered *Mère Blanche*. She was just old enough to spawn. That's why he was known as Xavier the Gold. Not because he... Actually, his fire was Lime Green. But he insisted everyone call him... Ah, here we are."

Véronique glanced at me. I crossed my eyes. I was getting whiplash from listening to this woman never finish a sentence.

We came into a larger tunnel with several rows of tables.

Twenty or so Reds had their hands in vats of what—in the dim light—looked like sludge.

"The salters massage the dendritic salt in carefully so as not to break the roe. Then it's canned and sent topside for curing. We use only women salters for... Anyways, manly hands are too clumsy."

Véronique smirked at me. I made an appropriate face of indignation.

A few feet beyond the tables, the tunnel opened into a large cavern. Around the room Red fires reflected off dozens of tiny ponds. The temperature seemed to drop twenty degrees.

"So tell me again why you can't make a confined combustion or something down here?"

"They won't spawn. Same if there's any electrical current nearby. Very temperamental."

"What are these people doing?" Véronique asked.

"Some of them are massaging out the ripe roe. That boy over there is administering a signaling protein. We do that every fifteen months to... Now see that one with a drinking straw? He's testing the roe to see if it's mature enough for... Anyways."

Véronique stepped to the closest pond and dipped in her hand. She recoiled and dried it on her shirt. "How long have you worked here, Letty?"

"Going on seventeen years."

"Did you know Troi DeGrave?"

Letty spun around and embraced Véronique again. "I knew you looked familiar! Troi loved these fish even more than... Are you a sister?"

"Why would he lie to us about digging for tin?" Her raised voice echoed in the cavern and several workers stopped what they were doing.

"Rules are rules, little bulb. Can't have the locals sneaking down to steal fish."

The locals. She meant the Reds. "Of course not," I said. "Much better that they starve to death."

"Troi had a special bond with Mère Blanche," Letty said as if I hadn't spoken. "He spent most of one shift helping heal a torn fin. Everyone else got out to avoid hypothermia, but he —"

"Lost the fingers on his dark hand," Véronique said in a tight voice.

"Not that it mattered. He went and attacked that poor Green... Anyways, I never would've believed it of—"

Véronique raised her fire so it shone directly at Letty's face, making the woman squint.

I'd seen kids do that to one another when their parents weren't looking, but never thought Véronique would be capable of such rudeness. "Neek..."

She ignored me. "You didn't know my father at all if you think he'd attack anyone."

Now even the salters had stopped what they were doing. Only the occasional sound of fishy splashing interrupted the silence.

"As I said, it hardly matters now—"

Véronique made a move to slap Letty, but the woman's hand came up like lightning and caught Véronique's wrist. "Need fast reflexes to work with fish. Now I'm going to need you both to take your clothes off."

Huh? I'd been about to ask for a coat.

Véronique twisted her arm free. "I want to see Mère Blanche."

Letty laughed. "That's what the new recruits do all day. Swim with the white mother and warm up the water with their body heat."

"Black that." I was freezing fully clothed. No way were they going to get me in that water.

Letty's eyes narrowed. "Watch your language, children work here."

"Obviously the fish are used to the cold. Mt. Tremper has melting snow most of the year. What's the point of giving everyone frostbite?"

"Someone is listening," Letty said with a smile.

I followed her gaze to the farthest corner of the cavern, where most of the area was taken up by a small lake. Nine or ten Red fires floated in the water around a pale island of rock.

"Who's listening?" I asked.

Then the island grew longer and began moving. "Son of a Violet."

Letty shot me another look.

Véronique was already moving toward the white behemoth. And what's more she was unbuttoning her shirt.

"That's the spirit," Letty said.

"Um, Neek?" I had to jog to keep up with her. The closer I got to the beast the less I wanted to be anywhere near it. It looked like an enormous white snake gliding through the blackness. It had to be twenty feet long. "What does it eat?"

"Not humans," Letty said. "Although if the tail hits you just right it'll break your arm."

This close I could see that the other Reds in Mère Blanche's lake were all moving silently through the water. Some had swimsuits, but the majority wore only underwear. And a couple were *au naturale.*

Definitely not sanitary. "Neek?"

But she was already in up to her waist, her outer clothes in a pile at Letty's feet.

"You've got a keeper, there," Letty said with a wink.

"I'm starting to wonder if all the lights are on upstairs."

"Troi was the same way. They must share blood with the fish folk."

I held my breath as Véronique reached Mère Blanche and laid a hand on its slimy back. There was a violent splash, then the enormous white shape was gone.

"Are you okay?" I called, ready to jump in and drag Véronique to safety.

She laughed. "She doesn't have any scales. Her skin feels like silk."

"Most workers go out of their way to avoid touching her,"

Letty said in an undertone. "I can tell I'm going to like this girl."

"She can't stay," I said. I was tired of this charade. Véronique had seen where her father worked, she'd even touched the dinosaur fish. Now it was time to—

"Bruno," Véronique called, "hurry up and take off your clothes."

Well, when she put it like that.

I stripped down to my gloves and briefs and jumped in.

"Holy Creation!" This wasn't cold water, it was glacial.

A round of laughter drifted from the salting tables. Letty joined them. "Now you see why we need to warm up the tanks a bit. The warmer they are, the faster they grow and the more they spawn."

By the time I made it to where Véronique was crouched I was pretty much convulsing.

"You get used to it," she told me.

"You've been in for thirty seconds."

"Okay, so I'm not used to it yet, but—"

"I thought you couldn't swim."

Véronique stood up. Even as short as she was, her head and shoulders were out of the water.

I stood up as well, hoping to warm up a bit. It didn't help.

"You look silly swimming with your gloves on," Véronique said through chattering teeth. "Not to mention that mustache."

I flexed my arms and chest. "How about now?"

"Better."

Véronique splashed me. It felt like she'd doused me with acid. I may have screamed again. I thought Letty might lecture us on disturbing the fish with our noise, but she just laughed at my pain. Apparently the fish weren't sensitive to sound.

I never actually got used to the water. It only grew slightly less excruciating. After a while I only shivered occasionally. And with Véronique to distract me, I managed to forget my discomfort for thirty seconds at a time.

The thought of Gaspard combing the estate for me also kept my brain occupied. I was pretty certain this would be my last jaunt into the Red slums without some kind of entourage, if Gaspard let me come at all. He was at least twice as overprotective as my mother.

Might as well make this outing worth it.

"I still haven't asked you my second question," I said.

Véronique stroked Mère Blanche with her fire. She was getting good at sneaking up on the thing and keeping it calm.

I shivered. The thought of eating something that came out of that sea monster made me queasy.

"She's beautiful," Véronique said.

"Sure. Gorgeous. Are you listening?" I kicked my legs to warm them up. "It's about breaking my promise."

"To take us to the mainland? Under the circumstances—"

"I want you to come live with me at the estate. You can

bring your mom and everybody. I don't care what Gaspard says. I'll tell him he can take you in or I'll live with you in the shelter."

Mère Blanche disappeared underwater again, and Véronique began swim-walking toward the deeper area. "I can't."

"Can't because your mom said no, or can't because you don't like me enough? You can still work in the fish mines if you want. It's actually closer."

"What would we do there?"

"Swim around. Pet fish."

"In the estate."

"Oh. You'll hang out, eat my royal food." I stressed the royal so she knew I was teasing her.

She didn't acknowledge the joke. "Leaving the island is one thing—but moving into an estate halfway across town just because you like me, is not going to work."

"Why not? I said your family can come. Would you rather stay in the Taudis?"

"What would we say to our friends? That we'll be eating veal and caviar while their children starve? Are my brothers going to leave the Feu Noir? La-la is a founding member."

La-la was also a Violet, thanks to me. And he promised he'd have a "talk" with his sister. Apparently, he wasn't as smooth as he thought.

"What about just you then?" Ack. She had me so flustered I was using awful grammar.

"And what happens when you get tired of me?" Véronique asked. "We don't actually know each other very well."

"Get tired of you?"

"Our relationship can't be based on anything lasting. I

treated you like river sludge when we met—still do sometimes. You put up with it for some reason. I assume because you're attracted to my face or body or both."

"I like your personality too."

Véronique laughed. "Yeah, okay. I don't mind being your 'special friend' for a while, but I'm not going to displace my family only to get them kicked back into the slums when a bright Blue catches your eye."

"Your shade has nothing to..."

A boy of ten or eleven swam between us. He raised his red fire. "Morning, thought I'd introduce myself." He faced Véronique. "Welcome to the Cool Pool. I'm Quinlin."

Cool Pool. Quaint.

"Why are there kids here?" I asked. "You can't have been classified yet."

"I need the money. Don't get paid as much as graduates, but it's a living."

Véronique glared at me as if I'd been the one to lower the boy's wages.

"Do you like it here?" she asked.

Quinlin shrugged. "Beats going to class."

"You don't get cold?"

"I stopped feeling the cold about a year ago. Gotta be careful not to stay in too long or else..." He lifted his foot out of the water. Or his heel, rather. The rest was gone.

Véronique put a hand to her throat but quickly recovered. "Why can't you feel the cold?"

"My grandma says nerve damage, but I think I'm turning into a fish."

"Can't they find another job for you?"

Quinlin shook his head. "Can't really walk, so swimming is about it for me. Besides, the fish like me."

"Quin," Letty called, "enough flirting. Back to your section, please."

"I'm Véronique. It was nice to meet you."

"Same here," he said without so much as a glance at me. If I didn't feel so sorry for the kid I would've been annoyed.

He limped back to his own pond. Véronique raised her eyebrows at me as if her point had been proven beyond doubt.

"Toi—or Taudis Rouge as you 'higher colors' say—is our home. It's not ideal, but why not focus on helping us fix things instead of making us your pets?"

That was rude. I was starting to rethink what I'd said about her personality. "So last month you wanted to leave the Taudis, and now it's your mission to fix it?"

"I was wrong. I never should have agreed to leave."

This was not going well. "Fine, I'll fix it. Then will you live with me?"

"Fix it how? Build some new houses? Close the tin mines? Lift the fishing ban?"

"For a start. You don't think that will work?"

"The awful living conditions are not the whole problem. It's how we're viewed by the Blues and Greens—how we view ourselves. Unless you have some way to individually force every single person in Télesphore to rethink their prejudices, life in the Taudis will never change."

Didn't she just say she wanted my help? "Well, then what do you suggest, brainwash them?" I hadn't meant to lace it with such hostility, but it was out before I thought better of it.

Véronique didn't look hurt—just sad. "I suggest you find

yourself a princess." Then she took a step and disappeared under the water.

She was insane. She was going to hypothermiate herself.

After a few seconds, I realized I couldn't see her fire under the water. Where had she gone? Had she stepped off a ledge?

"Neek?" I walked to where she had disappeared. It felt solid enough. I stuck my head under.

Holy black. My ears felt like they were being burned off, but I stayed under. Where was her fire? It couldn't have just disappeared. I pulled the glove off my light hand. The cavern floor appeared bright green all around me—no fissures, no pits. Something black caught my eye, but it was only my mustache. It had come free and was spinning in the current. I swam deeper and felt the floor with my dark hand. I had to be missing something. Had she stumbled? Had she punctured her fire somehow? Many pairs of legs stood at the edge of the lake. Why didn't any of them help?

I stood and lifted my fire into the air. White light flooded the cavern. Gasps erupted from the salting tables. Letty nearly fell backward into the water. One of the Red children in a neighboring pond yelled, "It's King Bruno!"

"I need help!" I screamed. "She can't swim!" I dove back into the water and kicked frantically toward the center of the lake. She'd been under too long.

Out of the corner of my eye I saw movement—but when I looked, it wasn't Véronique or my recently liberated facial hair. It was the white monster fish. And it was swimming a lot faster than it had been earlier—straight toward me.

With its mouth open.

CHAPTER THREE

ROYAL INTENTIONS

I knocked on the enormous blue door. Po answered, and his sculpted eyebrows nearly reached his wig.

"Your Grace, what are you doing outside in your underthings?"

"Someone locked my window. Can I come in?"

Po seemed to remember he was the butler and performed something halfway between a bow and a curtsy. "Chancellor Gaspard will be pleased to see you."

"Where is he?" I asked as I entered.

"In the entryway."

The voice did not belong to Po. Gaspard, the former Haut Commissaire, stood at the foot of the stairs in silk-embroidered pajamas. "Thank the Créateur you're safe." He rushed across the crystal floor and held out a hand for my fire.

It was an archaic practice. Besides luminogenic arrest, modern science showed no correlation between a child's health and the state of their glowing palm. I displayed my hand anyway. He squinted at the light and gently pressed a finger in the center of the raised, dome-like skin. "More glorious every time I see it."

The brazen contact startled me. Besides hand-clasp reactions, the only people to ever touch my esca were family. Not only was it exceptionally invasive, it was very un-Blue.

Still, I was probably lucky not to be locked in my rooms. "Sorry about sneaking out. I didn't want to wake anyone. I went for an early morning swim."

"And lost your clothes, apparently. At least you've been putting the weight room to good use." He extended his pale blue fire as if to get a better look at me.

Okay, as if touching my fire weren't enough, having an old man compliment me on my muscle tone was beyond creepy. And even weirder, Gaspard's gray-bearded chauffeur stood at the top of the stairs staring at me as if trying to read my thoughts.

"I think I'll get dressed."

"Your parents phoned. They're coming to visit."

"Granny too?"

Gaspard nodded with a strange expression I couldn't place. He took a deep breath as if clearing his head and pulled his long white hair into a ponytail. "But first, the seamstresses have arrived from Tjarta. They've been waiting in your room for several hours."

Ah, crêpes.

"And by the way, your window has been welded shut."

Subtle. "What if there's a combustion event?"

"One of the guards who is stationed at your door will carry you to safety."

"More than one guard at my door?"

"Two at all times. Can't have criminals trying to sneak in and steal your lovely fire."

He winked at me.

I grimaced and wondered how long it would take me to learn the ropes of this ruling business. And how to go about dechancelloring someone.

I found two Green women sitting on my bedroom floor surrounded by pincushions, scraps of fabric and silk tape measures. They both popped to their feet when I entered. "Good morning, Your Grace," said the older one. She removed a short, red fabric pencil from behind her ear. "Are you ready to start the measurements?"

"Uh... I'm kind of in my underwear."

"Good. That will save time."

The hour that followed would've qualified as the most awkward of my life had I not just run mostly naked through the streets of Télesphore. The worst part of the flight from the mines was that I had left my gloves and had no way to conceal my fire. People kept shouting "Long live the king!" as I passed.

When I told my parents, they didn't laugh as I had hoped. Dad covered his mouth and Mom looked like she might be sick on the carpet. Only Granny Jade had a small grin as she looked at me over her two-hundred-cuivre horn-rimmed glasses.

"Isn't this the second time you've run through town half-naked? I'm sensing a pattern."

I smiled. "I really couldn't get my clothes. It was chaos. By the time I figured out that Véronique had been standing on the bank the whole time, the Reds were converging on me. Most looked like they wanted my autograph, but a couple were shouting like they were angry about something. Véronique and Letty told me to run. I think I might have hurt one of the kids—rugby instincts."

Now that I was safe and dry I felt a bit silly. Nothing would've happened to me—most likely. But when you're underground and surrounded by a crowd of agitated Reds...

Not that their shade mattered.

Blank, I was just as bad as the rest of the Blueborns. That moment of panic showed me that my prejudices were still alive and well. Véronique was right. How do you change an entire city's way of thinking? It would take years of constant propaganda—and who knows if that would even work.

"Gaspard sure cleared out of here quick," Granny said.

"Just being polite, I guess—giving us some privacy."

"Must be it."

Dad put a hand on my shoulder. "How was your first month as a monarch?"

Typically, at this point I would have gone into detail

about my schedule, servants and especially the menus, but after telling about my trip to the Tin Mines, it all felt unimportant.

"It's been fine—but I can't help feeling that I'm not doing well."

Mom laughed and straightened a lock of her pink-streaked hair. "You haven't burned the city down yet."

"I mean, I don't think the last month has been very good for me. When I was sneaking around trying to avoid the pokers last month, I had all these ideas about justice and equality and showing the Dominateur what's what."

"And now?" Granny asked.

"Well, I got my comfortable bed back. And the food might have distracted me—a lot. Seriously, you have to stay for dinner."

"So your mission to restore justice to Télesphore has been put on the back burner."

"More like I spaced it completely. How could I forget something like that? I mean, my girlfriend lives in a community shelter because the government won't let her cross the river and get a real job—and I'm the government!"

Mom smoothed my hair. "You're safe and that's what's important. And your skin is mostly back to normal." She gave me a distasteful look, as if I'd covered my body with acid on purpose.

"I hope you're growing your hair out again. I'll never forgive that Mallory for cutting it all off. The blond tips do look nice, though."

I sighed—hopefully making it clear that the matronly examination was over.

"You're still learning how to be an adult," Dad said. "Give it time. You'll grow into this role and then you can start making some changes."

"While Véronique lives in squalor."

"It's what they're used to," Mom said. "I hate to say it, but if we moved the Reds into Ville Bleu, they'd trash the place in a week."

"Mom."

Even my own family.

Granny took my hand and squinted into my fire. "Your Grandpa Molyneux would've loved to see you now. This was his dream—find the secret to white fire, choose a worthy King that would better our country."

"You haven't told anyone, have you?" Dad asked me.

I shook my head. "I don't really understand how I got the white fire myself. I've been vague when people ask—just reacted with some of my friends around town, then almost popped it saving half the Taudis."

"Good," Dad said. "The last thing you want is someone else becoming White and challenging your rule."

"Oh," Mom said, "I almost forgot the reason we came to see you in the first place. Your father doesn't have any surgeries scheduled this week and we're taking a few days on the boat— maybe catch some sharks."

"That sounds amazing."

Dad grinned. "I'll let Monsieur Livius know—you won't be more than a week, and maybe—"

"I wish I could go—but it's time I got serious about my duties."

My parents both frowned, but Granny nodded. "This city is past due for some Bruno Nazaire. Three pieces of advice, though—be careful, follow your instincts and never trust a politician."

They didn't stay for dinner. Which was just as well because Gaspard was in a bad mood. Although it didn't show in his treatment of me or the staff, he kept glaring into his prawn soup when he thought no one was looking. Maybe he was disappointed in me. He'd been holding things together for nearly thirty years, only to be displaced by an incompetent sixteen-year-old whose main concern was sneaking out to see his girlfriend.

Of course Gaspard didn't know about the girlfriend—I hoped.

It was time to start acting like a king.

"Gaspard, I won't be exiting through the windows anymore. I'm sorry for worrying you."

Gaspard looked up from his bowl and smiled. "And I apologize for being morose this evening. There is much on my mind."

"Anything I can help with?"

"Perhaps. Eventually."

"That's the thing. I've been thinking I'd like to get serious about making laws and stuff."

Gaspard blinked. "You don't let the grass grow, do you, child?"

I wasn't quite sure what he meant by that, so I just stared at him.

"Then tomorrow morning we begin your training. Make sure to get a good night's sleep—and if you feel the urge to go swimming in the middle of the night, take a bath."

In the morning Gaspard gave me a pair of his own slacks and a button up shirt to wear until my tailored clothes were ready. They weren't too bad except for the old man loafers. Who knew I could miss a pair of sneakers so much?

"Just curious—does this mean I have to wear button-up shirts every day?"

"A prince might get away with casual wear," said Gaspard with a sly smile, "but kings do not wear jeans and hooded sweatshirts."

"They don't know what they're missing."

"Having second thoughts? We could delay your official training until you're eighteen or so."

"Nope. I'm good."

"If you don't mind me asking, what kind of new laws did you have in mind?"

"Oh, you know. The usual."

"The usual."

"I'm still figuring it out."

"Well, let me know. I'd be interested to hear your take on things."

I'm not sure why I didn't tell Gaspard right then what I thought of the current system. Probably because it would mean telling him he'd been doing it wrong all these years. What if he was even more shade-strict than Mom? Despite his general uptightness and old man smell, I liked Gaspard. I didn't want to make him mad at me. I would tell him—eventually.

The day was much less enjoyable than my typical lie-around-the-estate schedule. I didn't realize how busy Gaspard kept. Each time I opened my mouth to ask if we were finished—and whether lunch was ready—another servant would appear with an issue that had to be dealt with immediately. Zacharie the Blue chauffeur followed us everywhere we went, never saying a word. By mid-afternoon I was starting to understand why he didn't bother. Clearly, his job was to be there if the Chancellor needed him but otherwise stay out of the way.

The training itself, along with the avalanche of tradition and policy, almost made me want to trade places with the scruffy old servant. At least he didn't have to memorize the names of all the Télesphorian ambassadors or try to learn the protocol for electing a new Dom.

My clothing arrived before dinner, and of course the two-person wardrobe committee couldn't just hand them over. The women had to watch me try on every single item to make sure it fit properly.

I had to admit, in those perfectly-tailored clothes I didn't look half bad. One of the blue ties matched my eyes and I'm embarrassed to say I spent several minutes in front of the mirror. I couldn't wait for Véronique to see me in these clothes.

Véronique—who had two shirts to her name. She wouldn't be impressed by my new wardrobe—not when my three-piece suit could have fed her family for a month.

What was my problem? How did I keep getting distracted from my purpose? I wasn't here to enjoy the food or admire myself in my finery. I was here to run a country. And if I didn't start soon, I had a feeling I'd end up just like Zacharie, following Gaspard around like a puppy while he made all the decisions and nothing changed.

This cowardly delaying had gone on long enough. It was time to let Gaspard know where I stood.

The women were fitting me with a pair of custom-made translucent gloves when Gaspard stepped into my bedroom. "You clean up nicely."

The women bowed as if the compliment were meant for them.

"As soon as you're finished," Gaspard said, "our truffles are waiting."

I stepped off the stool. "Before we do anything else, I need to tell you something."

Gaspard seemed to sense my solemnity and excused the seamstresses. They looked a little disappointed to have dress-up time interrupted. Only Zacharie remained with us and he watched me closely with his deep brown eyes.

"I know I don't know much about running a country yet," I began, "and I don't want you to think I'm attacking the way things are done around here."

"Ah, we're discussing your new laws."

"When I lived in Ville Bleu I thought Télesphore was the greatest city on earth."

"Many share that opinion."

"But then there was that fiasco with me getting painted and accidentally killing that guard. Which I am truly sorry about. You know that, right?"

Gaspard nodded. "And now, how do you feel about your city—after becoming a Mélangé and making friends with Greens and Reds?"

"It's totally screwed up."

"How so?"

"Well, I may have made several visits to the summerlight side of the river recently. You wouldn't believe the living conditions. The shelter is getting better, now that Chief Collins and his son are in prison, but everything is not milkweed and ducklings. The laws are supposed to protect the people, but the only ones it really helps are the Blues. It's impossible for Greens to get a high-paying job and if you're Red, forget about it. The whole shade-based system needs to be eliminated."

Gaspard closed his eyes and breathed in.

"You have no idea how good it is to hear you say this, Bruno." He looked at me and there was genuine relief in his eyes. "This past month I've been beside myself wondering how to proceed. Things got so much more complicated when you appeared with your white fire and accepted the throne. Being Blueborn I thought you would reinforce the social hierarchy. But now that I know we share the same goal, it will be so much easier."

"Wait, you agree with me? Then why haven't you done anything about it? Why is the police force corrupt and incompetent? Why do you allow the Mélangé to be discriminated against and Reds to go hungry? I'm sorry, but it doesn't seem like you're trying very hard."

Zacharie's eyes had grown large behind his bushy gray eyebrows.

Gaspard, on the other hand, didn't seem surprised. "As a steward of the kingdom, my power was severely limited. The Dominateur held sway in matters of policy and law. My attempts to improve Télesphore have been met with much opposition."

I had a feeling I knew which Doms presented the opposition. Gravois had been willing to let his grandson take the fall in order to protect his own reputation. At the last minute, I had saved Aro by revealing myself as the killer of the Royal Soldier. But that didn't change the fact that the old man with a bad toupee wasn't exactly a pillar of moral courage.

"Can't we get rid of them? What's the point of having a king, if we let the Doms run everything?"

Gaspard put his faded blue fire on my shoulder. I stiffened at the casual action. I liked the guy, but it wasn't like he was my grandpa.

"I didn't say it would be the case now," Gaspard said. "As king, you will be the most powerful member of the Dominateur. You run the meetings and make the final decisions."

"Good," I said with that same feeling of anticipation I got before a rugby match.

"But you must remember that your joint leaders work hard in the affairs of the kingdom. Without their support, your job would be nearly impossible. It will be in your best interest to introduce your ideas cautiously."

I cringed, thinking of my first act as king the night I revealed my white fire. The Doms and most of the spectators in the stadium had seemed baffled by my decree. "You mean, like not releasing four Red prisoners for the fun of it?"

Gaspard chuckled. "The Dominateur are old men. They're set in their ways. They must be coaxed from their positions with concessions and small favors. Certainly don't bring up more than one change at a time—and try to keep the spontaneous pardons to a minimum."

I smiled, but inside, felt exhausted. So much for storming in and setting everything right. Véronique's refusal to live at the estate was starting to make more sense. It would show my hand as a "Red-lover" and probably set half the Dominateur against me from the start.

If I was going to help Véronique's family, I would have to be more subtle—at least until I convinced the Dominateur that Blues weren't the center of the universe.

"Do I have to plan some sort of meeting to get everyone together?"

"I can set up a meeting immediately. How does next Thursday sound?"

"Can we do it sooner? I'm afraid I'll get distracted again." Besides, even if Véronique liked working in the cold with that white monster, the quicker I fixed things in Taudis Rouge the better. No more amputated appendages on my watch.

"Fair enough. It might ruffle some hair pieces, but I could probably get them to meet you tomorrow following Sunday Services. Are you quite sure you're ready to lead a roomful of crotchety old men?"

Sunday Services? Did that mean he wanted me to go to church? That sounded even less appealing than babysitting old men. "What if I dissolved the Dominateur all together? Can I even do that?"

"Yes, you could do that," Gaspard said with a solemn expression. "But such an action would undoubtedly lead to a civil war that could mean the end of our island nation as we know it."

"Right," I said. "Baby steps."

CHAPTER FOUR

DOMINATURDS

Mom wasn't overly religious—overly social, yes. And since her friends attended the morning services, she never missed a Sunday. Dad, on the other hand, refused to set foot in the cathedral, frequently citing his hatred of hypocrites and hard glass benches. For a while Mom dragged me with her as a conversation piece—but once I was old enough to realize church was optional, I opted out.

Now, after ten years, the incense and echo of the choir off crystal walls filled me with nostalgia. I realized I missed Mom scratching my back during the services, and the smell of her Sunday perfume.

But when I made a move to sit with the audience, Sébastien took my arm.

"Your Grace, it is inadvisable to intermingle with your subjects." The man was huge—which, is probably how he got the job as head guard—that and his chin that seemed large enough for a bird to land on. Talking with him made me feel like I'd been sent to the principal. It didn't help that until recently he'd been trying to capture and execute me.

"Not even if my mom is down there?"

"Apologies, 'sieur, but crowds make it exceptionally difficult to keep you safe."

From what? A bunch of old ladies in hats? I allowed Sébastien to steer me toward a gaudy throne in an alcove to the side of the pulpit. Since this was my first official appearance in public—unless you count the semi-nude jog—I probably shouldn't be seen arguing with my guards. Besides, Gaspard had warned me to step on as few toes as possible. My agenda would earn me enemies soon enough.

The high priestess shot me a sly wink, then acknowledged my presence using a lot of flowery words I didn't understand —some of it sounded like the old language. Mallory then proceeded to the sermon, but the congregation was having attention problems. Instead of quieting down, they grew steadily louder. The biggest offenders were my mother and her friends on the second row. A steady line of people kept getting out of their seats to present their fires to Mom and whisper their congratulations. One pair of ladies with matching blue velvet hats started up the aisle as if to introduce themselves to me.

They met with two of my guards and settled for a wave before returning to their seats.

I was used to performing in front of crowds. As a starting forward, they used to chant my name at least once a match —but this was different. I hadn't done anything to deserve my kingly White status. Would my fellow Télesphorians still want me to be king if they knew it had all happened by chance?

"Blessings," said Mallory in a slightly higher voice than usual. "It is transcendentally rapturous to have a monarch with us after so many years. Let us thank the Créateur by showing a little reverence in His Holy House."

The guilt treatment worked better. The conversations gradually faded.

Mom caught my eye and smiled. Granny wasn't with her. Probably getting ready for the boating trip. The three of them would leave first thing in the morning. Crêpes, I'd give anything to go with them.

Anything except my chance to fix Télesphore. And hopefully that would also show Véronique I was serious about taking care of her and her shademates. But the thought that she might be right about me burrowed into the back of my brain. Was I really that shallow? Would I lose interest in her as soon as things got rough? Was I trying to help the Reds only to impress her?

They were questions I didn't enjoy pondering.

Once the cathedral fell silent, Mallory smoothed her pearl dress and continued her sermon, although she did pause occasionally to glare at the second row.

The service went on forever. I had admired Mallory as a person—she was beautiful, funny, and secretly led the Feu Noir to relieve Red suffering, but her sermons were as exciting as calculometrics homework. At one point I discovered drool on my royal church cape. Had I nodded off? This was doubly awkward since most of the congregation was watching me instead of the high priestess. Probably hoping I'd take off my gloves so they could see my two-hundred-watt appendage.

After what seemed like several hours, church finally ended. I thought Sébastien might let me say hello to Mom, but my legion of guards escorted me directly to an upper room of the cathedral. On every wall, large tinted windows looked out over the city. I wanted to play tourist and enjoy the view, but most of the Dominateur were already seated at a long cobblestone table in the center of the room. A thin slab of glass lay atop the pebbled surface, and at least two of the Doms were tapping their fingers on it when I entered. As one, the group stood and bowed, but I could tell I wasn't a popular addition to the team. Barely concealed scowls followed me as I took what was obviously my seat.

I expected to be nervous, but to my surprise the sight of all the blue gave me confidence. I'd grown up around Blues. I'd never suffered from lack of confidence and I certainly wasn't going to start, now that I was in charge.

Still, I had to tread carefully.

A few of the guards, including Sébastien, filed in behind Gaspard and Zacharie. The rest positioned themselves in the hallway. Was Sébastien paranoid or did I really have that many enemies?

Once we were all seated, everyone looked in my direction.

"Good morning, distinguished messieurs," I said in a respectfully grave tone. "I am grateful for the opportunity to learn from such experienced rulers as yourselves. I hope you will have patience with me as I try not to botch everything." Was that suck-upy enough?

Around the room, a few shoulders relaxed and some of the scowls softened. Out of the corner of my eye, I saw Gaspard smile. His approval meant I was on the right track. I realized the Chancellor was beginning to take my father's place as the person I wanted most to please. Yeah, he acted touchy and weird some times, but I got the idea he was lonely and excited to have a surrogate grandson around.

"Your Grace?" one of the Doms prompted.

"Yes, my apologies. Since I have no idea how this is supposed to work, I invite you all to disregard normal protocol and say what's on your mind."

The old men looked at each other. I couldn't tell if they were pleased or annoyed.

"And since we are partners in serving Télesphore, I hope you will call me Bruno and dispense with formal titles."

"Your Majesty," said what looked like the oldest of the bunch, "just because you prefer to be called by your first name doesn't mean we do."

"I will address you each as Dom, unless instructed otherwise," I said, hoping my elevated language didn't sound as false as it felt. "You may call me whatever you like as long as it's suitable for the ears of a minor."

The ancient man harrumphed, but several others smiled, including the dark-haired Dom Marcoux with gray streaks in his mustache. At the stadium when I'd revealed my white fire, he'd been the first of the Dominateur to recognize me as king. I'd have to thank him later.

With a little more obsequious flattery to grease their jaw-bones, I convinced the council members to introduce themselves. Afterward, we dove right into the administrative duties of running a country. Since Télesphore had gone without a king for the better part of fifty years, the Dominateur seemed as clueless about my role as I was, so I mostly listened and took notes with the intent to ask Gaspard's opinion later.

We discussed land development, finances, and upcoming festivals. I thought about bringing up the tin mines and brainstorming ways to improve working conditions, but I wasn't sure the Doms even knew about the fish—or cared that people were losing parts of their body. Later, Gaspard would tell me the best way to go about it. Maybe we could come up with a concrete plan before the next meeting.

I pasted on an interested face and continued to nod thoughtfully as they discussed updating the classifications tests and whether part of the forest should be cleared to construct a golf course. After an hour, I began to get hungry—after two hours, ravenous. Somewhere during the third hour, the paper I was taking notes on began to look tasty.

"One more item before we break," Dom Gravois said. He took a moment to reposition his blond hairpiece. He didn't look much like his grandson. Aro was brown-haired and had a generic button nose. Gravois resembled an old crow with a gnarled beak.

"As you know," Gravois said, "the police force is stretched thin and most of our calls come from the summerlight side of the river."

What? No Reds would actually call for police assistance. He was either flat out lying or referring to Greens calling about suspicious Reds. I almost spoke up to have him clarify, but my rumbling stomach twisted my windpipe closed.

"With Taudis Rouge still growing exponentially," Gravois continued, "we expected a few more graduates to be classified into law enforcement." He glared at a large-eared man I suspected was Dom of Education. It was somewhere in my notes, but I couldn't muster the will to look.

"The Green class was tiny this year," the man replied. "Do you want to do without food preparation?"

"The rapid growth of the Taudis populace is dangerous," Gravois continued. "I propose we give Reds an option. Either submit to a one-child per couple restriction or lose the protection of our officers."

"Our officers?" I said before I could stop myself. The room went silent and I noticed Gaspard watching me. I didn't want to make anyone angry, but hungry or not, I knew I had to nip this one-child nonsense in the bud. If they'd thought of it earlier, Véronique wouldn't exist. Not to mention her sister Jeannette, who helped me escape capture, and their brother La-la who regularly risked his life to feed starving children.

"Well?" I said, "are Reds Télesphorians or not?"

"They pay taxes," Gravois said. "But that doesn't mean they have a right to monopolize the police force. After a few generations, a one-child limit would cut Taudis Rogue down to a more manageable size."

I nodded vaguely and tried to think of a diplomatic way to tell him he was an idiot.

"How do you plan to enforce this limit?"

Gravois put up his hands as if it would be simple. "We examine the Red women every six months and terminate any second pregnancies."

The thought of Mama DeGrave taking her daughters to get "examined" twisted my stomach.

"So you'd need to classify some Green census officials. As well as more Blue gynecologists. Where will all these graduates come from?"

Gravois opened his mouth to speak, but I cut him off.

"Not to mention you'd need more officers to deal with any resistance. And I assure you, there would be resistance."

"Then we'll utilize the Royal Soldiers. Give them something to do besides chase juvenile delinquents around the city."

From a few raised eyebrows, many in the room thought the comment was out of line. I decided to ignore it.

"So you want to mobilize the soldiers," I said, my voice louder now. "Why not? Let's declare war on Taudis Rogue."

Gaspard gave me a warning glance, but I wasn't going to put up with such blatant stupidity.

"What would you suggest, My King?" Gravois said, twisting the title into a curse.

For a moment I faltered. I'd been so intent on ripping apart his idea that I'd forgotten there was still a problem to address.

What would my father do in this situation? Or better yet, Granny. If she'd been here, she could have explained exactly why the men were wrong and do it in such a way that they felt grateful to be corrected. I rubbed my gloves together, feeling the deep hum of my fire. I pictured Granny standing next to me, her tiny fist pounding on the table, and I could almost hear her voice in my head as I spoke.

"I agree that your officers are ineffective," I said to Gravois. "Whether that's because they are spread too thin or inadequately trained, I can't say. You certainly did a brilliant job with Chief Collins."

Gravois's jaw tightened.

Were we really arguing over who enjoyed the services of Claude-the-crêpe-bag? An idea came to me. "If you're so worried about the safety of your officers, why not let the Taudis create its own police force?"

That seemed to wake everybody up. Several people began speaking at once.

"Gentlemen," Gaspard called, "decorum if you please."

"A Red police officer?" said the Dom straight across from me. "It's lunacy."

"No one would take them serious," another added.

"Seriously," I corrected automatically. Luckily no one was listening to my grammatical advice.

"And what about tranquilizer guns?" Gravois asked. "You can't have them running around with—"

"Obviously, their jurisdiction would be summerlight of the river," I said. "We will train them to use darts. Would you want to try keeping order in Taudis Rouge with a nightstick?"

"We couldn't pay them," Gravois said. "It would have to be completely volunt—"

"Oh, we'll pay them," I said in a voice Mom often used with Dad, "if we have to cut the salary of the Green officers."

Gaspard opened a notebook. "All in favor of preparing a plan to train and employ Red officers?"

I waited for the vote, hoping I wouldn't have to veto the

first decision made by my council. But I needn't have worried. The only ones that voted 'Nay' were Gravois and the two sitting next to him.

"Motion passed," Gaspard said. "Dom Gravois, please bring a draft of your plan for us to vote on next month. And if there's nothing else, we'll adjourn until—"

"I have a question," said the coffee-skin man on Gravois's light side. "What happens when the Red officers get a taste of power and decide they're tired of taking orders? What would prevent them from leading a revolt across the bridge with their newly acquired weapons?"

Several men nodded. I had to admit it was a legitimate question.

"That will be something to discuss next month," Gaspard said.

"It's alright," I said. "I think I have an answer."

The men waited, a few of them all but smirking.

I decided to stand. "It's true the Reds don't feel a lot of camaraderie toward the government, or towards their winterdark neighbors in general. But I believe the problem can be remedied."

Gaspard gave a slight head-shake, but I pretended not to see. Gravois was an insidious disease in this council and the baby step stuff wasn't going to cut it. No way was I going to wait until Véronique lost half her fingers and toes for the Doms to finally agree to make some changes. It was time to be honest with them and see where they stood.

"Although I still have a lot to learn, I don't need special training to see what's right in front of me."

The old men could tell something was coming, and several readied their scowls in anticipation.

"Preference or discrimination based on shade is unethical and until we change the laws, the Taudis will always be a threat."

"Now hold on—"

"My first goal as King is to remove all restrictions and privileges associated with fire-color and distribute them equally based on training and individual capacity."

The reaction was immediate. At once I was back in the rugby stadium—except instead of cheering, the old men were shouting with outrage.

It took ten minutes for Gaspard to calm them down enough to proceed, and several of the men changed their vote on the Red Officer Plan, saying if desegregation was my end-goal, they would have no part of it. Even my mustached friend seemed angry with me.

The motion still passed, but just barely.

"I think we all remember the idealism of our youth," Gaspard said with a wink in my direction. "But even if there is truth to what King Bruno is saying, we can't consider any large changes until he's gained the public's confidence."

I rubbed at a smudge on the glass tabletop. I knew Gaspard was smoothing things over to keep the peace, but it felt like he was invalidating everything I'd said.

"Bruno," he said in a softer voice, "dismantling an entire infrastructure at once would be like pulling the boat out from under Télesphore. It would likely lead to economic collapse and riots. Perhaps even assassination attempts."

A few Doms grunted in agreement.

I lowered my head, suddenly acutely aware of my age. Why was he talking like this when he'd told me we had the same goal? He was making me look like a fool.

"Building credibility takes time," Gaspard said, "and before you announce any big plans you must make sure you can maintain control of the people."

"Maintain control? You mean with more officers?"

Gaspard shook his head. "You must learn to use the Crystal Scepter."

Several Doms scoffed. One with a bulbous nose laughed. "Those ancient witchcraft stories are—"

"They are not stories," Gaspard said. "It is documented science."

I glanced at Gaspard but decided opening my mouth at this point would further prove my ignorance. Thankfully, he seemed to sense my confusion. He stood, walked to me and removed my glove. White light flooded the room. Although the Doms had seen my fire only a month ago, the entire room snapped to attention. A cane clattered to the floor and one of the older Doms nearly slid out of his chair.

"You are the only one who can use the scepter," Gaspard said in a reverent voice. "When you have learned to wield it, your country's faith in you will be unshakable. They will follow you anywhere."

"Wield it? You mean like martial arts training?"

Gaspard reached into his robe, and pulled out a four-foot-long, clear rod topped with a diamond half the size of my fist. Did he carry it around with him like a wallet? Maybe he didn't trust it out of his sight. It had to be worth a couple million cuivres.

"The Crystal Scepter isn't a walking stick or a staff with which to hit people. It is what is known as a light manipulator."

I stared at him. Was he taking advantage of my ignorance to make the others laugh?

"Even after thousands of years," he continued, "we still have no idea what our fires are capable of."

He was starting to sound like my grandpa. And if I hadn't recently used my fire to burn people and shoot flames from my hand, I would've said Gaspard was crazy. Clearly we didn't know everything about the esca.

"The scepter somehow channels the light of your fire?" I asked.

Gaspard nodded.

"What exactly does it do?"

The Chancellor looked directly at my snowy hand. "It turns your dreams into reality."

CHAPTER FIVE

LIGHT READING

B elievers of magic can be separated into two groups—religious fanatics and the mentally deranged.

Gaspard didn't strike me as either of those, yet he had just handed me a book that would "unlock the secrets of the scepter." He claimed it was science, but I was pretty sure my science book didn't have a section on light manipulators.

I sat on my bed. Gaspard watched me from the desk as I examined the tome. It was cool to the touch and weighed a ton. The binding looked like copper or bronze. There was no title on the front. As I opened the metal cover it gave off a slightly rancid smell as if the pages had begun to decompose.

"You've read this whole thing?" It was twice the size of Mom's bible.

"Twelve times. Would you like me to train you in it or would you prefer to first read it through on your own?"

"I guess on my own." Having him explain it would've been easier. I didn't want to embarrass myself, though. What if I didn't understand it right away?

"Very well, since this is our top priority, I'll try to give you as much study time as possible."

I nodded. So much for being done with school. And why did I get the impression there would be a test later?

Gaspard stood and stretched. He was the palest Blue I'd

ever seen.

"Won't the light thingy work for you?"

Gaspard stared into his own glowing palm. "I thought the answer to white fire was purity. I mentioned at your classification ceremony that my fire age is zero. Even when my wife was alive we kept our light hands apart. All for nothing. You are the only person in living memory to channel light through the scepter's diamond. I wish I knew how."

I absently rubbed the bulge in my glove. I really wanted to tell him how I'd reacted with half of Télesphore on my impromptu humanitarian mission—but Dad had just warned me again to keep it secret.

"There was something," I said.

"Yes?"

"I was thinking about donating a little money to Arnaud's family. As a sort of apology. Could we do that?"

"I thought you killed that Lefebvre boy in self-defense."

"Well, yeah, but technically I was also breaking the law trying to protect that Blue-Green Mélangé. Even if Arnaud's death was an accident, I'd like to make some sort of gesture."

Gaspard nodded. "How does a thousand cuivres sound?"

"Make it ten." Arnaud had several younger siblings. The Blue I'd given them would help, but the money would make certain their futures were taken care of.

"Anything else?"

"Yes, actually. A police officer named Sheri Dupont helped me out a while back and it might have gotten her in trouble."

"If it's the Green I'm thinking of, she was sentenced to five years for tranquilizing a fellow officer."

"That's her. From what I've seen, she's the best cop on the

force. I want her released from prison and made Chief of Police."

"We have already promoted Officer Terry to Chief."

Claude Terry? Not while I was king. "He can be Dupont's assistant, if she wants. But she will do a much better job."

"I'll inform Dom Gravois."

"Thank you. I guess I'll try to get some reading in before bed."

"Wonderful—you should have the entire day free tomorrow. The courtyard is a very peaceful spot. Personally, I prefer the view by the river."

"Behind the estate? I didn't know I could go back there."

"You can go anywhere in Télesphore as long as you take a guard with you." He smiled at me. Did he know about Véronique? Would he let me parade into the Red slums and advertise my relationship? I did need to have a talk with her and patch things up.

"Could I make a request?"

"Certainly."

But at that moment I realized I didn't want to share Véronique with anyone just yet. She was a very private person and letting the whole city know she was the king's girlfriend would bring much unwanted attention to her and her family. Not to mention I still hadn't done anything to fix her neighborhood. And according to Gaspard, the first step toward Red rights was a reading marathon. My trip to the Taudis would have to wait.

"I... um. I'd like Sébastien to accompany me to the riverbank tomorrow morning."

Gaspard's white eyebrows rose. "Le Capitaine is a very busy man. Is there any reason you'd prefer him?"

I glanced toward the corner where Zacharie stood listening. Couldn't he leave us alone for ten minutes?

"The big guy didn't look too happy with me as we left the cathedral this afternoon," I said in a low voice. "I figure if I'm going to convince the nation to support Red rights, I might as well start by convincing my own house." And it wouldn't hurt to make sure he'd forgiven me for making him look like a fool on multiple occasions.

"I will inform Sébastien of your request. Good luck with your studies and let me know when you're ready to begin practicing with the scepter."

After the old men left, I locked my door, glad to finally be alone. The last thing I felt like doing was opening that stinky book, so I turned on the jets in my whale-sized tub and soaked for a good thirty minutes. Or maybe it was forty-five. What's the point of being king if you can't enjoy a little luxury now and again?

It wasn't until I went to the sink to shave that I noticed something strange about the condensation on the mirror. Although the room was cooling quickly and the glass had almost cleared, I could make out several marks, as if someone had written something with a finger.

My insides lurched. Someone had been in my fanroom. I threw a towel around my waist and made a quick search of my chambers—under my bed, behind curtains—I even peeked into the hall.

"Can we help you with something, Your Grace?" one of the Green guards asked.

"Um, have you been here all day?"

"We can be if you like. The Chancellor told us it's only when you're in."

"No, you're fine. You didn't happen to see anyone coming in or out of here?"

"No 'sieur."

I thanked them and locked the door again.

Back at the sink, I let the hot water run until the steam again fogged the mirror. Five letters appeared.

G S c a r

What did that mean? Was GS an abbreviation? Maybe initials? Who did I know who's name started with a G? Gravois came to mind, but that was his last name. Same with Gouroux, one of my royal guards. Gaspard was the only first name I could think of that started with G—but his last name was Livius.

I definitely would've noticed if the writing had been there since I'd arrived last month. That meant the message was new —and it was for me.

My first impulse was to call Gaspard, but would he think I was being silly? I didn't want to seem paranoid. Besides, whoever had written it obviously didn't want me to let anyone else know, or they wouldn't have been so mysterious—and cryptic. GS car? What was the point of leaving a secret message if I had no idea what it meant? Unless my guards were in on it, the writer must have sneaked into my room earlier, possibly during the council meeting.

GS car. Maybe one of the servants had a crush and wanted me to meet her near a car. Too bad I didn't speak acronyms.

I decided to wait and see if there was another less enigmatic note. Hopefully they'd use entire words next time.

In the morning I met up with Sébastien. With hardly a word, he led me though a part of the estate I'd not yet seen. I made a point to watch the servants as we walked, in particular the young females. Maybe GS would catch my eye and wink.

By the time we'd made it outside to the river, however, my step had lost its pep. Not only had no one winked at me, but most of the looks directed at me had been barely-concealed frowns. This was new. Word must have spread about my plan to equalize fires. Wouldn't the Greens be happy about that? Of course, there were a lot more Reds than any other shade. Equalization would increase the competition ten-fold.

With a sinking feeling, I thought of something else. What if that message had been a threat?

Sébastien wasn't any friendlier than the rest of the staff.

He deposited me on the grass with my book and stood next to a tree, as if he felt uncomfortable without some sort of cover.

I'd give him a few minutes before I started in with my questions—no sense in rushing things. I lay back on the damp earth and opened the Scepter Guide—or the Bulletproof Bible, as I'd begun to think of it.

The first two hundred or so pages seemed to be about the history of light manipulators and how they were thought to have a mystical connection with time itself. Yawn.

Maybe I'd start with section two—How to Prepare Your Mind in Order to Utilize a Manipulator. Yeah, right.

Section three was labeled Proper Care and Maintenance of Your Manipulator—eighty-three pages long. I skipped that part too.

The title of section four was Utilizing Your Manipulator. Finally, the good stuff. I scanned the content list.

Firelock

Flare

Illusion

Projection

Celestial Burning

Sacred Song

Why did I feel as if I should be in someone's basement dressed like a wizard?

I set the book on the grass and watched the water. I could see why Gaspard liked it out here. The sound of the river mixed with bird chatter made me sleepy.

A chorus of yips and growls startled me out of my trance.

I'd almost forgotten about Gaspard's enormous white badger hounds. From the disturbing sounds coming from the pens, I figured it was feeding time. Sébastien didn't react to the noise. He peered through the tree branches, shifting his weight too often to be natural. He was probably wondering why he was out here babysitting.

"Are you married?" I asked.

It took him a moment to answer. "I was, Your Grace."

"Oh." It didn't feel right to ask whether she was dead or simply didn't want to be with him anymore.

I glanced at the book. That first "spell" sounded a little less nerdy than the others. I read the summary.

FIRELOCK—When properly performed, this skill secures the manipulator to the user's fire in order to prevent it being wrested from the user's grip or otherwise coming loose due to poor dexterity.

Great. It was going to teach me how to hold my stick. Somehow I doubted that was going to impress the citizens of Télesphore.

I turned back to Sébastien. "Do you have any kids?"

"I have a son."

Oh, yeah—adisa's boyfriend. The two of them had pulled me out of the river at an opportune moment. I could never remember his name, though—Ellie something. I was pretty sure Sébastien didn't know about his son's late night rescue, and I didn't intend to enlighten him.

"How old is he?" I asked casually. "What's his name?"

"Twenty. His name is Eloi."

That's right. Eloi. Like Ellie with an "oh" in the middle. "So he's been classified. What does he do?"

"He's also a guard here."

"Nice, I hope I get to meet him."

"As there are only nineteen royal guards and you happen to be king, I imagine you will."

I gave him a stiff smile and went back to my book. The abilities appeared to be listed in order of difficulty, so I skipped to the last one.

SACRED SONG—The only physically profound and permanent facet of manipulating light lies in the ability to produce auditory perfection. Such an endeavor shall only be undertaken by one seraphic soul prepared to see heaven and nothing more. In direst of need, an act of violence will end the perfection and begin another.

Releasing the song shall annihilate all injustice, pain, and hatred on the planet until such time as the chosen trio spread new life and law.

Annihilate all injustice, pain and hatred. That would be some trick—sounded like a deadly plague. I turned to the page indicated, only to find the entire section missing. Apparently, someone took it home to work on it.

I glanced at Sébastien. He looked more bored than angry now.

"Why does Zacharie follow Gaspard around all day?"

"He is the Chancellor's most trusted servant."

"What does he do?"

"That is Monsieur Livius's business."

Of course it was. "What exactly does a Chancellor do?"

"He acts as an adviser until you wish to release or replace him."

I brushed grass off my slacks. "I don't think I'll do that. He's the only one around here that knows what he's doing."

"I couldn't agree more."

I ignored his jibe and turned back to the skills list. The summary for Flare said it created a bright flash that disoriented enemies, leaving them momentarily blinded. That sounded kind of cool. At least it was something that might come in useful—unless that section was missing too. I turned to the back. It was there but spanned nearly forty pages of tiny text. On top of that I had trouble understanding the older language—many of the words I couldn't even pronounce. Maybe I should have asked for Gaspard's help right off.

I started to close the book and a section fell open. Nestled between the pages was a frail bone broken in two. Was it a chicken rib? Must have been a late night studying for Gaspard. But there was no grease on the pages. The bone was dry. And what are the chances he'd drop it accidentally at the start of a new section. Could it have been a bookmark of sorts? Rather useless since you couldn't even see it except for a few pages away.

...Unless that was the whole point.

I began reading, but it was more boring stuff about how the mind is connected to the fire on a spiritual level.

The only thing of interest I found on the page was two lines of elegant blue script written in the margin.

Proximity is key

100m from fire's owner

Was that Gaspard's handwriting? Or had someone written me another obscure note?

Yup—still had no idea what they were trying to say to me.

Although something about the phrase "fire's owner" bothered me. Why would you have to specify such a thing? Your fire never got farther away from you than your arm. So what's all this hundred meters business? It almost sounded like they were referring to snuffing—the act of removing someone's fire for one's own use. But not only was that against the law, it was impossible. No one had ever kept someone's fire burning after it had been severed.

"Thanks for nothing, GS," I said.

Sébastien glanced at me long enough to ascertain that I wasn't speaking to him, then went back to gazing intently at the landscape.

I shut the guide and rubbed my forehead. My hands were constantly sweaty now, thanks to the gloves I hardly ever removed. I pulled them off and went to wash in the water. Sébastien watched me closely as if worried he'd have to jump in and save me.

"Why don't they let Reds swim in Green pools?"

"The Reds have the river," Sébastien replied, his voice cold.

"The river is too dangerous to swim in."

"I guess that's why none of them can swim."

"Some of them can. I've been to the tin mines."

For the first time, Sébastien seemed surprised. "How did you—" Then he remembered who he was talking to.

"Don't worry. I like caviar as much as the next guy, but there's got to be a better way to warm up those ponds. Making the Reds swim in that ice water is torture."

Sébastien didn't respond, but I noticed the corners of his mouth tighten.

Maybe a little flattery to grease the gears...

"I have to say, of all the people hunting me last month, you were the MVP."

No reaction.

"The Chancellor is lucky to have you—or I guess it's me that's lucky now."

He did a quick little eyebrow raise that I couldn't decipher. But at least he wasn't scowling now.

"Sorry about all that, by the way," I continued. "I know you were just doing your job and I didn't make it easy for you. Well, I supposed you were trying to—"

Clearly, I was no good at this flattery stuff. Better paint while the brush was wet.

"You heard my plan in the council meeting. Do you think I'm being pig-headed and naïve?"

"It's not my business."

"I want to know what you think." So I can change your mind.

"With all due respect, I value my position too highly to jeopardize it by speaking my inconsequential opinion."

I nodded. "You've probably been a guard longer than I've been alive. I'd say your opinion would be very pertinent."

He didn't respond. As far as I could tell he wasn't even breathing.

"I need all the advice I can get," I continued. "Even if I don't agree with your input, I'll consider it. And I promise nothing bad will happen to you if I don't like what you have to say."

Sébastien sighed through his nose. "There are those who think you an arrogant, ignorant idealist with no other qualification to rule besides a conveniently white fire, which you obviously stumbled upon accidentally. Others still hold you responsible for that Lefebvre boy's death."

I suppressed the urge to explain myself. "Would you be among those?"

"If it's all the same to you, Your Royal Highness, I do a lot better at guarding when I'm not distracted."

"Of course. I'd hate for some renegade anti-monarchist to come flying out of the river with a knife."

A flare of Sébastien's nostrils was the only indication that I'd angered him. "Some of us take our duties seriously," he said. "I trust there will be nothing more."

It wasn't a question. He was through talking to me. He took a few steps toward the river as if scanning the trees for mercenaries.

I went back to the Bulletproof Bible but was too frustrated to read. So much for convincing my own house. If all Télesphorians were this opposed to desegregation, no amount of flashing bright lights was going to convince them otherwise. I was just about to give Sébastien another piece of my mind when I felt a drop of rain. I doubted Gaspard would appreciate me getting his book rusty, so we went back inside. Sébastien and I were both glad to say goodbye.

That afternoon I told Gaspard about missing my family's trip. I was pleased that he recognized my sacrifice. He assured me that once things quieted down he would organize a royal fishing expedition I'd never forget.

The talk of fishing reminded me of my best friend. Dad had taken me and Marin out on several occasions. Marin who last I heard was still in therapy to deal with his post-traumatic stress.

"Why is Sergent Whisnant still head of the *L'armée du Roi*?"

Gaspard finished his letter to the Dom of Medicine and pulled it from the typewriter. "Le Sergent Whisnant has led the Royal Soldiers for years."

"He tortured my best friend."

Gaspard closed his eyes. "The Faringoule boy," he said in a sad voice. "I heard about that, but I didn't realize Whisnant was party to it."

I dripped wax all over the document I was trying to seal. "He's not a good person. He shouldn't be leading a choir, let a lone an army of trained soldiers."

Gaspard nodded, his clear blue eyes now open and staring intently into mine. "If what you say is true, he ought to be in prison with the ex-chief."

"Show me where to sign."

"Therein lies the problem," Gaspard said. "Currently the head of law enforcement makes those decisions—and he hasn't exactly warmed up to you yet."

"If Gravois would execute his own grandson to make a point, I'm sure I won't be able to convince him to do anything."

Gaspard furrowed his eyebrows. "Are you speaking of Aro Loup?"

"Yes." Seriously? How could Gaspard forget Aro? The kid had ruined my life to make a few bucks on a rugby game.

"How do I get Gravois out of the council?" I asked. "Him and his little sidekick."

"I've been trying for years. Unfortunately he owns most of Hameau Vert and has several influential family members. As for Whisnant, the sergent is something of a local hero. Remember last autumn when he caught those barrier jumpers?"

I nodded. The story had seemed exciting at the time, but now I realized why it had made Granny Jade sick. "He pulled those women out of the tree at Blue Garden, then tranq'ed them while they swam across the pond." If I remembered right, two of them drowned—the other broke her neck from the fall.

"He gets results," Gaspard said with a note of disgust in his voice. "Makes the Blues feel safer in their homes."

"Well, it sounds like I'm going to start a civil war whatever I do, so I might as well get it over with and dissolve the Dominateur."

"And have Gravois murder you in your sleep? No. The only way you're going to pull Télesphore out of his grasp is to become the White King of Legends and wield light as your weapon."

"You mean like temporarily blind them for a few seconds? What good will that do?"

Zacharie grunted, but Gaspard ignored him. "My child, if you had any idea what that scepter is capable of it would haunt your dreams day and night."

I'm not sure why I didn't ask Gaspard right then about training—probably too proud to admit I couldn't do it on my own.

"Whisnant betrayed all of Télesphore when he tortured your friend," Gaspard said. "I swear to you, Bruno—he and Gravois will pay for their atrocities soon enough. And the one to hold him accountable must be you."

For the rest of the day I studied in my room, periodically checking the window. As soon as the rain let up I was planning to take a group of guards and visit the Taudis. If Gaspard insisted, I suppose I could wait until dark, but I wasn't too concerned about secrecy anymore. I needed to tell Véronique everything that was going on with the Dominateur and Gaspard. And while I was there she could probably explain the manipulator instructions to me with no problem.

The hard part would be sneaking the Bulletproof Bible out with me.

It continued to rain all that night. In the morning it was coming down even harder. On the third day, I awoke to the sound of a waterfall outside my window.

After four days of nonstop deluge, I decided I was going to visit her anyway. I'd just have to wrap Gaspard's book up to keep it dry.

I determined to tell Gaspard my decision at dinner that night. Even if the entire guard had to run behind the glass car in the rain, I was going to see my girlfriend.

I was already seated at the table when Gaspard and Zacharie came into the dining room. Outside the front windows, branches flailed in surrender to the storm.

"Ah," said Gaspard with a grin. "Always punctual on caviar night."

"There is something I needed to tell you."

"By all means." He sat down and turned to Zacharie. "Water, please."

The robed old man removed a glass pitcher from a stand and filled Gaspard's cup. Then he moved to mine. I'd never been so close to him. Typically, I poured my own water. The thinness of his arm surprised me, and just as he finished pouring I noticed something else that sent a chill up my back. A thick scar stretched across his light wrist as if he'd tried to take his own life.

"What was it you wanted to tell me?" Gaspard said.

I couldn't answer—I'd just had a horrible thought. What if the note wasn't GS car but G Scar? What was Zacharie's last name?

"Bruno?"

"Sorry." I opened my napkin to lay it on my lap. A tiny piece of brown paper fluttered onto my plate.

"What was that?" Gaspard asked.

Once again, I was unable to answer. This time I was staring at Gaspard's light hand as he pointed at my plate. A thin scar circled his wrist. How had I not noticed that before? Had he always kept his wrists covered with his robe sleeves? Apart from the thickness, the scar was almost identical to Zacharie's. Were they in some sort of masochistic cult together? It was almost like the hand had been removed then reattached.

G Scar.

Gaspard's scar. Had Gaspard and his servant somehow stolen two blue fires? What shade had they been before? No, that was impossible. They would both be dead. Unless they had figured out a way to keep it from going out.

"Wake up, my boy," Gaspard said with a strange smile. "Something fell onto your plate. Is it a note?"

I picked up the tiny brown square of cardboard and flipped it over. At first I thought it was blank—but then I saw the single word scratched onto the surface.

ESCAPE

CHAPTER SIX

POISON

My mind went blank. I didn't know what to say or whom to trust. One thing was certain—Gaspard wasn't telling me everything. Was he a Red masquerading as a Blue in order to start a revolution? That would explain his unorthodox ideas about equality. But why would he lie to me? Wasn't I on his side? And how had he managed to keep someone else's fire burning after they had died? Was that why someone was trying to warn me about him? Until I answered some of these questions I figured my best defense was to play dumb.

I hmm'd in a mildly surprised way and handed Gaspard the note. He looked at the tiny piece of cardboard then back at me.

"Do you know what this is about?"

I shrugged. "Maybe one of the servants doesn't like my radical ideas and is trying to scare me away."

"Could be." Gaspard set the note on the table and pushed his white hair behind his ears.

I couldn't stand it anymore. I had to ask. "Where did you get that scar around your wrist?"

Gaspard extended his fire and traced the line with a vague smile. "Zacharie and I were childhood friends. We'd heard about the white sea monster that lived in the tin mines."

"Mére Blanche."

Gaspard chuckled. "I see her legend lives on. We sneaked in one night to see her but found it full of men who'd had too much to drink. They overpowered us and tried to remove our light hands. To this day I'm not sure if they were trying to steal them for themselves, or simply kill us."

"How long ago was that? What happened to the Reds?" It couldn't have been Véronique's dad, could it? He would've been too young.

Gaspard smiled. "You assume it was Reds that attacked me."

"It wasn't?"

"That was back when the old King took an interest in his caviar production. The men who attacked Zacharie and me were two royal soldiers."

"They were Greens?"

Gaspard nodded. "It was the Red salter women who came to our aid. They slaughtered the soldiers and fed them to Mére Blanche. I've been fighting for Reds ever since. The big fish also holds a special place in my heart."

I shuddered. "That thing gives me the creeps. You know it tried to eat my fire? It must be drawn to white light or something because I seriously thought it was gonna swallow me whole."

Gaspard sniffed. "Interesting. She is remarkably intelligent. Perhaps it was her way of saying hello to the new king."

"Whatever her intention, I've lost my fondness for golden caviar." I laughed, but it morphed into a sort of sob. I realized my head was throbbing. Perhaps from the anxiety of not knowing whom I could trust. Yet, somehow I knew I could trust Gaspard.

"There was another note on my mirror. I think it said something about your scar. Who could be trying to turn me against you?"

Gaspard sighed. "I have many enemies. I've long suspected Gravois of working against me. It's possible some of my staff are working for him."

"Then we're not safe," I said. "We should—"

Gaspard put a wrinkled hand on mine. "Although I can't speak for the rest of the staff, I trust each of the Royal Guards explicitly. You don't need to worry about your safety."

"I'm worried about you."

A look of surprise passed over Gaspard's face, then he pressed his fire against my ear. A low hum filled my senses. My first instinct was to pull back, but I forced myself to hold still. I closed my eyes and leaned into the warmth. Only then did I realize how nice it felt. Gaspard possessed a wisdom that I'd never have. If anyone were to be king it should have been him. All he needed was the power behind the throne and he could have fixed Télesphore years ago.

"Let me show you something," Gaspard said.

He dropped his hand and my face felt oddly cold.

Gaspard motioned a young guard over, borrowed his gun, and removed a tiny black dart. "Your royal protectors do not carry tranqulizers like the police or even charge gloves like the soldiers. Have you seen these before? They're filled with anoxium pentathol."

"Plague darts," I said. "My dad told me about a patient that died from ano-pent poisoning. It wasn't pretty."

"Your father is right," Gaspard said. "As the chemical spreads from the puncture wound it hardens and blackens the epidermis, making it incredibly painful to move."

Was he saying this to reassure me? Why was he so certain his guards wouldn't turn on him? Sébastien obviously didn't feel the same way about Reds as Gaspard did.

"When the poison reaches their fire, they eventually die. But it moves very slowly along the skin rather than through the bloodstream."

"Sébastien hates me."

"I trust Sébastien with my life—and with yours. If anyone tries to harm you, a few ano-pent darts will incapacitate them. Meanwhile, we'll have plenty of time to ask questions. No need for other methods of interrogation. Then, if we decide to keep them alive, we take them to the hospital to get their system cleaned out. Either way they aren't a threat to anybody."

The caviar and buttered toast arrived, but for the first time in my life I wasn't hungry.

"I promise you are safe here, Bruno."

"Thank you." I really wanted to believe him. I really wanted to trust his judgment—but what if he was as naive as I had been? I was going to have to keep an eye out for him—and I certainly wouldn't be able to leave him alone and run off to the Taudis. Not with Gravois's infiltrators possibly roaming the Estate.

Gaspard returned the guard's gun and unrolled his napkin. He made a big show of checking for hidden notes.

I smiled halfheartedly.

Gaspard watched me for a moment, then called one of the head servants over. "Please have a word with the young lady who set the places. Threats to the King will not be tolerated. You may dock her two days pay."

"No, it's okay," I said. "Don't dock her."

Gaspard looked at me. "As you wish."

After a moment of awkward silence, we both began eating.

"How are your studies coming?"

"I'm pretty far into the guide," I said, glad he'd forgotten about my announcement.

"Have you read about the four scepters?"

I pretended to think and then shook my head.

"There were originally four manipulators. Each one was given to a different priest of the Quintum."

"What's the Quintum?"

"It means The Fifth. As far as we can tell, it was an ancient religion founded by Blues."

"So where are the other three scepters?"

"Probably lost. Melted down into jewelry, buried under volcanic ash, or dropped into the ocean. For at least eight hundred years Télesphore has possessed the only remaining manipulator."

And I'm the only one that can use it. No pressure.

Lightning flashed outside. I glanced at the window. The storm seemed as bad as ever. When I turned back, Sébastien stood next to us.

"Apologies for interrupting your dinner," he said, apparently speaking to both me and Gaspard. "Police Chief Dupont has informed me the river is flooding."

Gaspard put down his fork. "How much damage so far?"

"Taudis Rouge is taking the brunt of it. But the police are having difficulty keeping the rabble on their side. They're trying to get over the bridge to higher ground at the park. The officers are directing them to the shelter."

"Good."

"Good?" I said. "Why can't they cross the bridge? It's an emergency."

Gaspard looked at me. "We built the shelter for just such an occasion. It's the highest point in the Taudis and big enough to fit several thousand."

"I still can't see why—"

"We are keeping Reds from the park for their own safety," Gaspard said. "There is no telling what Blues and Greens would do to get them out. People's prejudices are strong."

"You say that as if Sébastien isn't standing right here. He hates Reds. Why do you think we can trust him?"

Sébastien's expression darkened.

Good, let him be annoyed. Maybe I could provoke him into revealing his true colors.

"What if they're trapped by the water? They can't swim. Are you at least sending boats to help them get to the shelter?"

"Of course they are," Gaspard said.

"Mm, actually," Sébastien said, "the boats are being used by police to sandbag the park perimeter. If the river gets any higher, the Hameau Vert buildings could be in danger."

Gaspard nodded. "Have the officers take a few of the boats to help Reds get to shelter."

"Send all the boats," I said. "You don't need boats to make a sandbag wall. Get the Greens out there to protect their own houses. The officers' priority should be those in immediate danger."

Sébastien looked at Gaspard, waiting.

"Do as he says," Gaspard said.

Something inside me snapped. "Why does he have to be the one to give you permission?" I said to Sébastien. "Isn't it enough that I said it? Do I inspire so little confidence in you? Am I king or am I not?"

Sébastien opened his mouth, but Gaspard beat him to it.

"On behalf of the staff, I apologize. It is simply an issue of habit, Bruno. I've run the affairs for so long—they've grown... accustomed to me. They will come around, but it might take some time."

"I'm sorry. It's been a stressful few days. I just don't want to be the cause of any Télesphorian deaths—Red or otherwise."

Sébastien nodded, his expression unreadable. "I will see to the boats," he said with a bow.

After he'd gone, Gaspard and I finished our dinner in silence. I ate mechanically, not tasting a thing. It was a shame, considering someone probably lost their fingers to get me these fish eggs.

The mines! It was under the river. Was that flooding too? Would they be able to get everyone out with that rickety old elevator? I would have to send someone to check on Véronique immediately.

I really hoped she wasn't one of those trying to get across the bridge. Black, I could smack those stupid Greens. It'll be fifty years before small-minded people finally start treating their neighbors with dignity—still stuck on their shade. Why did there have to be colors at all? Why couldn't we all just be Blue or Green... or White.

My fork clattered to the floor.

"Is something wrong?" Gaspard asked.

I stared straight ahead, my heart drowning out the rain on the window. "Fine." In fact, I was ecstatic. I knew how to bring down the color barriers—and all it would take was a single equation.

Blue plus green plus red equals white.

I wasn't sure exactly how it worked, or if it was possible for Greens and Reds to become White the same way, but at the very least, Blues would be spreading their shade to anyone they could. The entire city would become Mélangé, and sooner or later Blues would become pure White. And I had a feeling the Greens and Reds could become White just as easily.

By telling my secret I was probably forfeiting my right to the throne. The minute there were more Whites, they'd have to have some sort of vote to pick the most qualified candidate. Which certainly wouldn't be a sixteen-year-old boy.

It made me a little sad to think about giving up my chance to improve the country—but what better way to do it than to destroy decades of prejudice with a single announcement? The citizens of Télesphore would need each other—and the more they served each other, the more they'd become alike.

"Bruno, are you feeling all right?"

"You remember I had something to tell you?"

"Of course."

"I've been king for almost two months. I think it's time I addressed the country."

Gaspard nodded slowly. "What did you have in mind to say?"

"Don't worry, I won't get into my political views or pardon any more prisoners. I just wanted to introduce myself—and now with this flooding, I can assure them we're doing everything we can."

"A wonderful idea. The Rainbow Festival is scheduled for early next month. Maybe you could also—"

"I'd like to speak to them tomorrow. I feel like I've forgotten why I'm doing this. I think this will help."

Gaspard looked at me for what seemed like forever. "I'll tell you what. Give me twenty-four hours to spread the word and on Saturday morning I'll have the entire city in the front courtyard ready to welcome you."

"Thank you, Gaspard. I know I've been a pain."

"Honestly I think Télesphore could do a lot worse than Bruno Nazaire."

As soon as Gaspard left the banquet hall with Zacharie in tow, I approached the young guard whose gun we had inspected. He looked to be in his early twenties and he shared Sébastien's strong chin and sandy hair.

"Are you Eloi?"

The guard seemed surprised and flattered. He nodded.

I had a lot to say to him. He'd anonymously saved my life on more than one occasion, but there was no time. "Can you do something for me?"

"Yes, 'sieur."

Why couldn't his dad be this agreeable? "Do you know how to get into the tin mines?"

He shook his head—then seemed to remember himself

and repeated, "No, 'sieur."

I quickly explained how to find the elevator. "Make sure the workers are safe. Especially Véronique DeGrave. Ask around and make sure she's safe. If you can't find her check at the shelter. Make sure her and her family are okay."

He glanced around, as if he didn't know what to say.

"I know your father probably wouldn't approve, but we don't have to tell him. At any rate, you won't be punished for obeying a royal order."

Again, Eloi nodded. This time he was grinning.

I looked for a napkin to write her name on before I realized I didn't even have a pen.

I had him repeat the name several times, and he assured me he would find the dark-haired girl named Véronique. Then he disappeared out the servant entrance.

Back in my room, I thought about studying the Bulletproof Bible but decided it could wait. I needed to prepare my speech for Saturday.

I worked on it all that evening, then showered. The writing on the mirror hadn't changed. Too bad, I could have used a little more information about who I was supposed to be running from and why. I wiped the glass clean so it wouldn't get any of the servants in trouble.

The next morning I awoke to the eye shining through my window—about time. I dressed and hurried down to breakfast. Halfway through my chocolate pancakes, I heard Sébastien shouting outside. I followed the sound of his swearing. I reached the street in front of the Green Barracks in time to see Sébastien punch a young man in the face. It was Eloi.

"Sébastien," I shouted. "I will not tolerate the abuse of my staff. I don't care if he is your son."

At the sound of my voice, the nearby guards sprang to attention.

Sébastien turned his poisonous expression on me. "With all due respect—"

"You speak of respect, so why not show it? To me, to your son—to those of us that have to witness your tantrum."

Sébastien's face glowed with rage. He stepped toward me and in the same movement, lifted his hand.

"No!" Four guards tackled him.

Eloi stood against the wall, nose and lip bleeding.

"I gave Eloi a command," I said. "He had no choice but to fulfill my request. If you have a problem, take it up with me."

Eloi's head snapped up as if he'd just remembered his mission. "They are well, Your Grace—all of them."

Véronique was safe. Until I felt the relief flood me, I hadn't realized how worried I'd been. "Thank you."

Sébastien threw off the guards and got to his feet. His massive frame loomed over me. "The next time you have a request, you come to me. I will deploy my guards as I see fit."

"Fine. But if I hear of you striking another human being for whatever reason, you'll be looking for another career."

It took me a few hours to calm down after that incident. By mid-afternoon I was finally able to relax and work on my speech again. I finished sometime after dinner. Before bed I picked out my clothes for the morning and hung them on my door handle.

I couldn't sleep. I got up and double-checked that the door and windows were all locked—two Royal Guards at my door.

Still, it wasn't until I wedged a chair under the doorknob that I was able to relax. Finally, I drifted off.

A noise awakened me.

I had no idea what time it was, but I was too disoriented to register the significance of the sound. I rolled over and went back to sleep.

When I awoke, the chair was still wedged against the door, but my clothes lay on the floor. Had someone tried to get into my room last night?

Sounds of a gathering crowd filtered through my window, distracting me from my paranoia. I got out of bed and peeked through the curtains. The public address was set for ten. It was only seven-thirty and the courtyard and front gardens were already half-full.

I dressed but was too nervous to go down for breakfast. Instead I stayed in my room and tried to memorize my speech.

By nine, every square foot of the front grounds was sardine-packed with people, and I gave up hope of memorizing anything. I was having trouble just holding the paper still enough to read it. What if I was making a mistake? Dad had warned me repeatedly to keep the secret to myself.

For the next forty-five minutes I tried to call my family —there was no answer. Weren't they back from their trip? Or maybe they were already standing outside, waiting to hear their boy address the nation.

Ten minutes to ten, Sébastien came to collect me.

"I think someone tried to get into my room last night."

"Impossible. Two of my best were on duty."

Somehow that didn't make me feel better.

The hallways were completely deserted. The entire staff must be outside too. Sébastien led me to an elevator with a polished wood interior and pushed the button marked penthouse. This was my first time in the elevator. I'd heard a servant say it was the only way to get to the upper balcony of the estate. As the doors opened onto the fourth floor, I noticed another button marked B.

"I didn't know we had a basement."

"We rarely use the basement," Gaspard said from just outside the elevator. "It's mainly a medical wing."

I pretended to find that interesting.

The Chancellor wore a dark blue suit with his white hair pulled back in a ponytail. The only other person in the room was Zacharie, who for some reason was sitting in a chair facing the wall. Was he in time out? What was going on?

"I think your subjects are getting restless," Gaspard said with a smile. "Wait here with Sébastien while I make an introduction."

He passed through a blue velvet curtain out onto the balcony. The sound of ten thousand people cheering nearly made me wet my pants.

I took a deep breath. I was going to be fine. I'd just read my paper into the microphone and wave. It would be easy.

"Brothers and Sisters of Télesphore," Gaspard's voice echoed across the grounds. "I'm afraid I have terrible news."

I looked up from my speech. What?

"This morning we found the king's chamber empty except for this note."

I looked at Sébastien. "What is he doing?" I moved toward the balcony, but Sébastien stepped in front of me.

"Just wait. He wanted you to hear this."

Who? Gaspard? Was this some kind of a practical joke? Was he trying to soften up the crowd for me?

"Citizens of Télesphore," Gaspard said slowly as if reading. "The responsibility you've given me is too great. I know that continuing to pretend I can do this will only hurt the nation I love so much. By the time you read this, I will already be on a ship to the mainland."

A fury like I'd never known filled me and threatened to tear me open. I sprinted past Sébastien and dove toward the curtain. "I'll kill that toilet-pouch, son of—"

Sébastien caught me from behind and slapped a hand over my mouth. I struggled to free myself, but the guard didn't even seem to feel my teeth biting down on his skin.

"To my friends and family," Gaspard continued. "I'm sure you realize why I can't say goodbye in person. I'm sorry I let you down. I hope one day to earn your forgiveness. Signed, Bruno."

I jerked my head back and connected with Sébastien's face, but he only held me tighter.

"I too, am sorry," Gaspard said from the other side of the curtain. "Of course, we will make every effort to find our king, but I believe if he truly does not wish to be found, any attempts to bring him back will be futile."

I kicked backward into Sébastien's knee, but this time he was ready for me and dodged. His grip grew so tight I was unable to breathe.

"This is a great blow to our nation," Gaspard continued. "But we will forge on. Until a new White king appears, we will continue as we always have. We ask for your patience as I attempt to get the affairs of the country back in order. Thank you, and may the Créateur smile on our island home!"

There was no applause. The curtain parted and Gaspard appeared. "Why is he not sedated? Take him to the basement. Have Émile begin the preparations."

Émile? Why did that name sound familiar?

I wiggled my head until I was able to get a hold of Sébastien's finger with my teeth. I bit down hard.

He swore and suddenly my mouth was free.

"That story about Reds saving you was a lie, wasn't it? You're probably the one who cut up the trespassers and fed them to—"

Gaspard backhanded me across the face. "Speak to me again, and I'll have Dr. Talbot cut out your tongue."

Now I remember where I'd heard the name Émile. He was the father of one of my classmates. Orie had often mentioned how he was one of the best plastic surgeons in the country and did most of the work for the Commissaire himself. I never wondered what that meant.

Until now.

My eyes watered, but it wasn't from my throbbing cheek. It wasn't even that my crown had been ripped off my head. The thing that nearly split me in two was the hatred in Gaspard's face. That same face that had encouraged me with paternal affection.

The thought that I'd started thinking of him as a grandfather made me physically ill. I should have listened to the note. I should have escaped. But I never would've believed it. What human being could be capable of such calculating cruelty?

Sébastien pulled a rag out of his suit pocket. I caught a whiff of chemicals.

"Lord Livius," Sébastien said, "are you sure this is necessary?"

"You of all people know why it must be done," Gaspard said. "Think of your son."

Sébastien hesitated only a moment before pressing the rag to my mouth. Stars formed at the edge of my vision. Before the blackness rushed up to take me, I heard Gaspard say one last thing.

"If I'm not down in five minutes, tell Émile to wait. I want to be there when he takes off the hand."

CHAPTER SEVEN

BLACK

I awoke in darkness. I lay on a hard surface, wearing only briefs and an undershirt. My brain pressed on the inside of my skull like it was trying to break free, and my entire light arm ached.

Light.

Where was my light? Never in my life had I experienced dark like this. I'd always had my fire. And now Gaspard had taken it. But why was I still alive?

With my good hand I felt down my arm. My light hand was still there. But for some reason it wouldn't move. The fingers lay curled in my palm like a dead spider. What had he done to my fire? What was I going to do with two dark palms?

I felt moisture on my face. Why did my eyes burn so badly? I rubbed at them, but it only made it worse. I needed to find a sink and wash them out.

I pushed myself up on one elbow. My temples throbbed with every beat of my pulse. For a long moment I had to rest my head on my arm, but then I carefully stood. My head hit the ceiling before I was fully erect. Was I underground? Not the faintest glimmer of light penetrated the darkness.

I pried up my useless fingers and felt the shape of my fire. It hurt like black itself, but everything seemed intact. I could even feel the slight vibration. So where was the light? Had Gaspard found a way to disable the fire without killing the rest of the body?

I needed to find a light switch so I could examine my hand. Not to mention get some water. My eyes felt like they were burning out of my head.

I found a wall and felt my way around the room. My balance was off. Something wasn't right with my body. My muscles felt strange and weak and my stomach was like a tiny brick in the pit of my belly. How long had I been out? It felt like it could have been days, or weeks.

My fingers touched a familiar shape on the wall. I clicked the light switch a few times. Nothing happened. Next to it I found a door handle—locked.

"Hello?" My voice came out as a hoarse whisper. "Can anybody hear me?" I banged on the cold metal door with both fists. Bad idea. The pain in my light hand jumped in intensity and the floor tilted under my feet. If I didn't lie down, I was going to pass out.

I stumbled toward the center of the room, searching for a table or chair to hold onto. My foot hit something that sounded like a bucket. A sudden heat brushed my face. I jerked back. What had touched me? Was someone in the room?

"Hello?"

No one answered. I reached into the darkness and felt what had burned my cheek. Hanging from the ceiling by a wire, was an artificial-light bulb. Had someone turned it off right before I awoke?

I touched the bulb again. It was hot—not the just-turned-off kind of hot, either.

But if it was on, that meant...

"No." I dropped to my knees. "No. No."

In a way, it was a relief to know my fire was still shining.

But what difference did it make?

I couldn't see it.

Another wave of dizziness washed over me and I fell onto my elbow. How had Gaspard taken my vision? Why hadn't he just killed me? I almost wished he had.

A wave of cold washed through me. I lay down on the stone floor in an effort to stay conscious. It was no use.

Before I passed out, I felt someone lift my head and slide a pillow under my ear.

When I awoke again, I was lying on some sort of bedroll. My mind seemed clearer, and the pain in my light hand felt slightly less agonizing. Maybe I wouldn't bang it on the door this time.

I gingerly felt my fingers—still useless. I was tempted to lie there and feel sorry for myself, but I needed to get out of this room. Although I had no idea why Gaspard would want to keep me as a prisoner, I was not about to make it easy for him.

The thought of Gaspard made me furious and sick at once. He'd been manipulating me the whole time. And I bought it— despite all the warnings. Until the very end all I wanted was to make that man proud of me.

I could still picture his face when he slapped me. His mask had finally come off and I'd seen what lay underneath—contempt.

He must have hated me the moment I told him about my plan to help the lower shades. Or maybe it was before that—when I made the scepter shine at the classification ceremony.

Now that I was out of the picture there would be no reformation or new laws. Gaspard was back in control and Taudis Rouge would only grow worse.

I had failed Véronique and her family.

I had failed Télesphore.

No.

Not yet. I could get out of here.

Maybe Gaspard thought blinding me would make escape impossible. That simply meant I had to prove him wrong. If I got to know my surroundings perfectly, sooner or later an opportunity would present itself. All I had to do was get outside the estate. I'd just have to get my message about white fire to one person.

One person and Télesphore would be saved.

A rustling startled me. I sat up. "Who's there?"

"Shhh," came a low voice.

"Who are you?" I said quietly.

A shuffling came toward me and I sprang to my feet—or at least that had been my intention. Instead, I lost my balance and fell against the wall.

A warm hand gripped my dark wrist. I pulled away.

The man made a soothing noise and again took my good hand. He pressed it to his face. I felt bristly hair and a wrinkled, sunken cheek—Zacharie.

I pulled back and punched him on the mouth. It wasn't nearly as satisfying as I'd hoped. My arm was so weak it felt like I'd tried to give him a high five.

I made my voice as menacing as possible. "You tell Gaspard to let me out, or I'll—"

Zacharie shushed me again.

"No I won't be quiet! What is going on? What did Gaspard do to my hand?"

Behind me, a key scraped in a lock. Before I'd heard the hinges squeak I was already diving toward the door.

I never made it. A heavy boot slammed into my stomach and sent me backward onto the floor. I clutched my abdomen, unable to draw breath.

"Your orders were to keep him quiet," a man's voice said —Sébastien. "Use the meds if you have to. He's awakened the Prince twice already."

From the other side of the room came a strange noise, like someone moaning and gargling at the same time. Was that coming from Zacharie?

"Lord Livius is not interested," Sébastien replied. "Do your job or I'll bind and gag you both."

I still wasn't fully recovered from the kick to the gut, but I managed to crawl toward Zacharie. I used his cloak to get to my feet and then as quickly as I could manage while breathing like an asthmatic, I wrapped my arm around Zacharie's tiny neck and pulled him into a headlock—but there was no force behind it. I had the energy, but my muscles wouldn't cooperate.

Hopefully, Sébastien couldn't tell the difference.

"Put your gun on the floor," I said.

Sébastien laughed.

"Do it now or I'll break his neck."

Something pricked my shoulder, and a cold liquid spread down my arm. I didn't even remember hitting the ground.

This time when I came to, I found myself on some sort of cot, with my hands and feet tied to the frame. My mouth ached from the cloth gag wedged between my teeth.

For a while, I struggled to pull free of my bonds but only succeeded in pulling an IV out of my arm. Shortly afterward, I felt another stabbing pain in my shoulder and fell into blackness.

The next time I awoke, I stayed perfectly still and tried to take in my surroundings. I was hungry but not as lightheaded as before. The IV must be feeding me. That meant I had probably been out for several days. Although my hands and feet were still tied, the gag had been loosened so I could close my mouth. I rubbed my cracked lips against the cloth.

My back hurt. I shifted my weight. Something didn't feel right in my below-the-belt region. After a moment of panic, I discovered I was hooked up to a catheter. I shuddered and once again wondered why Gaspard had bothered to keep me alive.

I could hear Zacharie moving around the room, but I remained still. The last thing I wanted was another trip to happy land.

For what seemed like days, I drifted in and out of sleep. I came close to asking for food a couple times but decided it was more important to stay alert and become aware of my surroundings. The key to escape would be patience.

Periodically, Zacharie made those strange gargling sounds. At first I thought he was speaking another language, but after a while I was able to recognize the rhythm and even catch a few words. He was speaking Téle—at least he was trying. Either he was born with some sort of serious speech impediment, or someone had cut out his tongue—and if his tongue had been mutilated, I had a good idea who was responsible.

After that I found it harder to hate the old man, knowing he'd been another of Gaspard's victims.

I wasn't sure how many days had passed when I woke up with Zacharie's hand over my mouth. My first thought was that he was trying to smother me, but then I realized I'd been screaming. Once I stopped struggling, Zacharie removed his hand. He said something in his garbled voice that I interpreted to mean, "You were dreaming."

The door creaked open. "What's going on in here?"

Zacharie spoke gibberish for a while. Sébastien must have understood because he walked toward me and removed my gag.

"The geezer says you've been on your best behavior."

I nodded.

"You gonna keep quiet?"

"Yes." My voice came out as a whisper.

"Not that screaming would help. You're two levels underground."

I licked my scaly lips. "Is there water?" It hurt to speak.

A wrinkled hand touched a cup to my face. I never knew anything so delicious.

"I'll untie you," Sébastien said, "but only if you stop diving for the door every time it opens."

I had only done it once, but I didn't correct him. Now was not the time to start an argument.

Sébastien tugged at my knots. "Even if you could get into the hall," he said conversationally, "there are three locked doors before you get to the stairs."

I could deal with locked doors. All I needed was the right moment to steal the keys. I would make Gaspard pay for what he had done to me. I would lead all of Télesphore against him.

Sébastien finished with the ropes and went on to my medical equipment. He could have been a little gentler removing the IV and catheter, but I was grateful to be free of the bed.

The moment I sat up, however, I could tell something wasn't right—even more than last time. My arms felt long and spindly, my chest oddly flat. Down my side I could feel each individual rib.

"How long have I been here?"

I rubbed at the loose skin of my belly and felt a vague sense of loss. Here I was, one-handed and blind, and yet what I missed most was my six-pack.

"It doesn't matter," Sébastien said. "What's important is for you to accept that this is your home for a while—might as well make it as pleasant as possible."

"Why didn't Gaspard kill me?"

"Lord Livius needs you."

"To work his stupid light stick?"

"No, the Prince will do that."

"Who's this Prince?" I said. "Am I not the rightful king?"

Sébastien's laugh pierced me through the center. "I forgot you can't see, so I'll take the liberty of describing your shade. It's turquoise."

"It can't be, I—"

"Yup, turquoise. And I was under the impression that only a White would sit on the throne. So much for your revolution of equality."

"But the Prince—"

"Once he's trained to use the scepter he'll be announced as the new king."

"What happened to my fire? Dr. Talbot couldn't have taken it out of my hand?"

"No, your fire's still in your hand. But your hand is now on the Prince's arm."

No. It was impossible. Once again I felt my light hand. This time I noticed medical tape on my wrist. I ripped off the bandages and traced the scar. It went all the way around. I felt the knuckles, the lifeless fingers—they were too small.

"This hand belongs to the Prince." I felt as if someone had taken my soul and replaced it with a cheap substitute.

"Lord Livius discovered the only way to steal a fire," Sébastien said, a note of pride in his voice. "It has to be exchanged. Cut off both hands and sew them back on before the lights go out. The only inconvenience is that you can't ever separate the fires."

"You mean…"

"For the past few months the Prince has been recovering

in the room directly above you. If you get more than a hundred yards from him, your fires will fade and eventually you'll both die."

I fell to the bed, suddenly hollow inside. It didn't matter how patient I was. It didn't matter if I ever got ahold of Sébastien's keys. If I ever left this house I would die and kill some unknown boy in the process.

As my hope for escape evaporated, I realized it had been the only thing keeping me together. The reality that I would never see my family again descended on me and for the first time since my grandpa died, I totally lost it.

Sébastien cleared his throat. "I tried to convince Lord Livius not to blind you, but he felt it was necessary."

I wished Sébastien would leave—but heard no door open or close. After a moment I was able to quiet my heaves.

"And I am sorry Talbot did such a sloppy job reattaching the bones and tendons." Sébastien's voice sounded different now. "Lord Livius insisted he focus on Aro."

My head snapped up and my grief gave way to fury. "Aro, the grandson of Dom Gravois?"

"That is a common misconception," Sébastien said. "Gravois is simply a friend of the family. Aro's grandfather is Gaspard."

CHAPTER EIGHT

KEEPING UP

T he bucket I kicked over on the first day turned out to be my toilet. I never thought I'd be comfortable vacating my bowels in front of a creepy old man, but losing your vision and your fire in the same day tends to rearrange your priorities.

Zacharie quickly became my eyes and my only friend. He helped me pick the moldy parts from my food and would wake me the second I started to cry out in my sleep. The nightmares weren't getting any better. Although I could never remember what I'd been screaming about, I had the feeling it was always the same thing.

Sébastien visited once a day to bring food and a clean bucket. The rest of the time I spent alone with Zacharie. At first, trying to understand his impaired speech gave me a headache—but then I learned it was easier to listen to the flow and rhythm of the whole phrase rather than try to pick out individual words.

After a few weeks, when our exchanges had grown into something resembling conversation, he suggested we begin physical therapy. I didn't see the point but agreed to try. Each morning Zacharie would work my crippled hand until I could no longer stand the pain. Then in the evenings before bed he'd drop a few coins on the stone floor and I'd try to pick them up. It took three days of this before I could move my fingers enough to pick up a single coin.

"Pahef," Zacharie said, which I understood as "progress."

I nodded. "Before long I'll be able to pick my nose."

The old man laughed, and the sound seemed unaffected by his lack of a tongue. It was a warm, low chuckle that made me strangely nostalgic. Had I known him somewhere before? It almost felt like he might have been one of my teachers in elementary school.

I sat on my cot. "Will you tell me how you ended up here?"

"Hehet?"

"Of course I'll keep it secret." Who was I going to tell?

And so the bearded man sat next to me on the bed and, in a soft voice, told me his story. He had to repeat himself often, since this required more vocabulary than our usual small talk, but I think I got the gist of it.

As a fire scientist, he'd researched genetics and why infants were only born with one of three colors. Unable to find funding or test subjects, he began experimenting with his own fire. What he learned was—unlike paint, the primary colors of light were red, green, and blue. And while any color could be derived from these, mixing the three together in equal portions resulted in a pure white light.

Zacharie's fire was powder blue when he realized the secret to becoming White, but he had no desire to be king. Instead of reacting with a few more Reds and Greens to complete the transformation, he showed his fire to one of his fellow scientists to get his opinion—a charismatic man named Gaspard Livius.

His colleague's reaction surprised Zacharie. Gaspard grew angry and demanded to know how Zacharie had done it. When Zacharie refused to share his research, Gaspard brought a chair down on his head.

Zacharie awoke the next day, locked in an underground

cell. His light hand was gone and had been replaced with Gaspard's blue fire. His fellow scientist, it turned out, had been doing his own research—but in a much darker vein. Gaspard had developed the first successful procedure to steal another's fire. Soon after the switch, Gaspard used his new shade and government connections to become Haut Commissaire of Télesphore.

Zacharie tried twice to escape. Before he was caught the second time, he managed to tell a cook what Gaspard had done. The Commissaire was not a merciful man. After killing the cook and cutting out Zacharie's tongue, Gaspard instructed a handful of guards to lock him away deep in the mountains.

Zacharie had only been gone a few hours when Gaspard realized his mistake. Without its original owner close by, Gaspard's fire was fading. By the time the Commissaire had caught up with Zacharie's group, both men were near death. And although they did eventually regain their strength, their fires never fully recovered.

"So, you're the real king," I said. "Or you would've been, if you'd kept going."

"No," Zacharie said in his strange language, "only scientist."

"Maybe you knew my grandpa," I said. "He studied fires, too. Big guy, probably three hundred pounds?"

Zacharie said nothing.

"It's funny because his name was also Zacha…" I trailed off, suddenly realizing why the man's laugh sounded so familiar.

"It can't be. You aren't my…"

Zacharie's breathing changed. I realized he was crying.

"You died in a chemical fire. I went to your funeral."

"Burned remains in casket belonged to cook."

I was finding it easier to understand him now. Maybe because I could almost hear the old grandpa underneath all the gargling sounds. I took a breath and slowly extended my dark hand. Zacharie grabbed it and pulled me into a weak embrace. I could feel his spine through his cloak. No wonder I hadn't recognized him. He was a shadow of the man he'd once been.

"Why didn't you say something before now?"

"Was ashamed."

"You have nothing to be ashamed of."

"My fault boy forced reaction with you."

"How was it your fault? Aro blackmailed some little kid so he could win his bet on my game. Baptiste came onto Blue Campus and tricked me into... how did you know about me getting painted?"

"Gaspard tortured for White secret."

"He tortured you? Why didn't you tell him? Who cares if he can make the light stick glow?"

Grandpa shook his head. "White Gaspard will use scepter —unstoppable. We can't let."

I didn't see what the big deal was. Even if Gaspard managed to make the scepter do a few tricks, it certainly wasn't worth being tortured over.

"What does all this have to do with Aro and Baptiste?"

"Torture didn't work. Gaspard threatened family. Said he would ruin their lives. I didn't believe—I thought bluffing— spit in his face."

"Couldn't you have warned us or something?"

"Many times I made call from Green barracks—but of course, no one understood. Only comfort was—Gaspard didn't know about you. But then you met in Blue Garden."

Crêpes. "How did he know who I was? Do I look like you or something?"

"Maybe," he said. "But also knew Brandt was my wife's maiden name."

I put my head between my knees. "It was my fault after all. I'm a toilet pouch."

Grandpa patted my back. "Don't know what that is, but Gaspard is one to blame."

"It had to be that same morning that Gaspard devised a plan to paint me. But why use his grandson, then turn around and try to execute him? And now suddenly he's the Prince?"

"To Gaspard, everyone tool—friends, family—only a way to get what he wants."

That made sense. Gaspard probably gave Aro step by step instructions on how to manipulate Baptiste into painting me. Then if something went wrong—as it had—Aro was the scape-goat. Gaspard could deny any knowledge of the crime and let his grandson take the fall.

I should have let him. Why didn't I listen to Véronique? She told me to choose her instead—that I couldn't save everybody. We would have been into our new lives on the mainland by now.

I carefully felt Aro's fire. I couldn't wrap my mind around the news—my painting had nothing to do with a rugby bet. The Commissaire himself had sent someone to ruin my life— and all to make my grandfather talk.

"You tried to warn me, didn't you? On the mirror, the scepter guide, and at dinner."

"Clumsy."

"You think he'll try to torture the secret out of me?"

"No need. Aro use scepter—Gaspard control Aro."

"Why didn't Gaspard just take my hand himself?"

"Must have same blood type."

Keys rattled in the door. I moved away from Grandpa.

So, if Gaspard and I had shared the same type of blood, I'd have a geriatric hand, Aro would be out of the picture, and Grandpa would most likely be dead. Gaspard would've had to take his hand from Zacharie and give it to me—or would he make a triple bond?

Sébastien opened the door. "Let's go geezer. Lord Livius wants you upstairs."

Had he been listening at the door? I sat motionless and tried to keep my expression neutral.

After Grandpa Zacharie left with the guard, I spent the next few hours trying to think of some way I could get word to my family that Grandpa was alive and we were both trapped in the estate.

I spent that night alone, worrying about what Gaspard might be doing to Grandpa. The next morning, I awoke to Sébastien throwing me over his shoulder. The sound of his boots echoing on tile told me we'd left the room. Cold sweat broke out on my back and arms. Maybe Grandpa had been wrong. Maybe Gaspard was going to torture the secret out of me anyway.

"Where are we going?"

Sébastien ignored my question and started up a flight of stairs. As I lay doubled over on the guard's shoulder, a strange thing happened—a point of light appeared at the edge of my vision. My first thought was that my eyesight was coming back, but the light didn't fade or move as Sébastien continued down the corridor. It remained perfectly stationary.

I concentrated on the bright spot and opened my eyes wider in an effort to let more light in.

Sébastien stopped, set me on my feet and knocked on a door. The point of light disappeared, and I found myself wondering if I'd really seen it at all. The door must have opened because I heard feet shuffling past us into the hall. I smelled Grandpa's cloak.

Someone gasped. "That can't be him?" came a familiar high voice. I'd forgotten how young Aro was. Thirteen or fourteen at most.

"Don't dawdle," Gaspard said. "We've much to do."

The footsteps receded down the hallway and Sébastien led me into the room. Carpet rustled under my bare feet. My hand touched a wooden bedpost.

"What am I supposed to do in here?" I asked.

"Whatever you do, do it in the toilet. I'm through disposing of your excrement."

"I get to stay with Aro?"

The guard scoffed. "This was the Prince's recovery room. Now that he's recovered he'll be staying directly above you in the specially prepared king's quarters."

I felt my way over to a wall but found only painted cinder blocks. "No windows?"

"You're still underground. Although if you did scream, the staff might actually hear you."

"Why are you telling me this?"

"Because you're a smart boy and can imagine what would happen if you did."

I felt my way back to the bed and sat down. "Gaspard would tell everyone Aro had a nightmare and then he'd send you down here to gag me."

"Gag and beat you."

"I guess I'll save you the trouble."

"Thank you," Sébastien said. "There's a razor at the sink. Use it to shave your head but not your face. If you screw this up Lord Livius will make me shave you from now on, and I promise I will make it unpleasant. I'll be back in three hours to take you upstairs."

"Upstairs? You mean I'm going to the surface? Do I have to wear a hood or something?"

"There's no need."

Did he mean the entire staff was in on the plot? Shaving my head was not much of a disguise.

"Aren't you worried I'll use the razor to kill myself and take Aro's life force with me?"

"You're welcome to try. As dull as the razor is, you'll be sawing for a while."

I sighed.

"Act like a prisoner and they'll treat you like one," Sébastien continued. "Act like an adult and maybe you'll last as long as the mumbling geezer."

I fought the impulse to defend Grandpa. Picking a fight with Sébastien wasn't going to help our situation.

He left and I managed to find my way into the fanroom. The hot water felt like heaven, and getting rid of my tangled mess of hair was actually a relief. It had grown into my eyes. Too bad Granny wouldn't get a chance to see it. She'd always begged me to grow my hair longer.

Granny. My Parents.

The knowledge that I was as good as dead to them swallowed me with crippling ferocity. I sank to the floor. I was so tired of this suffocating blackness—it pressed in on me from all sides.

Where was my father? Why had he left on that trip? If only he had stayed. I could have told him about the note on the mirror and at dinner. He could have gotten me out of here. Why hasn't he found me? Surely he didn't believe that story about me running away. That must have been months ago. What were they doing now—moving on with life as if I'd never existed?

I felt my newly shaved head. I'd always wondered what I'd look like without hair—now I would never know. Maybe if I got out of here I'd ask Véronique if she liked it. The thought of not being able to see her face again brought my head to the tile.

Black, I was pathetic. Wallowing in a pile of my own hair.

Eventually, I pulled myself to my feet and wiped my face. It wouldn't do me any good to cry about my vision and wish I were home. Sébastien was right—I was here, so I might as well make the most of it.

I found a bar of soap and rubbed it on my face. The coarse hair along my jaw and upper lip had grown but not much. Dad always said I inherited his baby face. At any rate, the sparse growth certainly wasn't going to hide my identity. I was tempted to trim it a little, but the thought of Sébastien going at me with a blade changed my mind.

When he came to fetch me I had managed to get my pants on, but I still hadn't found my socks and was pretty sure I had the robe on backward. I thought Sébastien might help a blind brother out—instead he led me barefoot into the hall. I trailed my dark hand along the wall as we walked. We passed several sets of double doors—probably the medical areas. Just as we stepped into the elevator, the tiny light reappeared. It startled me at first, and I dodged as if it were coming toward me.

"What's your problem?" Sébastien said.

The elevator jerked into motion.

"Being blind isn't exactly convenient. It takes some getting used to."

I thought he might smack me, but instead he laughed. He certainly hadn't been this jovial at our river outing.

"Don't make a scene in front of the staff. They believe you've been hired as the Prince's page."

"A blind page? How stupid are they?"

"They've learned to mind their own business—but I'm sure you realize it's in your best interest to remain inconspicuous."

"So, don't go telling them I'm the lost king?"

"Not unless you want to end up like Mumbles."

"If you wanted me to be inconspicuous you could have let me get my shoes on."

The elevator chimed and the doors opened. My breathing quickened as Sébastien led me into the main lobby of the estate. Any number of staff could be watching me at that very moment. Would anyone recognize me? What would they do?

The point of light flickered occasionally but oddly out of sync with my movement through the estate. I squeezed my eyelids closed, but it didn't affect the light at all. Was it some random connection firing off in my retina?

We moved with long strides through the corridors. I heard doors opening and people walking past us, but there were no cries of recognition. Surely someone must be wondering why I looked so much like the missing king. Was everyone too scared of Gaspard to say anything?

"Capitaine, you've kept us waiting," Gaspard said.

The Chancellor's voice instantly brought up the fury and hurt I'd been drowning in these last weeks. "Such an inconvenience," I said. "Try getting dressed with your eyes closed and see how late it makes you."

I regretted the words as they left my mouth.

We stood there for what seemed like an entire minute, the silence heavy in the air.

"Aro, please inform your servant that unless he's asked to speak, perfect silence is required."

"You got that?" Aro said.

I nodded, resisting the urge to tackle the little twerp. I wondered how hard I'd have to pull to get my hand back.

"Now strike him," Gaspard said.

Apparently Aro needed no more encouragement than that, because something slammed into my mouth, sending me sideways into Grandpa. I tasted blood.

"In time, you'll learn to correct him without making a mark," Gaspard said. "For now, that will do."

"Apologies for our tardiness, Lord," Sébastien said.

"No matter," Gaspard said, his voice almost cheery. "I've decided the Prince's room is too cramped anyway. We'll be moving the session to the courtyard."

"Would you like me to—"

"No, thank you, Capitaine. You've played nursemaid long enough. You may return to your leadership duties."

At once, people began moving and I couldn't tell who was going where. But what distracted me most was that the point of light had begun to dance in front of me.

A soft, wrinkled hand gripped my forearm and guided me

forward. I tried to concentrate on the footsteps ahead of me, but they already sounded too far away.

"Zacharie get this door," Gaspard called from down the hall.

Grandpa moved past me. I quickened my pace and tried to catch hold of his robe. I missed. With no eyes, my reflexes were somewhere between senior citizen and zombie—but just as I got some momentum going, the tiny light went out completely.

A clattering sound echoed down the hallway. I came to an uneasy stop. Had I knocked something over?

"Keep hold of it, child. It's not a toy."

The light reappeared. I began feeling my way along the wall, keeping one hand extended to avoid bumping into anything.

"And tell your servant if he can't keep up he'll go without dinner."

Aro repeated his grandfather's threat and I moved toward the sound of his voice. By this point I was moving so recklessly I actually bumped into him before I was able to stop.

Another blow to the face sent me stumbling backward. I could tell from the force of the strike that it had been Gaspard.

"Inform your servant that this is his only warning. The next time he touches royalty he loses a finger."

I held my cheek where his ring had cut me.

Aro repeated Gaspard word for word, and it was all I could do to not interrupt and say—I heard him, you crêpe-head.

Grandpa Zacharie once again took my arm, and somehow the two of us made it into the courtyard without any more slaps or threats of mutilation. Gaspard directed Aro to take a seat on a bench while Grandpa and I stood a few yards away pretending to be invisible. I carefully shifted my weight, trying to ease the aching in my legs. I hadn't been this long on my feet for months. Grandpa reached out a hand and stilled me. I stopped fidgeting but couldn't resist the urge to touch my swollen lip. Was this life really worth it? How had he done it for so many years?

As I stood breathing the scent of the gardener's soil, Gaspard began his instruction on the properties of light manipulators. So, Aro had starting training. The clattering sound must have been the Prince demonstrating his skill with the scepter.

"Your mind and your fire are connected in ways we don't understand," Gaspard said. "According to the Guide, the scepter can take the light from your fire and bend it into any image you're currently thinking of."

I felt an irrational pang of jealousy. The guy was a crêpe-bag. Why did I miss being his protégé?

"Imagine an object," Gaspard said, his tone excited. "Your pet fox for example."

"Which one?" Aro said. "I have four kits."

"It doesn't matter. Picture one of them in your mind—really visualize it."

"Okay—but when can I bring them to the estate?"

"Soon. Now, that image of the fox is in your head, but it's also in your fire."

"So my hand turns into a picture?"

"No, your fire still appears white. But when the light passes through the scepter, the diamond somehow translates it into a visible projection of the fox."

"Why is it still the same sparkling lights, then?" Aro said. "You think the scepter's broken?"

"The scepter is fine," Gaspard said, for the first time sounding impatient. "The skill just takes practice."

I almost chuckled to myself. Served the old guy right for spawning dumb grandkids.

Gaspard droned on. I grew bored and turned my attention back to the light at the edge of my vision. The bright spot was stationary again, barely changing. The more I watched, the more I was convinced it wasn't a trick of my nerves.

"I can see light," I whispered to Grandpa.

He didn't respond. Was he actually listening to Gaspard's speech? At least the Chancellor didn't threatened to cut out my tongue. That probably meant he couldn't hear me from this far away.

"The light changes," I continued without moving my lips, "disappears sometimes. In fact, it went out for a minute back in the hall when Aro dropped the scepter."

Instead of answering, Grandpa grabbed my dark hand, pulled it behind his back, and began tracing his finger on my palm. It took me a second to realize he was writing letters. I remained perfectly still, my brain working furiously to understand his message. It helped that he pressed all his fingers into my palm to indicate a space.

M-I-N-D A-N-D F-I-R-E S-T-I-L-L C-O-N-N-E-C-T-E-D

My back already ached from maintaining the awkward position, but I held it. Good thing Gaspard was so engrossed in the sound of his own voice.

T-H-A-T W-H-Y Y-O-U D-I-E I-F G-E-T F-A-R F-R-O-
M A-R-O. S-T-A-F-F A-B-S-O-R-B-S F-I-R-E-L-I-G-H-
T A-N-D P-R-O-J-E-C-T-S I-T O-U-T D-I-A-M-O-N-

D. R-E-V-E-R-S-E C-O-U-L-D A-L-S-O B-E T-R-U

By this point my entire arm was killing me and my spine felt seconds away from snapping in two. At the very least I was going to fall over and attract Gaspard's attention. Grandpa would have to give me the rest of the message later. I tried to pull my hand away, but he held it tight, tracing letters with such speed I could hardly keep up.

M-A-Y-B-E D-I-A-M-O-N-D C-A-N A-B-S-O-R-B O-U-T-S-I-D-E L-I-G-H-T A-N-D T-R-A-N-S-M-I-T I-T I-N-T-O F-I-R-E A-N-D T-H-U-S I-N-T-O T-H-E B-R-A-I

"What is going on there?" Gaspard said.

Grandpa withdrew his hands, and any hope I had of remaining upright went with them. I landed in a particularly thorny bush and cried out.

"Hard stand long time," Grandpa said in his garbled voice.

"I'm not interested," Gaspard said. "If either of you interrupt the lesson again you'll be very sorry indeed."

Grandpa reached down to help me up, but I couldn't move. From the moment I'd deciphered that bit about the scepter transmitting light into my fire, I had focused on that bright spot in my vision, willing it to grow closer. Even as I felt Grandpa tugging on my arm, I began to see the light more clearly. Now I noticed that the flickering was caused by shadows moving across the surface. But no matter how hard I concentrated on that dot, I couldn't get it to grow any larger. It almost felt like the tiny light was fighting against a tide.

Of course! The light from Aro's white fire was already sending so much light through the scepter that there was no room for any more light to come in.

"You are trying my patience," Gaspard said. "Get him up this instant."

Was it possible to somehow reverse the flow of light? If the fire controlled the scepter, maybe it could also control the direction the light was traveling.

Grandpa grabbed my arm and hissed into my ear. "Up!" But it was as if someone were speaking to me in the middle of a dream and I knew I had to ignore the voice or the vision would disappear.

Gaspard swore and called for a guard, but I was miles away, remembering an evening in the stairwell of the Red Shelter. The day I'd accidentally burned Véronique's back. And when I'd burned the boy at Green Park. And again when I was suffocating in the fanroom of the shelter—hadn't I somehow made my fire brighter or hotter? Maybe it was also possible to dim the fire, make it accept light, rather than emit it. If only I could get Aro to try. His white fire was simply too bright.

I could hear the guard stepping into the bushes behind me. As the fabric at the back of my cloak tightened, I realized I was wrong. It wasn't Aro's white fire—it was mine. And if Grandpa was right, I still shared a connection with it.

The guard yanked me upward. Thorns tore at my arms, but my mind didn't register the pain. I was already preparing to try again. This time, instead of focusing on the tiny light and trying to force it nearer, I concentrated on my fire. Not the weak thing at the end of my arm but the ball of energy that I could suddenly sense just yards away. I clenched my fist and imagined all that power in the palm of my hand instead of across the courtyard. I could almost feel the thrumming between my crippled fingers.

When I had burned Véronique, I'd somehow drawn my body's warmth into my palm. But this time I took the energy pulsing in my hand and pulled it deeper inside me, letting it fill my entire body with heat. For a split second, my fire felt strangely empty. And then the vacuum was filled.

It was as if someone had flipped a light switch. I could see Grandpa as clear as anything but from a distance and at a strange angle. Next to him, a guard held up a skinny boy by his cloak.

With that single image I immediately knew two things.

One—I had discovered how to use the scepter as an eye.

And two—the hideous bald creature being lifted from the bushes would never in a million years be mistaken for the former king of Télesphore.

CHAPTER NINE

STUDY PARTNERS

W alking down a corridor while my eyes were ten feet away watching Aro's every move, took some getting used to. I'd actually run into less furniture when I was blind. Now I averaged two or three slaps an hour for my clumsiness. Aro had gotten better at causing pain without making a mark. He'd recently discovered that by twisting my light hand he could make involuntary tears spring to my eyes. Watching myself cry was a little unsettling, but it beat the unchanging blackness I had grown accustomed to.

Looking through the scepter was unlike anything I'd ever experienced. Not only could I see clearer and farther than before, surfaces changed color when viewed from different angles, and light would often play off random objects, making them sparkle. It was as if the entire world were a shifting kaleidoscope of precious stones—and if that wasn't enough to overload my senses, I could also see a full three-hundred-sixty degrees at once.

However, since the Prince's enormous face was usually taking up half my field of vision, I learned to block him out and concentrate on what was in front of him.

The best part was that Gaspard and Aro had no idea what was going on. Even that moment in the courtyard when the scepter's light went out, Gaspard had blamed Aro's inexperience. Before the Chancellor could grow suspicious, I figured out how to balance the flow of light, bringing enough in for me to see but letting enough out so the scepter could function.

At least I hoped that's what I had done. For some reason Aro was still having trouble making it work.

"Concentrate," Gaspard said for the umpteenth time. It was nearly a week after I'd regained my vision and so far the only thing Aro had been able to do with the scepter was make those sparkly lights come out the top.

"I followed my notes exactly," Aro said.

He threw his notebook across the bedroom. It landed on the floor not two feet from my shoe. If Gaspard hadn't been facing me, I probably would've picked it up and slipped it under my cloak. Grandpa Zacharie had told me paper was hard to come by in the estate. After cutting out Grandpa's tongue, Gaspard had removed all the writing materials to prevent Grandpa from slipping notes to the staff or throwing messages out the window for the gardeners to find.

"Forget trying to record everything and listen," Gaspard said.

"I thought you said Firelock was the easiest skill."

Gaspard took a seat next to Aro on the bed. "It's not going to come all at once. Light manipulation is an art that has been lost for hundreds of years."

I rolled my sightless eyes. I'd heard it all countless times. In fact, I'd gotten good at tuning out the incessant babbling and typically used the time to think. Today my thoughts were on Véronique. Was she still taking care of Mére Blanche? Did she still have all her fingers and toes? La-la was home, so at least she had that. Helping her brother out of prison was pretty much the only worthwhile thing I did for her. Did she wonder where I'd run off to and why I hadn't taken her with me?

I was standing against the wall, imagining how I would

break the news of my blindness if I ever got out of here, when Grandpa grabbed my dark hand and began tracing letters. Even though he knew I could read his lips through the scepter, we'd decided it was less obvious to communicate behind our backs.

N-O-T-E-B-O-O-K

"I see it," I said without moving my mouth, "but he's watching."

D-I-S-T-R-A-C-T-I-O-N

"I could throw up."

Grandpa shook his head.

T-R-Y F-I-R-E-L-O-C-K

"Seriously?" Using the scepter to see was one thing, but how was I supposed to do magic tricks from the other side of the room?

Grandpa lowered his chin a half nod.

I took a deep breath. At least by this time I had memorized Gaspard's instructions. I was supposed to tighten my fingers around the staff. Obviously, I couldn't do that. I needed to relax my hand, then imagine the crystal rod passing into my palm. Simple, right? So what was Aro's problem?

"Can we be done for today?" he asked.

Since I was seeing everything from the viewpoint of the scepter, Aro's white fire appeared directly below me, just beyond my field of vision. I focused on the glowing aura, imagining his fire was my fire. I pictured the staff, extending below me and imagined the white fireball pressing deeper into the crystal.

"I promise I'll practice hard tommoaaaAAAH!"

My whole world pivoted as Aro turned the scepter sideways.

Gaspard jumped to his feet. "What's wrong?"

"My hand feels like it's melted into the crystal."

"You've done it!" Gaspard said. The elation on his face brought me a rush of pride before I remembered the smile wasn't for me.

But then I noticed Grandpa. Although his expression remained stoic, I could see a glint of triumph in his eyes. I scanned the carpet for the notebook. It was still there.

But it did look a bit thinner.

For the rest of the afternoon we practiced securing the scepter. Releasing it was more difficult, but by dinner I was able to do both without any trouble.

The next day Gaspard moved on to Flash. This time when he began his lecture he had my full attention. Even though Grandpa insisted finding a pen was our top priority, I knew learning to use the scepter could only help our dismal situation. If Gaspard discovered that the notebook was missing pages or we failed to steal a pen, the scepter might be our only means of communication. I decided Grandpa could work on getting the pen from Aro's desk—I'd concentrate on being at the top of my class.

It turned out easier than I expected. In fact, I nearly hopped up and down like a little boy when Gaspard described the process of drawing energy from the body. I'd done it three times already. I had thought I was freak, but according to

Gaspard, anybody could gather the body's natural energy into their fire. If he was right, the same power I'd released as heat could be converted into a burst of light. All I needed was the scepter.

I didn't wait for Gaspard to finish the instructions. I imagined I was back in the shelter fanroom, surrounded by dying Reds. I remembered the panic. The tingling sensation that seemed to wash through me as if all the energy were moving in the direction of my light hand. I remember my fire had grown warm, but it hadn't released until I'd fallen to the floor. I'd been half out of my mind from holding my breath so I still wasn't sure exactly how I'd done it.

And now, standing in Aro's bedroom with no immediate danger, I was having trouble recreating the feeling. I focused on Gaspard's voice. He was the reason I was here. He'd taken away my vision, my family, and my entire identity. He'd taken away my chance to fix my country and doomed Véronique to a life of hunger and pain.

I felt my temperature rising.

That warped old man had taken everything from me and given it to his spoiled, blackhead of a grandson.

My attention turned inward. I felt the tingling pins-and-needles through my limbs. Like a rush of adrenaline during a rugby game, my body throbbed with bottled energy. For a moment, I let the warmth wash over me, then I willed the energy down my arm and into my fire.

Instead of a blinding flash, everything went black.

It wasn't until my vision returned and I saw Gaspard blinking wildly, that I realized what had happened. I'd done it right, but the outward surge of light had cut off the flow coming in, momentarily blinding me.

Gaspard clapped his hands and told Aro how magnificent

he was.

I was tempted to grab the scepter and smash them both over the head with it. But Grandpa Zacharie took my hand.

L-O-N-G O-N-E

I made a few more flashes, trying to make one long enough for Grandpa to slip over to Aro's desk and find a writing utensil. Rather than getting longer, however, my flashes were getting shorter and weaker. Grandpa hadn't moved from his spot. I leaned against the wall. I was starting to get light-headed.

Gaspard rubbed at his watery eyes. "Why don't we take a break. Your parents will be joining us for lunch."

Aro nodded. He didn't seem too thrilled.

Little idiot. If he only knew what I'd give to see my parents again.

Normally we stood by the wall and listened to our stomachs growl while Aro and Gaspard ate. But with company, Grandpa and I were literally shoved into a closet just off the dining room with Sébastien guarding the door. I guess Gaspard didn't want to have to answer any questions about the pair of creepy skeletal servants.

I looked forward to these times. There was just enough space for us to sit together on the closet floor. And although we had to whisper so Sébastien didn't hear, it was the only time we got to speak freely.

"Sorry I couldn't do the long flash," I whispered.

In the darkness Grandpa found my head and pulled me to his chest. He was always trying to snuggle me. At first I told him I was sixteen and too old for such things—and it reminded me too much of Gaspard's fake overtures—but recently I'd relented. It didn't take long for me to enjoy being held.

We each lived in a stark world of isolation. These short periods once or twice a month were like morphine. They dulled the pain and filled me with an indescribable feeling of safety.

It was only during these times, leaning against Grandpa's chest with his hand rubbing my shoulder that I thought I might be able to make it to adulthood like this. But Grandpa was at least seventy. He wouldn't be around forever. Would I be able to survive without him?

The thought that Grandpa's death would also kill Gaspard made me feel a little better.

It revolted me that such warmth and goodness could be permanently tied to such hatred and evil.

"Remember dragon dreams?"

I smiled. Grandpa's beard ticked my bald head when he spoke.

"Yeah, Mom was so mad at Dad for getting me that knight book."

"Ice Cream."

I chuckled and nodded. Grandpa used to hold me until I stopped crying, then take me downstairs for a treat. Granny would get so mad in the morning when she found all her butter pecan gone.

"When did my dreams finally stop?" I asked.

"When Ro died."

I nodded. It felt like months since I'd thought of my little brother. The one I couldn't save. He'd died of a fire infection and afterward I was a different person—stronger, more careful—until Grandpa left. That's when I stopped praying. Maybe it was time to start again.

Grandpa pressed his fire into my ear. The sound and warmth washed through me. I was halfway between crying and falling asleep when Grandpa abruptly sat up.

My head fell into his lap. I righted myself. "What is it?"

"Research. I hid before I confront Gaspard."

"Where? Granny could never find it. We thought it burned."

"Andre's office. Bottom filing cabinet. Inside Hospital Emergency Procedure Manual."

It had been in Dad's office the whole time? They had torn Grandpa's room apart looking for his papers.

"I think they replace those manuals every ten years or so. Hopefully we're not too late."

Listen to me—as if we could just waltz out the front door and stop by the hospital.

"What's in your research that's so important? We already know the secret to white fire."

"More. Clues to communicate other worlds."

"How would our fires help us talk with other worlds?"

Grandpa shrugged.

"Are you the one who stole the instructions to that final scepter skill?"

Grandpa shook his head. "Lost long ago. There is story."

"Of how it was lost?"

"No, about jellyfish."

Before I could ask what in the rainbow he was talking about, Sébastien opened the door.

"Out."

I helped Grandpa to his feet and he gave my hand a squeeze. I had to get him out of here—somehow.

We followed Aro back to his bedroom where Gaspard went straight into Illusion. This one was a little harder since it involved holding Firelock while creating an image in my mind and willing it to appear in front of me. But the break had given me time to recuperate my strength.

"Outstanding!" Gaspard said.

"How come I couldn't see anything?" Aro asked.

"It's impossible for light to actually make a physical object," Gaspard said from across the room. "The scepter sends the light forward in a wave. Since I was standing in front of you, the light hit my eye in such a way to make me think I saw a dark-haired girl standing in front of me. I must say, you do have an eye for beauty."

Aro's face crumpled in confusion. "But I didn't—"

"Don't be ashamed my boy. If you really like her we can have Talbot switch her Red fire for a Blue."

I could have kicked myself. The image of Véronique had come so easily and I certainly hadn't expected it to work on the first try.

"I made a Red girl?" Aro asked carefully.

"The level of detail was incredible. I could see individual freckles." Gaspard shook his head in amazement. "You my son, are a natural."

Aro smiled. "Thanks."

"With practice you can cast an image up to fifty yards away. But keep in mind it's a two-dimensional image, so only those directly in front of you will be fooled. The farther a person moves to the side, the more distorted the image will become."

He asked Aro to try a few more and thankfully made requests this time. With Gaspard now facing Aro, his back was to us. As I shot image after image through the scepter, Grandpa sidled closer to the desk. When he was almost within reach, Gaspard asked to see Great Aunt Renée. Since I had no idea what Renée looked like, I took a chance and envisioned a walrus instead. Gaspard laughed so hard he began coughing. I almost started laughing myself when I saw Aro's look of utter bewilderment.

During the coughing fit, Grandpa stepped in front of the desk and opened the top drawer.

"Are you sure this thing is working right?" Aro said.

"Sometimes it doesn't do exactly what I want."

"You'll get better at it," Gaspard said.

Aro's eyes darted to the corner of the room. "What are you doing in my desk?"

Without pausing to think, I harnessed my panic and shot a bolt of energy down my arm. Even before it reached my fire, I knew it was going to be the most powerful flash yet.

When it hit, three things happened at once. Aro screamed. Gaspard fell backward, pinning me against the wall. My vision went dark.

And this time it didn't come back.

CHAPTER TEN

A FAMILIAR FACE

"**C**loak caught on drawer," Grandpa said in his gargle language. "Didn't want damage furniture by yanking free."

Gaspard huffed. "That wouldn't happen if you'd just stay in one place. And as for you, young man. Next time you're going to pull something like that, you could at least warn someone."

"Sorry," Aro said. "I guess I just got excited and…"

"I know it's late, but let's try Projection. Pick up the scepter."

A wave of relief washed over me. When my vision hadn't returned after the super-nova flash I thought I'd somehow ruined my connection with the scepter. Apparently butter fingers had dropped it.

The room swam back into view. Gaspard had the Bulletproof Bible open and was squinting at the tiny text. He tapped the page. "Just as I thought. Unlike an illusion, a projection must come from memory. It has to be something you've actually seen." He grinned. "So marine mammals in dresses are out."

Aro gave him a blank look.

I watched Grandpa through the scepter until he gave his head a slight shake. His excursion to the desk had not been successful.

Maybe we could write notes with our blood. Hadn't people been doing that for centuries? Of course they'd probably had quills or something. I would likely bleed to death before I managed to write anything legible.

"You've mastered Illusion," Gaspard continued, "but Projection sends out light in all directions and in a much more complicated pattern."

"Does that mean I'll be able to see it, too?"

"Yes, but you'll see it from behind."

"I don't get it."

"Instead of sending one image straight forward, the scepter sends out a million images, each one a drawing of the object from a slightly different angle."

Aro nodded, but his vacant expression betrayed his confusion.

While Gaspard tried to explain it again, I rubbed my foot absentmindedly over a bump in the area rug. These fabric shoes were so thin I felt every pebble and—

With a start I realized the bump was long and thin. About the size of a crayon.

"So if I was in front of you," Gaspard continued, "and moved to the side, the image would change as I walked, making the object appear fully dimensional. In addition, you can actually make the object move, whereas an illusion is always a still picture."

I silently removed my shoe and slowly massaged the bump toward the edge of the rug.

"*Chanmé*," Aro said vaguely. He hadn't understood a word. Hard to believe he won the Academy Mélangé color improvement scholarship last year. It was clear his grandpa had been buying his grades. The kid was an imbécile.

"So how do I do it?"

"It's similar to making an illusion, except you must send a greater quantity of light through the scepter—almost as if you're attempting a flash and illusion simultaneously."

Aro's face fell—he'd obviously been hoping for something simpler.

"I think the important thing is the visualization," Gaspard said, oblivious to Aro's distress. "The reason it must be something you've seen with your own eyes is because you have to experience it again. Just thinking about it isn't enough."

Aro looked paler by the minute.

The bump finally reached then end of the rug and slid onto the wood floor. I couldn't quite see what it was through the scepter so I pretended to trip on my cloak and grabbed it.

Gaspard glared at me but didn't pause the training session.

I almost laughed when I felt it—a pencil. I slid it into the band of my underwear.

"Then you give it a boost of energy and anyone within view of the diamond will be transported into your memory. You should pick a potent one so it will be easier to relive."

Aro swallowed.

Maybe it was because I was elated about having stashed a pencil in my undies, but for the first time I felt a pang of pity for the boy. I understood the pressure he was feeling. I knew what it was like to want so badly to make someone proud.

"I think I'll try the Naissance I got my foxes," Aro said in a small voice. His hands were shaking. I realized that even if he was a little idiot, he was only thirteen years old. And what kind of role models did he have?

Aro closed his eyes as if concentrating, and for a moment, I didn't know what to do. The one time I actually wanted to perform a skill for Aro's benefit, it was impossible. I couldn't create a memory I didn't have, and using one of my own would immediately give me away.

So I did nothing. I simply watched as Aro struggled with all his might to make the scepter work. After an hour, Gaspard took pity on him and ended the training.

"Don't be hard on yourself," he said as we walked to dinner. "Your progress is still extraordinary. In fact, I've decided to move your coronation up to next week."

Fabulous—by helping Aro I was only speeding up his ascent to the throne.

"Are you sure I'll be ready?"

"It won't take much to impress the rabble. Although I think I'll call a meeting of the Dominateur this Sunday. You could practice on them—show them what you've got."

I felt a soft hand on my arm and slowed my pace. When there was enough space between us and Gaspard, Grandpa hissed in my ear.

"What pick up?"

I produced the pencil and pressed it into his dark hand.

The feel of the corrugated, peel-off tip brought to mind a memory. I'd seen the pencil before. It was the small red fabric pencil my Tjardan tailors used for my fitting all those months ago.

"Good boy. I make message."

"Be careful," I said, "if the wrong person finds it—"

"Have person in mind."

"Zacharie, get up here and open this door!"

"Good boy," Grandpa repeated, his voice catching.

I knew how he felt. We had a pencil and several pages from a notebook. We could finally try to communicate with the outside world. The only trick now would be finding help without getting caught.

Since Grandpa and I only ate once a day in our rooms, we spent most of the time hungry. Early on I'd grown to hate the dining room. At breakfast, lunch, and dinner—in the absence of company—not only did we have to stand against the wall and watch the Prince stuff his face, if he ever dropped a fork or emptied his water glass Grandpa was expected to remedy the situation. Not even Aro was stupid enough to let a blind boy pour his water and hand him pointy objects.

"I can't wait to see Marcoux's face when you show them," Gaspard said.

Marcoux—wasn't that the dark-haired Dom with the gray-streaked mustache? It seemed he and Gaspard weren't on good terms.

"That last flash was something else. For a moment I thought you'd managed Celestial Burning."

"What's that?"

I had to imagine Aro's look of confusion this time, because Gaspard had put the scepter back in his cloak.

"It's exactly like a flash except you have to stare directly into the diamond."

"Seriously?"

"As the light enters your eyes, the energy moves down to your fire and fuels the scepter. It keeps looping like feedback in a microphone, each time growing brighter."

"Won't I go blind?"

"Eventually," Gaspard said. "If I remember correctly you can go a full two minutes before retinal scarring occurs."

"What's the point?"

"The point is that you can completely incapacitate an entire army. Even when the light fades, their vision will be impaired for several more minutes. Yours will return immediately."

"I guess that's pretty cool," Aro said with his mouth full of food. "What about the last one that's missing from the book?"

"How to make the scepter sing is the greatest mystery of our world," Gaspard said in a sad voice. "As far as I know, that knowledge has been lost forever."

Aro seemed to perk up after that—probably relieved to have one less skill to learn.

I, however, shared Gaspard's sentiments. If those missing pages really could have ended all pain and hatred in the world, they were priceless. But even with all I'd seen, it sounded pretty far-fetched that a shiny stick could magically make everything better. Apart from instantly killing every person on the planet, I didn't see how it could end all pain and injustice. Maybe that's why the pages had been taken, to avoid a complete annihilation of our species.

Over the next few days I didn't have much time to philoso-phize about world problems. Each hour that wasn't spent eat-ing, sleeping, or using the fan, was used for training. I quickly perfected the easier skills, but Celestial Burning was physic-ally impossible for a blind man, and I still refused to attempt Projection. I knew I would only get one chance to use it, and it would have to be in front of the Dominateur.

But what memory could I possibly show them that would explain who I was? The scepter didn't reproduce sound, only images—and I still didn't understand exactly how it worked. Since it was my memory would everyone see it from my point of view? Maybe I wouldn't be visible at all.

The night before the council meeting I had trouble getting to sleep. My mind was too caught up in what I'd just learned from Grandpa Zacharie. "Project Red Pencil" was underway. Through a series of notes, Grandpa had been in contact with a member of the staff and together they were planning a way to expose Gaspard.

The fact that someone else was on our side sent chills through me. I might get to see my parents soon! But first I had to do my part. I had to think of a way to tell the Dominateur who I was with a single silent memory. I kept coming back to that moment in the penthouse when Gaspard returned from the balcony and watched Sébastien drug me. But would it be clear enough? And even if they knew Gaspard had done something to the king, that didn't mean they'd recognize the bald, skinny kid.

"Hey Bag o' bones, get up."

I awoke to black. Aro was in my room, but he didn't have the scepter.

"Get dressed."

Without a word, I slid out of bed and pulled on my cloak. I didn't smell Gaspard's shampoo or Grandpa's musty clothes. I felt around on the floor until I found my robe and pulled it over my head.

"You're disgusting, you know that?"

I wanted to answer back but was too thrown off by him showing up alone. Once I'd gotten my shoes on, he told me to follow him. The sound of his feet led me down hallways and up stairs until two guards stopped us.

"I'm the Prince," Aro said in a voice that made me want to punch him. "I need to speak with Lord Livius."

The guards must have let him pass, because I heard a knock on the door. From inside, a female giggled and then fell silent.

"Grandfather? It's me, Aro."

"Not now," came Gaspard's voice. "I'm occupied."

Occupied was right. Unless Gaspard's wife had returned from the grave, I couldn't imagine who was in there giggling with him.

"I need your help." Aro said.

Gaspard muttered something about choosing the wrong grandchild and opened the door. "What is it, child? I'm in the middle of my oboe lesson."

Oboe lesson—right.

Aro cleared his throat. "The meeting with the Doms is in four hours and I need to practice."

"Fine, take the manipulator. Go practice in the courtyard. I'll be there in an hour."

My darkness fell away as Aro took the scepter and I automatically locked it to his hand. Grandpa Zacharie stood outside the room, a few feet from the guards. I needed to talk with him about our plan for the council meeting, but Aro had already begun trudging down the stairs. I rushed to catch up before he got too far away and I became hopelessly disoriented.

Practicing alone turned out to be completely useless for us both. Since I had no idea which skill he was attempting, I simply sat on a bench and watched him grow more and more frustrated.

After a few minutes, a thought occurred to me. This was the first time Gaspard had left me alone with his precious grandson. He knew I couldn't hurt him too badly without risking my own life, but what if I were to tackle him and force a reaction? Would his fire turn bluish? My palm would certainly grow brighter.

I decided against it. Even if a brighter palm might make me a little easier to recognize, I didn't want to screw up my chances to perform in front of the Dominateur. Besides, I needed to trust Grandpa and his contact.

I also toyed with the idea of confiding in Aro and appealing to his better nature but determined it wasn't worth the risk. What if he didn't have a better nature? Our escape plans would be ruined.

So, I sat back and watched him bang the scepter with his fist as if jostling the diamond would make it start working. My thoughts drifted back to my family. Were they still out looking for me or had they given up? I imagined the look on Granny's face when I walked through the front door with Grandpa. We'd go get his research together and find out what jellyfish had to do with fires.

The next thing I knew I was being slapped awake.

"What's your problem?" Aro said.

"Sorry, I must have fallen asleep."

"You think? You were screaming like a dying pig."

I realized it was true. I'd had that dream again.

"I think I got bit by a spider." Wow, that sounded lame even to me.

"Get up. I have to speak with my grandfather."

I followed Aro through the winding hallways. Why was he in such a hurry to talk to Gaspard? The kid had an enormous smile on his face and that alone was enough to twist my stomach in knots.

We entered the hallway leading to Gaspard's chambers and the two of us stopped dead.

Sébastien and another guard approached, escorting a pair of attractive Blue girls. One was a tall and dark with black hair, the other a petite cream-skin with hair the color of wheat—both carried instrument cases. Aro and I stared as they passed. There was something familiar about the blonde. If her hair had been shorter she would've looked exactly like one of my classmates from Blue Campus.

"Emma Raplapla?"

Both girls gave me a startled look as they passed.

"It's me," I said, before I thought better of it.

They had just disappeared around a corner when Gaspard stepped out into the hall, wearing a flowery house coat and holding an oboe. "What are you doing up here again? I told you I'd be—"

Aro ran toward Gaspard. "I did it! I made a projection!"

My bowels turned to lead.

"Are you sure?" Gaspard said, his anger forgotten. "Tell me everything."

Grandpa Zacharie furrowed his brow in confusion. I shook my head and felt like I might throw up.

"Well, first the scepter wasn't cooperating, so I decided to eat breakfast while I waited for you. Of course my lazy page boy was asleep. I gave his wrist a good tweak to get him up, but then he disappeared and I was in some sort of operating room. I could see myself strapped to a table and he was on a table too. Only he had hair. You were saying something to him, and then the doctor cut off both our hands and switched them."

"Impossible," Gaspard said. "You were out cold for the surgery. Your servant was the one who woke up just as we were…"

He fixed me with a calculating stare.

I swore several times in the privacy of my own head.

"When did the illusion stop?"

"Well, it started to fade after a minute. Even though I was back in the courtyard, I could still see the operating tables. This idiot's screaming was driving me nuts, so I slapped him awake. I guess that's when it faded completely."

"I see."

Gaspard approached me and I watched the blood drain from my own face. For the first time since he'd stolen my fire, he spoke directly to me.

"Do you have something to tell us?"

I froze, hoping Grandpa would interrupt with one of his brilliant lies. But before anyone could speak, shouts erupted from the hallway behind us. Emma appeared, followed closely by Sébastien. She saw me and skidded to a halt. Just before the guard clamped a hand over her mouth she got out one word.

"Bruno."

CHAPTER ELEVEN

THE MISSING LOCK

E mma was the first girl to send me a love note. She spelled my name wrong and the picture she drew made me look like a serial killer, but that note still sat under my socks, next to my baby teeth. Although our friendship never progressed into romance, the note still meant a lot. The six hundred that followed, not quite as much.

But now I had killed her. I should have kept my mouth shut as Emma passed. I probably would have seen her again. I could have slipped a note into her pocket. But now there was no way Gaspard would keep her alive. I felt as if a cold metal band was tightening around my torso, making it increasingly hard to breathe.

"Release her," Gaspard said.

Sébastien obeyed. Emma looked behind her as if debating making a run for it.

"Come here, girl."

Emma glanced at me and then approached the long-haired old man.

Gaspard glanced down at her empty hands. "I'd hate to waste a musical talent like yours. I really do need a teacher."

"What did you do to Bruno? He looks sick."

"Your friend has chosen to serve his country in a different way."

Emma scoffed. "I'm sure it was his idea to starve himself and change his fire back to Blue. What are those scars around his wrist?"

"Certain measures had to be taken for the good of Télesphore—and no, he didn't have a choice—but you do."

Emma eyed him and twisted an earring.

"You can either return to your family as a corpse, or you can keep my secret voluntarily and live here with me."

The band around my chest seemed to loosen a little. Gaspard would let her live?

"What about Bruno?"

"Either way, he will remain where he is."

Emma sighed. "I'll stay, as long as I can visit my family."

"There are no conditions—in fact, if you enjoy living, you will have to learn to do it without a tongue."

"What?"

Gaspard wet his lips. "You will most likely be confined to my chambers until my grandson is old enough to take a concubine."

"I'm old enough," Aro said.

"Be silent, child." Gaspard turned back to Emma. "Make your decision."

I had hoped Emma self-preservation would kick in, but the look on her face left no room for interpretation.

Gaspard's eyes grew cold. "Very well. Sébastien, take—"

"Run, Emma!" I launched myself at Sébastien and wrapped my arms around his knees. Before he could kick me away, I shoved a bolt of energy down my arm and imagined myself back in Madame Axelle's classroom on the day Emma tried to give me answers for the final.

Sébastien and Gaspard disappeared, and in their place my old classmates sat at their desks, preparing for evaluations. Strange—I had expected everything to go dark, but maybe I was finally learning to keep the light balanced.

The Emma from the projection leaned across the aisle and slid a note onto the desk of a muscular Bruno with hair. I read it, then put the small paper in my mouth and began to chew, just as Madame Loisible passed.

The scene only lasted a few seconds before I felt my energy fade. Although memory-Emma had turned bright pink in the face, I could now see the real Emma feeling her way along the walls.

"She's behind you, crétin!" Gaspard yelled.

Sébastien, who had stopped struggling the moment I'd begun the projection, now shook off his surprise and kicked me away. The memory faded completely and Emma took off at a run.

Sébastien caught her in three strides and stifled her scream.

"Feed her to the dogs," Gaspard said.

"Forgive me, Lord, but it would be harder to make it look accidental."

"Fine, pump her full of morphine—tell her parents she overdosed. Better kill the other one too, just to be safe."

Sébastien hesitated as if he wanted to say something but then disappeared down the stairs with Emma in tow.

Gaspard walked to where I lay on the floor. "It would appear the page still has some lingering connection with his fire."

"I can help you," I said. "Let those girls go and I promise—"

Gaspard kicked me in the stomach and turned to his

grandson. "Has he been doing it all along?"

"No!" Aro said. "It was me mostly—he just got in the way."

"Let's do a test to make sure you'll be able to perform to-night," Gaspard said. "Make an illusion."

Through the scepter I watched him mouth the word, "Father."

I felt like crying. I had no idea what his father looked like. When I didn't produce his image Gaspard would know Aro was a complete failure and cancel the meeting.

Aro walked to the other end of the hallway and held the scepter out like it was a gun. His lips twisted in concentration.

I was about to tell him to save his limited brain cells when I remembered something. After I'd confessed as the Blue Campus murderer and gotten Aro off the hook, his mother had embraced a man on the pitch.

It had to be Aro's father, but I didn't get a good look at him. Making an illusion was out of the question, but maybe if I made a projection of the moment, it would be enough to satisfy Gaspard.

The memory was easy enough to relive since it was the most terrified I'd ever been in my life. As soon as I could see the couple in my mind, I sent a wave of power down my arm.

The stadium appeared.

"Excellent projection," Gaspard said, looking out over the scene in wonder. "Not a very happy memory, but I trust you understand why the act was necessary."

"The act?" Aro said.

"You didn't think we were honestly going to execute you? It was only a ruse to get the Nazaire boy to reveal himself."

What a load of crêpes. I released the scene and the hallway

returned.

Aro narrowed his eyes at me, but bless his foolish pride, he didn't say anything.

"Well, that's a relief," Gaspard said. "For a moment I thought you might be completely incompetent."

"Let's not bring him to the cathedral," Aro said.

"We can't risk your fire weakening. There are other ways to keep him from interfering."

"Kill him?"

Gaspard rolled his eyes. "I'll have Sébastien drug him. I'm sure we have something that produces a dreamless state."

"Aro," I said from the floor, "when are you going to grow up and stop taking orders from this geezer?"

Gaspard's eyes bulged and even Grandpa Zacharie's mouth opened in surprise.

"You really think he knew I'd be at classifications? He was going to let you take the fall—and he's still using you. You're the one with the white palm. He can't—"

Gaspard stepped on my fire and dug his heel into my bad wrist. The explosion of pain nearly overloaded my consciousness. Just as I thought I would pass out, he removed his foot.

"We'll have to do something about his face," Gaspard said. "If the girl recognized him there's a chance the Doms could as well."

"You could cut off his nose," Aro said.

"Unfortunately there's no time. It'll have to be after the meeting. I'll have Talbot prepare the operating room."

I cradled my throbbing hand. "It doesn't matter what you do to me. I'll find a way to tell someone what you are."

Gaspard laughed. "I think you're underestimating my surgeon."

"You're not going to take out his tongue, are you?" Aro said. "Having one mumbler is annoying enough."

"His tongue he'll keep. Talbot will be removing his frontal lobes."

Grandpa Zacharie grunted something unintelligible— something about never allowing such a thing.

Gaspard stepped in front of him. "That's something for you to keep in mind as well. You don't need to be sane to keep my fire alive."

I pressed my face into the carpet. I had failed. My family would never see me again. Véronique would never leave Taudis Rogue. I'd handed Télesphore over to a murderer.

"Now get your serving boy off the ground and go dress yourself. We're needed at the cathedral in an hour."

"I'm not touching him," Aro said. "He'll probably bite me or something."

Gaspard motioned for Grandpa Zacharie to deal with me. When Grandpa leaned down to grab my arms I whispered, "I'm going to force reaction with Aro. Maybe it will change his fire enough to disqual—"

"Zacharie!" Gaspard said. "Why is he speaking to you?"

I had just made it to my feet when Grandpa slapped me. It wasn't hard, but it surprised me so much I almost fell over again.

"Ohk," he said in a loud voice. Don't.

"That's more like it," Gaspard said. "Aro, take him downstairs and lock him in the closet while you get dressed. If you have any more trouble with him, call Sébastien."

I followed Aro downstairs. Somehow I resisted the urge

to tackle him and force our fires together. Grandpa's slap had been for Gaspard's benefit, but I was pretty sure the warning was for me. It was too risky to try forcing reaction and probably wouldn't have much of an effect anyway. Maybe Grandpa had a plan.

Please let him have a plan.

Once we reached his room, Aro took his tux out of the closet and pushed me inside. As soon as the door closed, I lay down on the soft carpet. There was no point in trying the knob. The door only opened from the outside. It was the perfect place to stash me while the Prince was showering, using the toilet, or otherwise wanted his privacy.

Aro set the scepter down and my view of the room disappeared. As I lay there I knew I should be trying to come up with a plan of my own, but all I could think about was my family. If I ever saw them again I probably wouldn't recognize them. I'd be a husk of a person without any will or personality. A cold feeling descended on me. Maybe I should just choose death and take Aro with me.

A crinkling sound startled me. I felt around on the floor and discovered a folded piece of paper. Someone had slid it under the door. It couldn't have been Aro since the shower was still going.

"Is someone out there?" I whispered.

There was no reply.

"I might have some trouble reading your note," I said. "I'm sort of blind."

"Look up," came a male voice.

Look up? Hadn't I just told him I was blind? "Where did you get the paper? Did my grandpa send you?"

After a few seconds of silence I heard Aro's bedroom door click shut and I knew the man had gone.

I unfolded the paper and found a key inside.

A key! I was on my feet and feeling for a keyhole before I realized the water was no longer running. How long ago had it stopped? Panicked, I put the key in my mouth so I could feel for the lock with both hands. I was in that position when Aro opened the door.

"What are you doing?"

"I get claustrophobic," I said, trying to speak normally despite the large piece of metal under my tongue.

"Put this on and follow me." He threw a cloak at my face. It was nearly twice as big as my usual robe and once I got it on, I began tripping over it. If Aro noticed, he didn't slow down. Was he hoping I'd provide a little entertainment by face-planting onto the stone floor?

As we wound our way through the estate, I paid close attention to doors. Why did the key delivery-guy have to be so cryptic? He could have at least told me which door it was supposed to open. Maybe it was a skeleton key for any door in the house. The thought brought hope and panic all at once. Was I supposed to throw Aro over my shoulder and make a break for it? Somehow I didn't see that working out—as soon as Aro dropped the scepter I'd be as helpless as a bug in the toilet.

I followed Aro downstairs to the underground garage, every second thinking—Have I missed my chance? Should I knock him out while we're alone?

I was almost relieved when we met up with Gaspard at his improbable glass car. Whether I'd missed my opportunity or not, I couldn't do anything about it now.

"Go find it then!" Gaspard shouted at Sébastien.

The guard left, his face a pale red.

Gaspard pulled at the door handle and growled. "It starts in fifteen minutes and he's lost the key."

I tightened my grip around the piece of metal in my palm. Was it a car key? What was I supposed to do, deposit Aro in the backseat and take off? I had no idea how to drive. Once again, I lamented that my instructions hadn't been clearer. Look up. What did that even mean?

That's when I noticed it. Through the scepter I saw a note taped to the ceiling of the parking garage. In the dim light I could just make out the letters written in red pencil. The best part was I didn't even have to lift my head to read it.

B, Tell Z I replaced G's drug with less potent. Fake sleep. Use glow stick.

"We could walk," Aro said. For a moment, his big face distracted me.

"And arrive sweaty and disheveled?" Gaspard said. "I'd rather be late."

I returned my focus to the ceiling. It was hard to read the tiny lettering with Aro jostling the scepter every couple of seconds.

Z and I discussed you reacting with A. Fires could recognize true owners and fuse together permanently. Also might cause megareaction. A chance it will kill you both. Use as last resort!

Footsteps echoed through the garage. A sweaty and disheveled Sébastien appeared.

"My Lord, I can't understand what could have happened to it."

Was this an act? Could Sébastien be the one Grandpa had been writing notes to? Was I supposed to give the key back, now that I'd had time to read the note?

I decided before I did anything I should let Grandpa know about the drug-switch. While Gaspard yelled at Sébastien, demanding to know who'd had access to his key ring, I sidled over to Grandpa Zacharie. After I whispered the general contents of the note he grabbed my palm and wrote.

P-R-O-J-E-C-T G-A-S-P O-N B-A-L-C-O-N-Y

I nodded. I'd gone over the scene in my mind for days. The balcony had been the first moment I saw Gaspard for who he was. The Doms would have no choice but to confront him and ask what he'd done with the king. That's when I would jump up and identify myself.

It was a great idea.

It had to work.

CHAPTER TWELVE

ATOP THE CATHEDRAL

T he refrigerator was one of my best friends growing up. So, you can imagine my excitement when—as a nine-year-old—I discovered a mini-fridge in my parents' closet. That afternoon I feasted on cheesecake, éclairs, and sour soda. When my parents got home they found me passed out in the hallway.

For years after that the slightest smell of champagne would send me running to the fan. Between the time I started drinking and when I lost consciousness, I experienced some really weird sensations—severe confusion, loss of motor function, and a horrible case of the giggles.

The drugs Gaspard had shot me with were having much the same effect, except instead of giggling I was trying desperately to process what was going on around me. I knew I was tied to a chair but couldn't tell if I was asleep, or if my body was paralyzed. Whatever the case, I kept swimming in and out of consciousness, never quite able to distinguish dream from reality.

My memories from the estate were still pretty clear. I had pretended to find the key on the ground. Shortly afterward Gaspard stuck a syringe in my neck and shoved me onto the floor of the glass sedan. We pulled out of the garage. Through the scepter, I saw a hospital crew loading two lightless girls into an ambulance. Chief Dupont tried to wave down the car, but Gaspard sent Sébastien to answer her questions.

Once we pulled onto the street, the rest of the Royal Guard exited the Green Barracks and began running behind the vehicle. After that, the drug started to take effect and things got hazy. I remember being carried up the stairs to the top floor of the cathedral. Currently, I was pretty sure I was stuffed in a corner with a hood over my face.

Doms arrived and shook hands. Every once in a while I remembered I was supposed to be doing something but for the life of me couldn't think what it was. Occasionally, Grandpa Zacharie tickled my palm with his finger. I tried to ask what he was doing, but my mouth hung slack, unable to form words.

At one point I thought I was in a stairwell with a pair of caramel-colored eyes watching me. Then Gaspard was walking toward me with an angry look on his face. He yelled that I was not to touch the scepter until I was ready to perform. Or maybe he was talking to Aro. After that my vision went black. Someone lifted my eyelids and prodded at my neck. Gaspard said something about needing more time to take effect.

I was in the middle of a dream about an all-you-can-eat shrimp and lobster buffet when a voice came over the loud speaker of the restaurant.

"Gentlemen, months ago I informed you I had a project I'd been working on. In light of our last incident with pubescent royalty, I'm sure you can see why I delayed revealing the details. But now, my protégé is trained and ready to accept his role."

A murmuring rose from a few tables over. I shrugged to myself and continued smearing butter on my crab cakes.

"Presenting Aro Algernon Loupe—my grandson and future King of Télesphore."

"Another white fire!"

"How can this be?"

I was about to tell the people to shut up and let me eat, when the mec on the speaker said, "Show them why Télesphore will follow you, son. Let them see what you can do."

At this point things really got weird. In the middle of the restaurant a long, cobblestone table appeared, surrounded by a group of old men in robes. Each wore an expression of complete astonishment that morphed into confusion when they saw me stuffing my face.

"It's the Nazaire boy!" one of them called.

"Drop it, you idiot!" came a familiar voice. Was it Gaspard? Yes, I could see him by the buffet trying to rip the scepter out of Aro's grip.

"I can't," the boy cried, "it's stuck."

Several of the elderly men got to their feet.

Grandpa Zacharie watched them for a moment, then took off toward a back corner of the restaurant where a hooded figure sat motionless in a chair. "Do it now!" he shouted as he ran. "The balcony!"

I had the vague notion he was speaking to me, but I wasn't sure what it was I was supposed to be doing.

"Sébastien," Gaspard yelled, "come get this scepter free. Zacharie, stay back or you'll share his fate."

Grandpa must not have heard because he kept running. I wanted to invite him to eat with me, but as soon as he reached the hooded figure at the back he grabbed the guy's turquoise palm and twisted. A jolt of pain shot up my arm and the restaurant disappeared.

Two young patients lay in a brightly lit operating room. One of the boys—handsome with a white palm—lay awake, while the other—a Turquoise Mélangé—slept. Once again the old men in robes were smack in the center of the room. Gaspard passed through them like smoke and approached the conscious boy. After a brief unheard conversation, Gaspard motioned to a man in scrubs and a surgeon's mask.

The robed men watched the scene with expressions ranging from extreme confusion to fascinated wonder.

"Remarkable."

"Are we seeing the future?"

"Don't be daft, he said the scepter only shows memories."

"Isn't that the boy king?"

"It's both of them!"

"What is the meaning of this, Livius?"

That's when I realized there were two Gaspards. One was watching the doctor apply a tourniquet above the boy's wrist. The other was slowly making his way along the floor of the operating room, his eyes locked on the hooded figure in the back corner.

Several people cried out. I looked to see the doctor holding a machine with a tiny spinning blade.

"Is this some sort of joke?"

Now the old men were all on their feet. I suddenly remembered they were members of the Dominateur. Wasn't I supposed to show them something about Gaspard on a balcony? If only I could concentrate enough to remember.

The crawling Gaspard was now in the middle of the room, wrestling on the floor with Grandpa Zacharie. A few of the Doms seemed to notice, but most were still watching the doctor as he raised the blade. The handsome boy shook his head. His wild eyes darted from the saw to the door, his mouth forming unheard pleas.

"Stop this at once!" someone shouted.

Gaspard kicked himself free from Grandpa and scurried toward the back corner like a white-haired beetle. Right to the cloaked figure.

The doctor brought down the blade. A chorus of screams rent the air. One Dom was sick. Several hid their faces. I watched Gaspard put the glowing white hand on a tray while the doctor moved to the other boy and removed his fire just as quickly.

The screams turned to shouts of outrage. Aro had stopped trying to release the scepter and now stood with his mouth hanging open.

The doctor began sewing the white hand onto the Mélangé. Gaspard approached the other boy. The handsome one with the dark brown hair.

I knew him. I had known all along who he was, but my mind had simply refused to acknowledge it. Gaspard produced an aerosol bottle covered with corrosive chemical symbols and the reality of what I was seeing finally broke through.

Gaspard was going to take my vision midway through the surgery so the last thing I'd see was the stump on the end of my arm. No wonder my conscious mind had blocked this memory.

Gaspard pointed the can and sprayed. I felt the pain in my eyes all over again. It was worse than losing my hand. An inhuman shriek tore out of my throat and echoed off the walls of the cathedral.

Cold fingers wrapped around my neck and cut off my air.

I was awake. The operating room vanished, leaving only a group of old men and a long, cobblestone table. I couldn't breathe. Through the scepter I could see Gaspard on his knees at the back corner with his hands around my throat. All at once the Doms seemed to realize what was going on and rushed forward to pull him off me.

"Get back, fools." Gaspard released his grip and pushed the old men away. He stood to his full height and faced the Dominateur. "Can't you see I did only what was necessary to ensure the future of Télesphore? The boy's naïve vision of equality would have thrown our country into civil war."

I tried to open my mouth to defend myself, but my brain felt fuzzy. Whether it was the drugs or my recent near-strangulation, it was all I could do to keep Aro's fire locked to the scepter.

Sébastien finally stopped trying to pull it from Aro's grip and moved to stand behind Gaspard. I hadn't seen him come in. Evidently he'd finished lying to the police. I realized he was the only guard in the room.

"So you blinded our king and stripped him of his white fire?" Dom Marcoux said, his mustache quivering with fury. "You are a traitor to the crown."

"I am a patriot to the crown!" Gaspard screamed. "I refused to hand it over to some idealistic child who would've destroyed all we've worked to build! It was through criminal acts that he stumbled upon the secret to white fire. The boy no more deserves to be king than my grandson. Except that Aro recognizes his own ignorance and welcomes the wisdom of those who have gone before him."

"The Haut Commissaire is right," Dom Gravois said. "He made the decision so none of us had to. He shoulders the responsibility while we benefit."

"He should have brought it before the Dominateur!" someone shouted. "He had no right—"

"I bring it before you now," Gaspard said. "I know it is late, but let us vote and see where we stand. I will abide by your decision even if it means my removal from office and trial for treason."

A few Doms took their seats amid murmurs of approval.

"There is no need to sit," Gaspard said. "This is a momentous vote that deserves more than a simple raise of hands."

Grandpa Zacharie slowly began creeping along the marble floor toward me.

"On the light side of the room let us have all those who accept my decision to create a worthy king. Those who oppose my actions please move to the far dark wall."

After a pause, old men shuffled around the room to make their opinions known. Grandpa reached me and began untying my ropes.

"Eh reay," Grandpa said.

Get ready for what? Were we going to make a break for it? We were three stories up and the hallway was lined with guards. "I think I could probably carry Aro," I whispered, my head feeling clearer, "but what are we going to do about Gaspard?"

Grandpa shrugged like we'd do whatever we had to. My hands came free just as the last Dom took his place along the far wall. The vote was actually pretty near even. I felt a deep respect for the men that were standing up to Gaspard. Was it enough?

Grandpa stood and edged his way along the glass windows toward Gaspard at the front of the room. I hoped he knew what he was doing.

"I am saddened," Gaspard said to the Doms on his dark, "that so many of you have let concern for minor points of law cloud your vision."

"Fire theft is not a minor point of law," Dom Marcoux said. "The punishment is death."

Grandpa stopped a few feet behind Aro. Was I supposed to make another projection? What was he waiting for?

"You are quite right," Gaspard said. "I can see the majority has spoken against me." He crossed his hands behind his back as if waiting to be cuffed. "Sébastien."

Sébastien approached Gaspard from behind—but since Aro stood slightly behind the Chancellor, I had a clear view of Gaspard's hands. Sébastien, instead of securing his wrists, produced a pair of dart guns and slipped them into the Chancellor's waiting palms.

"Get down!" I yelled.

Before anyone could react, Gaspard strode toward the old men against the far wall and began firing.

Chaos erupted. Several Doms lunged at Gaspard, but he was too quick. They stumbled to the floor, plague darts already releasing poison into their skin.

My vision tilted. Aro's mouth shot open in surprise as he was lifted into the air and carried toward the back corner of the room. Before it occurred to Aro to struggle, Grandpa Zacharie had already deposited him in front of me. With a fierceness I'd never seen in him, Grandpa grabbed Aro's wrist and thrust his fire in front of me, scepter still attached.

Aro finally found his voice. "Grandfather!"

But his call for help was drowned out by Dom Marcoux's battle cry. Even with a dart protruding from his light arm, the dark-haired man threw himself again at Gaspard. Sébastien knocked him aside. Marcoux's head hit the edge of the stone table and he crumpled to the floor.

Grandpa slapped a hand over Aro's mouth and with the other, shook the boy's wrist. I wasn't locking his fire to the scepter anymore, but Aro had a death grip on it.

Shouts of outrage became cries of pain as one after another, the Doms who had defied the Chancellor fell into twisting heaps. Gaspard must have reloaded the weapons, because
he continued to shoot dart after dart into the fallen men.

The Doms standing on the light side shuffled toward the
doorway and slipped out into the hall. Although obviously
uncomfortable with what they'd witnessed, they seemed relieved to have made the correct choice.

Cowards—if only they would stand and fight. There was
no way Gaspard and Sébastien could take them all.

There wasn't much time. Grandpa and I needed to get out
of here while the battle still raged. In the confusion of people
escaping, we may be able to make it past the guards in the hallway—but the thirteen-year-old Princeling was making things
difficult.

"Aro," I said into his ear. "I know your grandpa manipu-
lated you like he has everyone else. It's not too late to be a real
man. Also, if you don't let go of this stick I'm going to shove my
thumb in your eye."

The scepter clattered to the floor. My vision went dark. I
thrust my fire against Aro's palm and held it there.

Nothing happened—no frozen joints, not even a slight tingling sensation. It had been a while since I'd reacted with anyone. What was I doing wrong?

"Fiaoch" Grandpa said.

Firelock? But that was for securing the fire to the staff. Was
he saying I should secure my fire to Aro's palm? What would
that even do?

The sounds of struggle had faded, leaving only the anguished cries of dying men. How long would it take for the
poison to reach their fires and finish them off? It was supposed

to work slowly, but they'd all received multiple darts.

"Aro!" It was Gaspard's voice. He had seen us.

I tightened my grip on Aro's hand and imaged my fire pressing deeper into his—that they were occupying the same space. Something slipped into position and the pressure between our palms slackened. I relaxed my grip and pulled. We were stuck.

"I think I did it."

But Grandpa didn't answer. I realized I could no longer smell the musty scent of his cloak. Where had he gone?

"Grandfather," Aro called, "help me!"

Gaspard's fingernails dug into my arm. "Release him."

"Our fires are fused," I said. "If you force us apart, you'll kill us both." I'd meant it as an idle threat, but it probably wasn't far from the truth.

Gaspard's cold hand disappeared.

Now what? Staying attached to Aro wasn't an option. Gaspard could still lobotomize me—and I didn't relish the idea of having a whiny brat for a conjoined twin, with or without my brains intact.

But releasing firelock wasn't working. It was as if my body recognized my old organ and refused to relinquish its hold.

That gave me an idea.

"Your orders were to stay in the hallway!" Sébastien said. "Get back in the... It was you—you stole my key."

Who was he talking to? And what was Gaspard doing? At least for the moment he'd given up trying to pry us apart. I focused on my hand. Although I'd thought I had pressed the firelock as far as it would go, I could still feel Aro's white fire pull on my palm as if it were anxious to return to its place in my body.

I focused my will and slowly tightened my lock on Aro's fire. The pressure increased until I thought it would burst. Aro cried out, but still I pulled, tighter and tighter, no longer caring if it killed us both. This had to end.

Now.

With one last mighty pull, something gave way. An ocean of pain slammed into me as my palm split open. With the force of a lightning bolt, our fires changed places, cauterizing the wounds with white-hot heat.

I fell backward, my hand suddenly free. It was in there—I could feel my fire back inside me. It was like coming home to the smell of pies in the oven.

"Thank you for showing me how to do that," Gaspard said from somewhere to my dark. "I'll be performing that on your grandfather shortly."

I tried to pull myself off the floor, but my body wouldn't cooperate.

"Your family has been a thorn in my side for generations. My first act as Emperor of Télesphore will be to hunt down and root out the entire Molyneux line."

I felt something hard under my arm—the scepter.

"Yes, I remember the day we met at the Gardens. When you didn't react to the Ulfish insults I hurled at you, I knew you were pretending—but it wasn't until you used the name Brant, that I realized who you must be."

I grabbed the scepter with my light hand. Gaspard appeared before me, his expression panicked. I tried to gather the energy to make a projection, but the ordeal with Aro had completely sapped my strength. I couldn't even manage a little flash. Useless dancing lights passed across Gaspard's face, just as they had at the classification ceremony.

Twitching bodies covered the floor. Sébastien stood near the door, holding one of the guards by the hair. It was his son, Eloi.

I made one more attempt at a flash, but it was no use—my body had given all it could give.

Gaspard smiled. "You should feel privileged. You'll be the first political assassination in the Molyneux family." He picked a dart gun from the floor, pointed it at my face and pulled the trigger.

He would've hit me between the eyes if I hadn't jerked my head out of the way. Instead, the plague dart grazed my ear and hit the wall.

Gaspard stared at me. "How did you see that coming?"

I touched my bloody ear. "Maybe your blinding chemicals aren't what they used to be."

"Well, it hardly matters now." He pushed the gun barrel into my cheek.

"Hey, Gas!"

Gaspard turned. Grandpa Zacharie stood in front of a large window overlooking the city. In a voice that only Gaspard and I—and possibly Sébastien—could understand, he said, "Time for bed."

Then he bit into his own palm, puncturing the fire.

"You daft fool," Gaspard shouted.

Grandpa only smiled and threw himself through the window.

I couldn't cry out. I couldn't move. All I could do was watch him disappear in an explosion of glass.

The room grew silent.

"Sébastien," Gaspard said through ragged breaths. "Bring

me that hand."

Sébastien released his son. "I'll have Talbot prepare the operating room."

"There's no time, tell him to bring his equipment here."

Sébastien opened the door.

"Gouroux and Abbott, follow me," he said. "Marwig, bring the car around. Mallette, have your squad escort Dr. Talbot back here immediately. I don't care if you have to pull him out of surgery. In fact, the rest of you accompany him, in case the hospital gives you trouble."

The sounds of their boots faded down the stairs. Gaspard fell against the table as if his strength had abruptly left him. I knew what that meant.

Grandpa Zacharie was gone.

An inhuman sound tore from my throat—it felt like a black saw cutting me up from the inside. The more I screamed the more it sliced through tissue and bone, shredding organs and soul until there was nothing left but broken glass and the gaping hole where Grandpa had vanished.

Aro got up from the floor and ripped the scepter from my hand. My vision went black, but it was nothing compared to the darkness already smothering me from the inside.

I almost smiled at the thought of death.

Nothing was worth enduring this ripping, bone-shattering pain. I would be with Grandpa Zacharie soon.

I held my head up and waited.

But instead of cold hands around my throat, warm hands slid under me and lifted me into the air.

"Leave him where he is, Eloi," Gaspard said in a weak voice.

I felt Eloi turn. "Long live the king," he said.

And with me in his arms, he sprinted through the door and into the empty hallway.

CHAPTER THIRTEEN

TIME TO THINK

"Y ou eat it."

"I swear I'm full." I pushed the remains of the charred rabbit toward Eloi.

"Nice try," Eloi said over the crackle of the fire. "I've seen you pack it in at the estate."

"That was before my surgery. My stomach shrunk."

The truth was I hadn't had much of an appetite since I'd watched Grandpa jump out a third story window.

"Looks like it's snowing," Eloi said. "I should have grabbed a couple blankets."

We'd been holed up in a mountain for nearly a week now. According to Eloi it was the same cave Gaspard had prepared to imprison Grandpa Zacharie all those years ago—and for some reason it smelled like the community pool.

"You need protein," I said. "How are you going to protect me if you lose all your man strength?"

Eloi scoffed, but I heard the clink of the metal camping plate as he began eating.

I smiled and pulled my blanket tighter around me. Not for the first time I wondered if hiding out was really necessary. I wanted to see my parents. Gaspard was probably dead. What if the entire country was waiting for me to return and take the throne? But Eloi assured me that if Gaspard had survived, or if one of the other Doms had taken his place, pokers would be searching for me everywhere. And since I'd recently made myself expendable with my little fire-switching trick, we were lying low—at least until things calmed down and I recovered some of my strength.

"Lucky you know how to hunt," I said.

"My father's an outdoor nut," Eloi said with his mouth full.

"Mine too. One time he took me shark fishing and I almost got eaten by a great white."

"You're making that up."

"Okay, it just flew out of the water and hit the boat. But you know what did try to eat me was that creepy prehistoric fish in the tin mines—tried to swallow my fire. Good thing it didn't have any teeth."

"My Dad prefers big game. Taught me to skin a deer before I could..."

Eloi trailed off, as if memories of his father were too painful.

"He'll come around," I said. "I don't think he's a bad person. He's just trapped by his loyalty to Gaspard."

Eloi said nothing. I hated being blind. I couldn't see if he was crying silently to himself or glaring at me.

To my surprise, he laughed. "You sure irritated him."

I smiled. "Did he hate me that much?"

"No, he hated my Yellow girlfriend. He just took it out on you."

"So it's Adisa's fault he's against Red rights."

Eloi sighed. "How's your ear?"

"Still hurts." I brought a hand to the dark side of my head

and winced. Although the plague dart had only scratched me, some of the poison had gotten into my skin. "Does it look bad?"

"A little discolored," Eloi said. "Your exposure to the anopent was minimal. Your body should have no trouble fighting it off."

Unfortunately my body didn't share his optimism. Whether it was due to the months of malnutrition or the exposure to the cold, my immune system seemed to have given up. After two more days, the pain had spread to my face. In another week it was into my chest, making it hard to breathe.

"I'm taking you back to the estate," Eloi said one windy morning in late Novembre. "We have to get you on dialysis."

"You know he'll kill us both." I closed my eyes and tried to ignore the shooting pain in my head and neck. "My dad is a doctor. If we could—"

"Impossible—Gaspard will have someone watching your parents around the clock."

"If Gaspard is even alive. We need to find out what's going on. I know you don't want to leave me like this, but you have to."

"Where would I go?"

"Just far enough to get some information. Is the Emperor still alive? Are they looking for me? Then if it's good news you can bring my dad back. It's our only option."

"I'll go tonight."

"Good."

"Try to stay as still as possible so it'll spread slower. I promise I won't be more than a few hours."

I nodded. "Before you go I need to tell you about white fire."

"No. If they catch me, they—"

"The knowledge is too valuable to die with me. Please just listen."

"Fine, but don't blame me if Gaspard tortures it out of me and becomes a white-handed demigod."

As soon as it was dark, Eloi left. Although I was still nervous about being alone, I didn't feel as much pressure as before. Eloi now knew everything I did about mixing fires and using the scepter. If I died, at least he might be able to change Téles-phore for the better.

I waited up as long as I could before drifting to sleep. When I awoke, birds chirped outside the cave. It was morning.

"Eloi?"

Nothing—I was still alone.

Maybe this was good news. Maybe it meant he had found help and was organizing a rescue party.

Who was I kidding—it was definitely not good news.

I started on our stores of food and waited. The hours wore on. I felt the cave grow warmer and then cooler as the eye set. The birds fell silent again and I began to cope with the reality that Eloi might be dead. I thought about leaving to find help, but something told me to stay put and trust him. I waited another night and day. My firewood ran out, followed by my water. When my thirst got severe enough, I crawled out of my sleeping bag and collected snow in my mouth.

For two more days I waited while the ano-pent spread through my body. By the time it made its way to my light shoulder I had run out of food.

Eventually I accepted the fact that Eloi wasn't coming back—but by then it was too late. The pain was so consuming I could barely crawl out to get water, much less hike down a mountain to look for help.

On the fourth day alone, I awoke to find a snake curled in my sleeping bag. The fear only lasted a moment before hunger took over. My attempts to catch it were clumsy and it struck me several times, but its teeth were so small I barely felt it. I finally managed to beat its head against the cave floor until it went limp.

I immediately bit into the belly. The sensation of warm liquid in my mouth was a welcome change. It tasted horribly metallic, but I swallowed it quickly and suppressed my gag reflex. The flavor of the raw meat was harder to ignore. It was like rotting fish. If it hadn't been for the scales getting stuck to the back of my throat I probably could have finished it. But after a few bites, everything ended up on the cave floor.

I rolled onto my back and moved to wipe the spittle from my mouth, but it wasn't worth the effort.

How had I come to this? I should have gone out looking for Eloi the day he didn't come back.

If Eloi was dead it meant Gaspard was looking for me, which meant I probably would've gotten caught anyway. At least that would have been a quick end.

Another wave of nausea overtook me and I clamped my hand over my mouth. I couldn't afford to lose any more fluids.

When had my life become this nightmare? I longed to be back on the rugby pitch where everything made sense. If I became injured during a game, the crowd would fall silent, my teammates would carry me to safety.

But I had no right to want that. I had cost Eloi his life. Marin had been tortured for me. I'd gotten Véronique's hopes up just to abandon her family to a life of poverty and disease. And Gaspard had been behind it from the very beginning. Had he gone straight from the Gardens to find Aro? The thought of Grandpa giving his life for nothing brought a strangled cry to my throat. Gaspard lived and I was going to die anyway.

I should have left with Véronique when I had the chance.

I cried out again. There were so many people I ached to see —to be held by. Most of all Grandpa Zacharie. In those months at the estate he'd been everything to me.

The rest of my family was lucky. They never knew he was alive, and didn't know of his horrific death—they'd go on living.

In time they'd forget me too.

Black, I was pathetic. But at least my self-pity distracted me from the pain engulfing my body.

After what seemed like an hour of bemoaning my fate and imagining what I would do to Gaspard if I ever saw him again, the snake flavor in my mouth began to taste good again, and I picked the carcass clean.

It was a few more days before I could bring myself to finish the puddle of vomit as well. By then it was frozen and I had to chip up pieces with my teeth. Eventually I grew too tired and cold to continue.

I spent the next several days in and out of fitful sleep. When I could manage it, I screamed for help. When I couldn't, I cried softly and prayed for my life to end. I grew dehydrated and confused. I could no longer leave the sleeping bag, and my urine-soaked clothes sapped my body heat. After what must have been two weeks following Eloi's disappearance, the poison reached my fire.

I screamed until my voice gave out. I finally understood why the old men had writhed on the cathedral floor. It was the pain of death, yet my body refused to die. When I thought the torture had reached its peak—that it couldn't possibly get any worse—it did. Doubled over from agony, I heaved until not even bile remained.

The disorientation that had plagued me since I'd lost my sight now swallowed me whole. I lost all sense of the world around me. All that existed was the agony.

Each second felt like an hour. There was no day and night, no time. There was not even me.

Only pain.

Then.

Finally.

Mercifully.

My mind shut off, plunging me into blessed darkness.

"Thank the Créateur—he's still with us."

It wasn't Eloi. I knew instinctively I was no longer in the cave. For one thing it was warmer, for another I was dry and wearing clean clothes. Best of all, there was no pain.

"Who's there?" I said, my voice barely audible.

"He can talk. That's a good sign."

"Where's Eloi?"

"I'm here," Eloi said.

Tears sprang to my eyes. "I thought you—"

"Save your energy," Eloi said. "I'm sorry I put you through that."

"What happened?"

"I made the mistake of approaching a Green. He answered my questions but must have gone straight home to call the police. Gaspard is very much alive and had offered a sixty thousand cuivre award for tips leading to the arrest of two missing servants."

"So we're at the estate?" It was the only explanation for my sudden recovery.

"No. I finally escaped and brought you to the only place I knew you had friends."

"I give up. Where am I?"

"We are currently in an non-functional sewage pipe."

"What?" I said. "What about the shelter?"

"Gaspard shut that down a while back. Too much money to run, apparently."

So if the DeGraves had moved back into their old sewage pipe, did that mean…

I suddenly found it difficult to breath. "Véronique?" Did I want her to see me like this?

"She's gone," another person replied. I knew the voice but couldn't concentrate enough to place it.

"Gone?! She's not—"

"She moved into a house."

Now I knew who it was. The ten-year-old boy whom Aro

blackmailed into painting me. The boy whose life I'd saved, only to have him save mine in return. "Baptiste."

"You know, so far you haven't been a very effective king."

I grinned. "Nice to see you too—or it would be if I could see."

Baptiste and Eloi filled me in on what I'd missed—which was a lot.

No sooner had Gaspard's hand been restored than he proclaimed himself Emperor and began making decrees. He dissolved the Dominateur and appointed the surviving Doms as sub-rulers in charge of hospitals, schools, and law enforcement. All Mélangé were declared inferior and sent to live in Taudis Rogue. For some reason the DeGraves had moved in with a Red named Luc. They had bequeathed their concrete pipe to Baptiste and his father. When Eloi showed up in the middle of the night with my limp body, Monsieur Wedel ran to Hameau Vert for a nurse and Baptiste slipped away to tell the DeGraves I was alive.

The nurse, a soft-spoken Green woman with cool hands, had gotten me re-hydrated and apparently given me something potent for the pain.

"So I'm not healed?"

"Sorry," the woman said. "In fact, from the look of your fire, I'd say it's only a matter of hours."

"Can I get a second opinion?"

"Apart from taking you directly to the Emperor, I'm afraid there's nothing we can do."

"That's inconvenient." At least I knew where I stood. I turned toward the sound of Baptiste's breathing. "Can you get my family here? What about Véronique? Why didn't she come back with you?"

"Everyone's on the lookout," Monsieur Wedel said, "hoping to get a piece of the reward money. We took a huge risk bringing Madame Lefebvre here. Had to wade through the river since Pont en Pierre is locked down."

The nurse was Madame Lefebvre? I wondered if I should say something about her son. When I'd confessed to murdering Arnaud at the classification ceremony, I'd also mentioned it had been an accident. Did she believe me? If anyone had reason to turn me in, it was her.

"The DeGraves are getting a bed ready for you at Luc's house," Baptiste said. "We're supposed to bring you up as soon as you can be moved."

"Then what are we waiting for?"

"My husband," said Camille. "He's collecting our children from the Taudis Orphanage."

For a moment I didn't understand, then I remembered. In a fit of guilt, I'd reacted with all four of her kids. Rather than giving them a brighter future I'd ended up separating them from their parents.

"I'm sorry my gesture turned out to be worthless."

"No one could have known. It was your gift of ten thousand cuivres that helped us out the most."

What do you know, Gaspard actually honored my request —of course that was back when he thought I'd be a good little puppet.

"That's how I paid for my nursing recertification, giving me access to pain-killers, which you've no doubt found useful."

I nodded. "I'm really sorry about Arnaud."

Camille pursed her lips. "For a while I hated you. I almost threw the money back in the messenger's face. But then my husband reminded me of the time Arnaud had come home from school with a cut above his eye. After questioning him, I filed a report against one of his schoolmates. The family had to pay a large fine and the child got a public lashing.

"Six months later I found out that Arnaud had mercilessly taunted the boy about his crooked teeth." She put a hand on my arm. "I didn't raise him to be like that."

"I know."

"I'm a good mother." Her voice broke on the last word.

"I know."

"It's better if we go a few at a time anyway," Monsieur Wedel said. "I'll take Bruno and Baptiste in the handcart."

It was nearly an hour later and Camille's husband had still not returned. Eloi had already left to sneak into Ville Bleu. He said he'd try to get to my parents without being seen. I had told him about Grandpa's research hidden in my dad's office, but he didn't think it likely they'd be able to stop by the hospital.

Probably for the best—they could always grab the research later, but I wouldn't be around all day. Strange that I felt so indifferent about my own death. Maybe because anything was better than rolling around in that cave without anyone to hear my screams.

"Be careful," Camille said to Monsieur Wedel. "We'll follow as soon as we can."

I wanted to ask why she had to bring her entire family to the DeGrave's house but instead thanked her again for the pain meds. I was glad I could enjoy my last few hours—especially if Véronique was involved. I still wasn't excited for her to see me in my deathbed glory, but she would certainly make the passing easier.

Soon Baptiste and I were lying under a blanket listening to wooden wheels creaking along the cobblestone street.

"The Emperor tortured Eloi to find out where you were," Baptiste whispered. "Eloi said he would take them to you, but as soon as he was outside he broke his thumb and slipped out of the handcuffs."

"You know, I think I might give him a raise."

Baptiste laughed and Monsieur Wedel shushed us.

"Oh, I almost forgot," Baptiste said, softer. "I got a letter from my mom. She wants me to come visit her in Deatherage."

"How did you find her?"

"It was Jeannette's sister. You know, the one you're obsessed with. She called four mental health facilities on the mainland until she found her."

"That's great."

"It would be, but now Mélangé can't leave the Taudis."

"Quiet," Monsieur Wedel said. "Pokers."

Baptiste and I fell silent.

"Hello gentlemen," Monsieur Wedel said.

"Out a little late, aren't you?" came a gruff voice.

"Got to get the presents hidden while the kids are asleep. You know how it is—they get smarter every year."

"Make it quick."

Presents? I must have been out longer than I thought. "What day is it?" I whispered after we'd passed the patrol.

"Forty-second of Decembre," Baptiste answered.

We were quiet after that, both of us likely thinking the same thing. I wasn't going to last three days and that meant I was going to ruin my family's *Jour de la Naissance*.

When the cart finally came to a stop Baptiste helped unload me. Even though I wasn't hurting, my limbs were stiff and useless.

A door creaked open. "He's here!" came a familiar voice. It was Mama DeGrave. She put a hand on my face. "You poor thing. Bring him inside."

The house was warm and smelled of food. Hushed voices gathered around me—many more than I'd expected.

"At last."

"Bring him to the bed."

"What have they done to him?"

I felt like I should apologize for looking like a recently animated corpse. Is that why Véronique hadn't made her way to me yet? I wouldn't blame her for being disgusted. At least I wasn't bald anymore. It was amazing how much warmer my head was with a half inch of growth.

"Welcome Bruno, Rightful King of Télesphore," came a soft male voice from somewhere near the floor. "My name is Luc and this is my home. You'll have to excuse me for not standing to greet you—I have no legs."

An unusual introduction, but at least he was nice enough

to take me in. "Thank you for having me," I said once they'd laid me on the bed. "Although I'm afraid I'm putting you all in danger by being here."

"You give us all hope by being here," Luc said. "When Baptiste told us you were coming we began gathering your troops."

"My troops?"

"Those you will lead against Emperor Livius."

What? Hadn't anyone told them I'd be dead in few hours? I couldn't even walk, how was I supposed to lead an army?

"Let me introduce my family," Luc said. "You probably remember my mother-in-law, Rosette."

Rosette? It didn't ring a bell.

"Bruno?"

My entire body went numb with pleasure. I knew that voice. Just hearing it took away my fear and embarrassment. However long I had to live, at least I would have that voice to keep me company.

"Oh, yes," Luc said, "I think you know my wife, Véronique."

CHAPTER FOURTEEN

A LAST REQUEST

A s a kid, watching my parents argue had always been entertaining. Whether it was because they knew I was listening or because they wanted to impress each other with their intelligence, they'd use big words and pile on the sarcasm. I used to eavesdrop from the next room, occasionally keeping score.

Listening to a house full of frightened strangers quarrel was another thing entirely. Not only did they all try to speak at once, they were prone to name-calling and tended to repeat their arguments ad nauseam.

"As long as he lives we're required to protect him with our lives."

"You're a fool if you think that means walking directly into—"

"I'd rather be a fool than a coward."

"Just because you're Green doesn't mean you're in charge."

I'd lost track of who was saying what. If I hadn't been the topic of conversation I probably would've asked that they leave my room so I could rest.

"The bottom line is we need him to wield the scepter. How can we hope to defeat Livius without it?"

"If he would tell us what he knows about creating white fire, maybe one of us could use it. Does he want the secret to die with him?"

Having them talk about me as if I weren't there was getting irritating. I thought about telling them Eloi knew as much as I did but decided he must have had a reason for keeping it quiet.

"White fire isn't going to solve anything," Mama DeGrave said. "Bruno is the only one who knows how to use the scepter anyway."

"According to your daughter, that's not exactly true."

"Jeannette?"

"If you're going to endanger us all by keeping her little friend in the house the least we could do is utilize him."

"Aro can't be trusted," came Luc's voice.

The hair on my arms prickled. "Aro? You mean he's here?"

"He's been disowned by the Emperor," Luc said. "He was sent to the Taudis with the other mixed fires."

"Jeannette convinced us to take him in," Mama DeGrave said. "He's been here a couple weeks now. So far he seems cooperative. At least he's answered our questions."

Was this for real? It seemed every time I turned around Aro was weaseling his way back into my life. And now I was supposed to believe he was on our side?

"You'll forgive me if I don't run to embrace him," I said.

"We understand," Luc replied. "We don't trust him either. He has been confined to the smallest bedroom and interacts only with Rosie and Jeannette. He doesn't know you're here and we plan to keep it that way."

"He's a spy," another voice said. "Give me ten minutes and I'll have it out of him."

"You would torture a thirteen-year-old boy?" Mama De-

Grave said.

"Why don't we ask Bruno what he thinks," Luc said. "After all, he is still king."

The room fell silent. I could feel their eyes on me.

"Aro doesn't know anything helpful," I said after a moment. "Still, if you wanted to torture him for the fun of it I wouldn't stop you."

Someone gasped.

"He's kidding, for blank's sake."

"We don't need the scepter," I continued. "Now is not the time for illusions and light tricks. The royal guards and soldiers are out looking for me, leaving the estate vulnerable. I think—"

"Then the dialysis machines will be unguarded!"

I sighed. "It's too late. Trying to save me now would only waste the precious time we have left. You need to gather as many men as you can and march against Gaspard."

"Where will we get weapons? Who will lead us?"

"Eloi could do it," I said. "He's young, but he knows the estate and has been trained in combat. He's also quite resourceful."

"Not to mention gorgeous," someone whispered.

A few women giggled.

I felt a pang of sadness. At first I didn't know why, but then I realized I missed being talked about like that. I missed being the one girls giggled over and passed notes to. Of course I was being ridiculous. The only thing that mattered was that they be willing to follow Eloi into battle.

Still, after everyone left the room, I lay on my bed feeling the place in my arm where my bicep used to be. Véronique hadn't attended the bedroom meeting. After Luc had introduced her, she kind of disappeared. It was probably for the best that she was avoiding me. Anything I said to her at this point would just make things more awkward.

She must have known how I felt about her. Obviously she didn't feel the same way. More than likely, she'd been in love with Luc before she met me. There was nothing to discuss.

But that didn't keep me from holding my breath every time the bedroom door opened. Usually it was Camille coming in to check on me, but occasionally Luc would enter with questions about the layout of the estate.

I was drifting off when the door flew open again, this time hitting the wall.

I sat up in bed. "What is it?"

"You're alive!" came a hysterical female voice.

Before I could react, I was being violently squeezed. The smell of the girl's expensive perfume was enough to identify her.

"Orie." The blond girl who had been willing to give up everything to help me escape justice. Ironic that after I rejected her, it was her surgeon father who removed my hand for Gaspard.

"I'm so sorry. They told me what happened."

"How did you know I was here?"

Orie disentangled herself from my neck. "I was there when Sébastien called Daddy to perform the emergency hand transplant. I heard him say you escaped with one of the guards."

"But that was months ago."

"I've been making regular visits to Baptiste's pipe to see if he had any news. This morning Monsieur Wedel told me where I could find you."

"Well, it's good to see you, too… you know what I mean."

Orie didn't laugh. "I almost didn't recognize you."

"I know —I'm scary."

"No," Orie said with sudden ferocity. "I didn't think it was possible, but you're even more beautiful than before."

I scoffed to hide my embarrassment. "I'm sure the anopent discoloration really brings out my eyes. Have you heard anything about Marin? Is he still okay?"

"His family has been gone for months. They took Drea to the mainland to search for you, right after the Chancellor read your letter."

"I didn't write that—obviously."

"Is it true you're dying?"

I nodded.

Orie began to cry. "What was the point?"

"Uh…"

"Why did I spend my entire life loving you for it to end like this? I mean, maybe if you had loved me back it would've been worth it, but—"

"I do love you." The words came out faster than I could stop them. Although they were true, I knew Orie was not talking about the same kind of love I was. After all she'd done for me, I was starting to think of her as a member of the family.

"You love me?" she asked.

I opened my mouth to explain but stopped. Was there any real point in telling her I only loved her as a friend? Véronique was married. I was as good as dead. Would it really hurt to let Orie feel loved for a few minutes?

"Don't sound so surprised," I said. "You're a thoughtful, beautiful girl. I'd be a fool not to love you."

Orie sobbed even louder and suddenly I felt her salty lips on mine. I kissed her back, silently thanking her for every sacrifice she'd made on my behalf, for every moment she'd spent despairing that I was out of reach.

I have to admit it wasn't all that bad. Although the drugs were starting to wear off and her caresses were hurting my ear, I could think of worse ways to spend my last few minutes. My only regret was that it wasn't—

"Oh, I'm sorry," came a quiet voice from the doorway.

My heart stopped.

Orie pulled herself off me.

"I heard someone crying," Véronique said. "I didn't mean to—"

"It's okay," Orie said. She sounded flustered. "I need to get home anyway. Claudette thinks I'm playing Firearchy at Blue Garden."

The bed creaked and Orie's weight disappeared.

"Be careful leaving the Taudis," I said. "Keep your fire in your pocket."

I felt another quick peck on my cheek and then Orie's footsteps faded down the hall.

"I really am sorry," Véronique said. "I thought you were alone."

My first impulse was to explain myself—tell her I didn't really like Orie—but I knew it didn't matter. There was no point trying to impress Véronique. She belonged to someone else now.

I decided to be happy for her. "Congratulations on the marriage. Luc seems nice."

"He is nice. I'd better go."

"Wait," I said, desperate to keep the conversation going. "So you thought it was me doing all that high-pitched sobbing?"

"How was I supposed to know what your crying sounds like?"

"I don't cry—and when I do, it's very manly sounding."

Véronique's laugh gave me the chills.

"Can I ask you a question?" I said.

After a pause, she answered in the affirmative.

"And I want a completely honest answer," I added.

"Okay."

"What do I look like?"

"Skinny."

"I'm talking about the ano-pent. Is it bad?"

"Well, the side of your head is black, and dark tendrils are shooting out and spiraling down your arms. It's kind of chanmé actually."

I winced and adjusted my weight.

"Do you want me to get Camille?"

"No—she'll have to go back to Hameau Vert for more medication. It's not worth the risk."

What I didn't say was that I couldn't bear to have Véronique leave me.

"Luc opened a bottle of champagne. That might help dull the pain a little."

"Champagne?" My stomach churned.

"It was left over from the wedding."

"I'm actually not a huge fan of the stuff."

"Bruno," Véronique said in a completely different tone, "I owe you an explanation."

"You don't owe me anything. It's none of my business."

"I want to explain why I married Luc—please."

I braced myself for a tidal wave of disappointment.

"A few weeks ago Livius decreed that all single girls ages sixteen to twenty-five attend 'musical auditions' at the estate."

"Do you play an instrument?"

"The auditions had less to do with talent and more to do with aesthetics if you get my meaning. A creepy old man was looking for pretty young women to keep him company."

I balled my hands into fists.

"The only way out of it was to get married. Luc was the only single Red not living at the construction site. He agreed to become my husband."

"Of course he did—you're the most amazing girl on the island."

Véronique fell silent. I would've given anything to see if she was blushing. I had to stop flirting—I was only making this harder for myself.

I decided to change the subject. "What construction site?"

"Gaspard sent all able-bodied Red men to build a stupid castle. My brothers say they work around the clock with no safety equipment and hardly any water."

"I bet La-la hates me for getting him out of prison to do hard labor."

"No, you saved his life," Véronique said. "A month ago Livius executed the inmates and demolished the prison."

"He demolished it?"

"So he could build his castle there. He killed Adisa." She sniffed. I regretted both being blind and not having a tissue to offer her.

"Why would he do that?" I asked after a moment.

"Her dad refused to organize the massacre of the prisoners, so he and his family were executed as well. I think that's part of the reason Eloi betrayed his father."

"What about LaClaire?"

"Who?"

"Did Adisa's dad remarry?"

"I don't think so."

I regretting having this conversation. Hearing about all of Gaspard's crimes was not only severely depressing—it was making me much less content to lay down and die.

"What does he do with people who break the law?"

"What do you think? Luc says more citizens have died of plague darts in the last month than in the entire history of—"

She broke off as I sucked in breath.

"What's wrong?"

"My light hand," I said. "It's burning cold."

"Your fire doesn't look so good. It's almost like the black scales are eating away at the light. I'll get Camille."

"No," I said. "I don't want a doctor. I don't want more drugs. I want you to stay here."

"How can I help you, Bruno?" Véronique said. It sounded like she was speaking carefully to keep the emotion out of her voice. "Tell me what to do and I'll do it."

With everything in me I wanted to reach out and bring her into my chest. I wanted to die with my face in her hair.

But I couldn't ask her. Especially not after she'd just caught me making out with Orie.

"Just talk to me." Preferably something interesting to distract from the growing pain in my fire.

"We are talking."

"No, we're having a serious discussion. I want to talk."

"Okay…"

"Can't we pretend we're back in the lobby of Baptiste's apartment? Like the last six months never happened? I just want to get to know you."

"Usually the way that works is you ask me questions."

"Okay. What's your biggest regret?"

I thought she would say getting into the boat with those boys, which resulted in Lala's imprisonment, but instead she told me a story about her dad rescuing a Green woman who'd fallen from the bridge.

"Jeannette was just a baby, so Papi forced her to react—but I was too scared."

"So you missed your chance to become Orange," I said through gritted teeth. The drugs had almost completely worn off and it was all I could do not to cry out.

"It gets worse. I freaked out and attracted the police. They charged him with murder and forcing reaction. They executed him on Mama's birthday."

"I'm so sorry." By this point my whole body was shaking.

"So what's your biggest regret?" Véronique said in a forced happy voice.

I struggled to speak. "Not being able to say goodbye to my parents. Which is funny because I hate goodbyes."

"Eloi will be here," Véronique said. "He called Luc a few

hours ago and said he'd made contact with your parents. They were going to stop by the hospital."

Sweat broke out on my face. My light hand felt encased in ice. I lay back against the bed and tried not to let the pain show in my expression.

"Véronique?"

"Yes."

"If things had turned out differently, do you think we could have been happy together?"

The was a pause. Then her hand was in mine, our fires touching.

"No!" I clumsily yanked my arm away. "Camille said the poison will transfer."

"That's what I'm counting on." Véronique grabbed my hand again. Her grip was too strong—I couldn't muster enough energy to pull free.

"Help!" I yelled.

Within seconds, I heard running in the hallway.

"Véronique?" Mama DeGrave said. "What's happening?"

"She's trying to react with me!" I said, still twisting my hand to avoid contact with her fire.

The next instant, Véronique's fingers were ripped from mine, and I pulled my trembling palm to my chest.

"Mama, I was trying to give him more time. If I take some of the poison maybe he'll be able to say goodbye to his parents."

"What if they never get here?" Mama DeGrave said in a loud voice. "Meanwhile you'd both be dead."

A few more sets of feet shuffled into the room.

"No," Véronique said. "I can go to the estate. Gaspard will heal me."

"For what price?" Mama DeGrave said. "I'll not have you become one of his female entertainers."

"I have to do this," Véronique said. "I've caused enough pain in people's lives. I think it's time I took some away."

"I love the boy, too," Mama DeGrave said. "He saved my Nicolas. But I will not let you throw your life away."

"Neither will I," I said.

There was a commotion in another part of the house. Baptiste was shouting. Was Aro trying to escape?

"I'll be the one making a trip to the estate," said Mama De-Grave. "I'm sure the Emperor is not interested in adding me to his harem."

Baptiste was still chanting something—it sounded like, "They're here."

Who was here?

Mama DeGrave slid her hand into mine and pressed it against my fire. The smell of champagne on her breath and Baptiste's chanting distracted me just long enough that by the time I tried to pull away, my fingers were already locked in place.

Mama DeGrave cried out.

The hallway erupted in a flurry of feet.

"He's in here!" Baptiste said from the doorway.

"Bruno?"

It was my father's voice.

"What are you doing to my boy?" I heard Mom say through a sob. "Get your filthy hands off him!"

With a burst of pain the reaction completed. Mama De-Grave's hand slipped from mine and she landed on the floor with a thump.

"Help her, Dad."

Quiet voices gathered around us.

"Are you okay, Mama?" Véronique asked.

"I think so—there's a lot of pain."

"I apologize for my daughter," came Granny's voice. "She's short on tact but long on emotional outbursts."

I grinned—my family was here. I swear I could feel them in the room. It was like they were giving off heat.

My hand felt less cold. I realized I was no longer shaking. But my relief was nothing compared to my guilt. Why hadn't I just kept my mouth shut and died like a man? Now Véronique's mother was infected too.

Fingers moved across my forehead. "I know I sound like Granny Jade, but your hair's too short."

"I'm dying, Mom."

"Eloi told me."

"Rosette was trying to take some of the poison."

Mom's hand stiffened. "Did it work?"

"I think so. It doesn't hurt as much."

Dad examined my fire, and then Mama DeGrave's.

"We need to get her to the estate," Véronique said. "She needs dialysis."

"Those old machines haven't been used in years," Dad said. "And anyway, she's taken a lot of the anoxium pentathol into her fire."

"Are you saying it's not worth trying?" Véronique said.

"I'm saying it's a long shot."

"Well, I've already lived my life," Granny said. "I might as well give her a few more hours. It's a long walk to the estate."

"Oh, no you don't, Mother," Dad said.

"Stop fussing, Andre. It's my life and I'll cut it short if I please."

After a moment of complete quiet, Granny said, "Oh, dear, that does pack a punch, doesn't it."

"How does it feel, Mama?" Véronique asked.

"Better," Mama DeGrave said. "Much better."

"I just had an idea," Dad said. "Our immune system produces antibodies against the ano-pent. Maybe if we dilute it enough, our bodies can overtake the poison."

"That's a big if," Mom said.

"I think he's right," came Camille's voice from the corner. "The ano-pent reproduces at a strictly controlled rate. If we dilute it fast enough we should be able to keep any one person from getting too much. If we're going to do this, we'd better hurry though."

"We'll need as many fires as we can get," Dad said. "Everyone has to take some of the poison if it's going to work."

A loud banging sounded from the front of the house.

Everyone fell silent. Someone was at the door.

A single pair of feet raced down the hall toward us.

"It's the police," said Eloi. "They followed us."

CHAPTER FIFTEEN

IN BED

E loi described the three officers outside the front door.

"The red-faced one is Claude," I said. "The coffee-and-milk-skin guy, I call Dimples. They're both crêpe bags."

"The third is no better," Camille said. "He once kicked my six-year-old for making fun of his long hair."

"We need to hide Bruno," Mom said, "maybe under—"

"No, we fight," Eloi said. "Even if we could hide him, half of us smell like champagne. They could arrest us just for having alcohol."

Another violent knock seemed to shake the entire house. Whispered arguments broke out amid prayers and quiet sobs. I had never felt more helpless. Being blind was bad enough, but to be confined to a bed while my friends took on three large men with weapons? If only it had been Officer Juenes at the door. Overpowering an eighty-year-old woman would've been a piece of cake.

"Wait," I said. "We need to turn out the lights."

"No good," Eloi said. "They already know we're in here."

"Yeah, but they don't know why we're here."

It only took a few seconds to explain my plan, and a few more to get everyone into position. Véronique and I were the only ones left in the bedroom, but with the door cracked we could hear what was going on.

Another knock. The police yelled something about entering by force. Hurry, Mom. Any minute she would open the door and flip on the lights. Eloi had advised everyone to stand back in case the officers were trigger-happy.

After what seemed like forever, a chorus of voices yelled, "Surprise!"

"What the—"

"Where's Yvette?" Mom said.

"What's going on here?" Claude bellowed. "Where are you keeping the fugitive?"

"I'm sorry officers," Dad said—he would be holding the bottle of champagne. "We were expecting Officer Juenes. This was supposed to be her retirement party."

"Yvette's retiring?" said one of the other officers.

"She's a close friend of the family," Dad said. "She was keeping it quiet. You don't happen to know if she's on her way?"

"You expect us to believe that Blues would sneak across the river to throw a party?" Claude said.

"What of it?" Granny said. "Since the Self-Proclaimed Emperor of the Universe sent all our Mélangé friends here, it's the only way we could include them."

"You're lucky none of the Royal Guard or soldiers are with us," Claude said. "They wouldn't take so kindly to slurs against the Emperor. Now, I want everybody on their faces with their hands on their heads. We're going to search every square inch of this house until we find that Nazaire boy and if anybody so much as sneezes they get a dart to the back."

Across the room, Véronique's breathing grew louder. I wasn't feeling overly peaceful myself, since my plan had just backfired.

"Who's in this room?" Claude said from the hallway.

I nearly fell out of the bed.

"Oh, my daughter's in there, sick," Mama DeGrave said. "The doctor hasn't figured out what it is yet. Don't know if it's contagious." Real subtle.

Without warning, my pillow slid out from under my head and was replaced on my face. I thought someone was trying to smother me, until I felt Véronique slide under the covers.

"Don't move," she whispered. In a matter of seconds she had positioned herself directly on top of me with her back flat against my chest.

With every brain cell that hadn't been completely overloaded by this turn of events, I strained to keep my limbs directly under hers. Was there any chance of making it look like there was only one person in the bed? Véronique relaxed and I felt the weight of her head on the pillow. By turning my face I found a pocket of air and took in quick shallow breaths. It was a good thing I'd lost sixty plus pounds—I took up much less space now.

"Check the closet and under the bed," Claude said. He was in the room, but his voice sounded muffled, as if he were holding a hand over his mouth.

"Be careful not to wake her," Granny hissed from the hall. "She tends to vomit when she's awake."

I pressed my palm into the mattress. Hopefully the blankets were thick enough to hide my white light.

The closet door opened. I heard grunting next to the bed as one of the officers managed to get a look underneath. Then the room grew silent and I realized they'd gone. Véronique and I listened as the officers checked the remaining rooms.

I had a mini-heart attack when I remembered Aro was in the house, but the kid must not have caused any trouble. Soon, I heard the policemen back in the front, laughing and telling about how "the old bird" had once tried to arrest a man for walking in on her in the fan, only to discover she was the one in the wrong fanroom. My father laughed the loudest and offered the policemen another glass of champagne. By the time they'd had their fill and wished everyone a happy Naissance, most of the feeling had left my arms and legs.

"They're gone," Granny said from the doorway. "And Bruno, you know if your father finds you like this you're going to get a lecture."

I tried to laugh, but it came out as a whimper.

"You still alive under there?" Véronique said as she climbed off the bed. "Sorry I'm so bony."

"I barely felt you," I lied.

"That couldn't have come at a worse time," Dad said. "Everyone get in here, quick. We need to start diluting the ano-pent."

Everyone including Aro, my parents, and Camille's entire family crowded into my tiny bedroom and began shaking hands. One would react with me, and then three others would react with that person. Some got less ano-pent than others, so they ended up coming back for another round from someone else. With each new reaction my hand felt warmer, less stiff. I kept waiting to feel Véronique's hand in mine, but after eight reactions my pain disappeared completely and my exhausted body fell into a deep sleep.

I awoke with a stiff neck and a horrible taste in my mouth. My eyes hurt more than normal. I reached up to rub them and somebody caught my wrist.

"Don't touch," Granny said. "You'll disturb the salve."

Salve? With a jolt of surprise I realized I could see her. Okay, maybe "see" was a little optimistic, but I could make out a blob that was probably her face and I had to squint against the light from her brilliant white palm.

"You're White," I said.

"It worked, Andre!" Granny called. "Get in here!"

Another white fire entered the room. "He can see?" Mom said.

"Either that or he's psychic," Granny said. "He knew my fire was white."

Two more white fires entered.

"It's probably okay to remove the ointment now," Dad said. "How are you feeling?"

"I've been worse," I said with a laugh. "What did you do?"

"How's your vision?"

I waved a hand in front of my face. "Still can't see anything out of my dark eye, but the light is way better."

Dad sat down on the bed and pressed a cold cloth against my eyes. I winced, but my mouth was stuck in a permanent grin.

"Ready?" Dad said.

I nodded. Please, please, please let this work.

He removed the cloth, and there they were, beaming at me. My father looked older than I remembered and Mom was crying.

"I can see. It's pretty cloudy and I have no depth perception, but I'll take that any day."

I looked past my parents, and there by the door, stood Véronique, her hands pressed together at her mouth as if praying. The light from her white fire made her caramel eyes almost luminescent. She briefly returned my smile, then disappeared into the hallway.

Mom took my hand. "When Eloi told us you were blind, your father called an eye surgeon. That's why it took so long to get up here."

"Did you get Grandpa's research?"

"We found his metal folder," Granny said, "but we haven't been able to open it yet."

I reached up and grabbed Granny's light hand with mine. She smiled, but I could tell she wasn't quite over the shock of learning her husband had been alive.

After a respectful moment Dad cleared his throat. "Eloi said Gaspard used corrosive chemicals in an aerosol can—any idea which?"

I shook my head.

"I thought you might need a corneal transplant," Dad said. "But the specialist suggested a topical steroid to reduce inflammation. I'm glad we tried it."

"Any chance those steroids will beef me up a little?"

"You'll be lucky if it doesn't cause glaucoma. As it is you're going to have to stay inside for a few days while your eyes are recovering."

"Do I get an eye patch? The girls will love that."

From the foot of the bed, Granny laughed. "By the way, your secret's out."

"Secret?"

She lifted her fire. "It seems this is the first time Reds, Greens, and Blues have indiscriminately mixed their shades. All this blazing white light certainly saves on electricity."

I grinned. "Is everyone okay?"

"They're fine," Dad said. "We were mostly worried about you. Especially when you didn't wake up for two days."

"Two days?"

Dad looked at his watch. "In ten minutes it will be Eve of Naissance."

"Aren't the police wondering why you're not home yet?"

Dad yawned. "We told them we'd be spending Naissance here with our friends. I also told them that if they asked, Yvette would probably deny she was retiring."

"They won't ask. From what I've seen they go out of their way to avoid her."

"We should get some sleep, Andre," Mom said. "Luc and Véronique offered their bed again."

I flinched. The words "their bed" ripped a hole somewhere in my chest.

"We'll sleep on the floor with everybody else," Dad said.

Mom nodded and after many more hugs and kissed fires, my parents left. I offered Granny my bed, but she claimed she wasn't tired.

"You know your mother wanted to name you Luc," Granny said, once the door had closed. "Then when you came out with a thick head of brown hair, I suggested Bruno. It was the first and last time she ever took my advice."

"Thanks—Luc is a toilet-pouch name."

Granny gave me a strange look.

I examined my fire. For the first time I saw the scar around my wrist and noticed how small and frail the fingers were compared to my dark hand. The linear burn bisecting my fire brought back the horror of that day in the cathedral.

"I'm sorry you didn't get to see Grandpa."

Granny took a paper out of her pocket. It was a note written in red pencil. "I got this the same day Livius took over the government. Eloi had mailed it for your grandfather."

"What does it say?"

"Mostly mushy stuff you have no business reading. But he did tell me you would've made a great scientist. And that he knew he would probably not live to…"

Granny made a show of carefully refolding the paper. After

a moment she said, "Would've been nice for him to include the code to his box of research."

"It must be something easy if he didn't even think to tell you. Is it letters or numbers?"

"Numbers—I tried his birthday, my birthday, your birthday, everyone in the family's birthday. Our anniversary. I even tried the date of his disappearance. Nothing opened the blessed thing."

"At least we know it's safe. At some point I'm sure we can hire a welder to melt the edge off or something."

"It would be a miracle if it didn't damage his documents."

"Six digits in the lock?"

Granny nodded. "Might as well be six hundred. The old fool writes me a love letter and forgets the important stuff." But she was smiling. I guess it occurred to her as well that maybe his priorities weren't so warped after all.

Still, a little post script is all it would've taken. I tried to think what numbers grandpa would've used. Maybe the ages of him and his wife and daughter at the time? Or maybe the years they were all born.

"I've been meaning to talk to you about that little blonde," Granny said. "She stopped by yesterday to check on you—said you two were 'an item' now."

I put my face in my hands.

"What did you say to her?" Granny asked.

"I thought I was dying. I just wanted to make her happy."

"Well, she's happy all right. Are you prepared to make good on your promises now?"

I closed my eyes. "I guess I have to. It's not like I could be with—"

"Véronique?"

"Is it that obvious?"

"Child, the way your face lights up when you hear her voice—you'd have to be blind not to see it. No offense."

"I'll try to make it work with Orie."

"You'd better make up your mind quick. You play with that girl's emotions any longer, she's likely to turn into a homicidal maniac."

I stared at the peeling wallpaper. "When did my life get so complicated?"

"When you decided to do the right thing."

"Does it ever get easier?"

"Hopefully after tomorrow we can all take a vacation."

"Tomorrow? We're invading the estate on Naissance? That doesn't seem very neighborly."

"Eloi's idea. The guards will be down to a skeleton crew. Livius will be at his most vulnerable."

"How many do we have?"

"We'll figure that out in the morning," Granny said with a stretch. "I think I'll take you up on that bed offer. Another night on the floor might do me in."

Granny helped me out of bed. It took a few tries, but eventually I stood on my own and hobbled around the room.

"One last thing before you turn in," I said. "Can you direct me to the refrigerator? I'm starving."

CHAPTER SIXTEEN

ARO'S CHARGE

There's something about eating in the middle of the night that feels wrong. Especially when everyone else is asleep. It was nice to have a little time to myself, though. After I'd filled up on leftover *cassoulet*, I spent the early morning hours learning to use my legs again.

Mama DeGrave woke before eyerise. She applauded when she realized I could see, which woke most of the others sleeping on the floor.

Shortly after breakfast someone knocked on the door. This time it was Véronique's brothers La-la and Philippe. According to them, the guards at the construction site wanted to spend La Naissance with their families so they gave the workers a two-day vacation. Véronique's brothers were a little surprised to find their entire family White, but once Philippe heard the plans to storm the estate he wasted no time in gathering people for the meeting. He brought back several local Feu Noir gang members, including the three Reds—now Violets—with whom I reacted in the shelter when we thought we were dying.

Luc presided, but really it was Eloi running the show. He knew the estate and the guard shifts. The plan seemed fairly simple—the only real point of disagreement being whether to try and secure the scepter.

"Tell me honestly," Eloi said to me, "will it benefit us to get the light stick?"

"It might. Now that I have the use of one eye, I might be able to do the celestial blinding thing. That would prevent Gaspard's men from being able to shoot anybody for a bit."

"Is that all?"

"Well, there's supposed to be a way to stop all injustice and pain, but no one knows how to make the scepter sing."

"What?"

"Exactly."

"This entire conversation is moot," Luc said from his stool. "Even if we did send someone in to steal the scepter, they wouldn't even know where to look."

"Aro knows," came a small female voice.

The Red, Violet, and White men turned to regard Jeannette. Several seemed to be wondering what a little girl was doing in the war room.

She ignored their scowls. "Aro knows exactly where his grandpa keeps the scepter and he could get it for us."

"That's an idea," Eloi said. "Gaspard would probably take him back when he saw his white fire."

"Wouldn't he ask how his fire got that way?" Luc asked.

"He can make something up," Eloi said. "He only needs to stay long enough to grab the stick and get out."

"If he betrays us, we're all dead," Monsieur Wedel said.

"He wouldn't!" Jeannette said. "He's not prejudice like the rest of his family. That's why he's a Mélangé."

Philippe rolled his eyes. "It's time to grow up, sis. The kid's a worthless piece of crepe."

"He told you how he became Mélangé?" I asked.

Jeannette nodded. "He had a Green nanny and was just

awful to her, so a few years ago she got fed up and spanked him."

"Do we really need to listen to this?" a bald Red said. "We've got a siege to plan."

"Let her finish," I said.

Jeannette glared at the man and then continued. "When he complained to his parents they fired her, which made Aro sad because he liked her better than his own mother. Anyway, he ran away from home to find her."

"Then he reacted with her?" I asked.

"No, she'd already left for the mainland, but Aro spent four days looking for her in Hameau Vert. He traded his Blue for food and information."

"We're wasting our time," the bald man said.

"I'm sorry to say I agree," Luc said. "Even if Aro sacrificed for a Green once, that doesn't mean he hasn't turned out like his grandfather. He was handpicked to succeed Livius after all."

Luc nodded at La-la, who took Jeannette by the shoulder and led her toward the door.

Jeannette pulled away. "Aro was the only one in his family with Bruno's blood type. He wasn't picked for his toilet-pouchy-ness."

"Did Aro tell you that about the blood type?" La-la asked in a soft voice. "Because it's possible it could all be scripted by Gaspard in order to earn our trust."

Jeannette looked ready to cry.

"Bring him in here," I said. "We'll figure out whose side he's on."

Jeannette ran out of the room. Eloi smirked at me and

began distributing gloves taken from the construction site. We would attack before dawn on the morning of Naissance and the thick leather would hide our fires from the guards.

Eloi had pulled out a hand-drawn map of the estate when the door opened and Orie entered.

"Sorry, they told me Bruno was—" She stopped when she met my eye. I waved. Her mouth fell open. Then with a squeal she ran and flung herself on me. A few of the men looked amused, but most were rolling their eyes at the interruption. I endured an awkward kiss before Jeannette finally returned with Aro.

"I need a few minutes to finish up here, okay, Orie?"

Orie nodded but didn't remove herself from my arm. I felt doubly uncomfortable continuing the meeting with her hanging on me, but I had told Granny I'd try to make it work.

I turned to Aro. He looked skinnier than I remembered, and he might have grown a little taller. At least he didn't look quite so generic as he used to.

"We'd like to believe you're with us," I said, "but you can understand why we're having trouble."

Aro nodded, keeping his eyes on the floor.

"You've got thirty seconds to convince us you'd betray your entire family for our cause or you're going back into that room until it's all over."

Aro swallowed. I expected him to vent about how unfair it was that his grandfather had disowned him, but instead he apologized.

"Sorry."

"Is that all?"

"Everything I did, I knew it was wrong. I just wanted my grandfather to be proud of me."

Philippe scoffed. "You stood by and watched him commit murder. Don't tell me it was because you wanted him to be proud of you. No one needs approval that bad."

I looked at Philippe. "You'd be surprised."

Philippe narrowed his eyes until they almost disappeared beneath his bushy black eyebrows.

Aro sniffed. "And I was thinking about what you said—about me taking the fall for my grandfather. I really think he would've let me die. The only thing I don't understand is why you gave yourself up to save me at the stadium."

"Look at me."

Aro raised his head. His nose and eyes were red.

"You've done a lot of stupid stuff—but I think you're learning from your mistakes."

He nodded.

"And you're learning who you can trust. We want to fix everything your grandfather has broken. Will you help us, even if it means disappointing your family?"

"They aren't my family," Aro said. "When I didn't have a place to go it was Luc who took me in. Jeannette treated me like I was still her best friend even though I only used her as an accomplice in the Academy. And Mama DeGrave... no one's ever hugged me like that. Like I was worth it."

He wiped at his face. "These people are my..."

He couldn't finish.

I stared at him a long moment, then nodded.

"Get the kid some gloves."

After the meeting, Orie led me into an empty room and shut the door.

"Why do you have to go with them?"

"I might need to use the scepter."

"But your dad said bright light could damage your good eye. You should wait."

"I'll bring a blindfold in case we're out after dawn. I can't stay here while my friends and family risk their lives."

"Why don't they recruit more Reds? The Emperor can't stand against the entire Taudis."

I cleared my throat. This had been discussed at the meeting. "It would take time to convince them. So far we've confided in people we're sure we can trust. It only takes one Red to turn us in—and there are many who'd be tempted by the reward money."

Orie shook her head. "A few dozen people trying to storm the estate is suicide."

"Not with Eloi's help. If we keep our numbers small we should be able to slip in quietly and make it to Gaspard with very little fighting."

"Don't go."

"I'm sorry, I have to."

Without warning Orie pushed me against the wall and kissed me—and not gently. I tried to reciprocate, but this time I couldn't get into it. Whether I was stressed or distracted, the longer I kissed her, the more uncomfortable I became. I realized I'd felt that same discomfort the other times I'd kissed her as well. Maybe all the talk of giving our lives for a cause made me realize how important it was to know myself and be honest about what I truly believed.

And I truly believed what I was doing to Orie wasn't right. I did not love this girl. I thought it unlikely I ever would, at least in the way she wanted and deserved. I couldn't pretend anymore.

I turned my head to the side—but Orie continued kissing my cheek and jaw. Finally she slowed, and stopped.

"What's wrong?"

I closed my eyes. There was no way I could say this without killing her. But I had to—for her good as much as mine.

"Bruno?"

I opened my eyes and looked directly at her. "You have no idea how much I wish I loved you."

"I thought you said—"

"You're like a sister to me. I know that sounds meaningless, but…"

"I don't care if you don't love me. I mean, I do. But I can live without it. I just can't live without you." She tried to kiss me again, but I held her back.

"You can do better that this. You're gorgeous. You could have anyone else in Télesphore."

"I want you."

"I can't."

"You mean you won't."

"I mean it won't work."

"Let's just try." She reached to embrace me.

"Orie," I said firmly. "I'm sorry. It's over."

Tears appeared on her cheeks. I hadn't even seen them fall.

"Then I have no reason to live."

She opened the door and disappeared into the hall. I swore under my breath and took off after her. In the main room over twenty-five people turned to look at me.

"Where is she?"

"Outside," Philippe said, "but you shouldn't follow her."

I strode to the door and flung it open. She was running down the hill.

Toward the bridge.

Before I could get through the doorway, Philippe's giant hand clamped over my mouth and yanked me back inside.

"Not a good idea," he said. "They've been watching the house for days."

"The patrols didn't see him," Eloi said. "If they had, they'd already be trying to break down the door."

"Someone has to stop Orie," I said. "She's..."

I realized they'd probably all heard our shouted conversation.

"Aro is at the estate by now," Eloi said. "None of us can risk being seen."

Someone knocked.

"Son of a Violet," Philippe said. He released me and peeked through the curtain. One of the Violets cast him a dirty look.

"What is it?" Luc asked.

"It's a poker."

No one moved. The knob rattled and the door swung open.

Eloi grabbed an empty champagne bottle from the trash and strode toward the female solider standing in the doorway.

"Stop," I told him. "Don't hurt her."

"Hello, Bruno," Officer Dupont said.

"Sheri."

Why was she dressed like a poker?

"I've been trying to keep the patrols away from this street, but it would be a lot easier if you'd stay inside."

Everyone looked at me as if waiting for me to explain why a royal soldier was suddenly in on our little *coup d'état*.

Sheri straightened her black uniform and glanced at her gloved dark hand. She obviously wanted me to ask about her new position, but there was only one thing I wanted to ask her right now.

"Sheri, that girl that just left might try to jump from the bridge. Would you mind running after her and making sure she doesn't do anything stupid?"

"At your service, Your Grace—even if I didn't owe you my job."

I thanked her and she took off down the street.

I prayed she was as fast on foot as she was on her bike. If she arrived too late...

Eloi shut the door.

"As much as I hate to say it," Luc said, "a suicide would distract the pokers, making it easier for us to—"

I punched Luc in the face.

CHAPTER SEVENTEEN

AN UNLATCHED
WINDOW

A collective cry went up from the room as Luc flew from his stool and landed on his back. Although I was also surprised by what I had done, I'd been aching to do that since he'd introduced me to his wife.

"What's wrong with you?"

Véronique's words went straight into my chest like one of her javelins.

"I'm sorry," I muttered.

But I wasn't. I now knew with certainty that my attraction to Véronique hadn't been fleeting or shallow. I didn't care what she looked like. I loved her because she was wise and kind, strong, yet fragile. I wanted to be with her as much as Orie wanted to be with me—and neither Orie nor I was going to get what we wanted. Suddenly she didn't seem so melodramatic.

We spent the rest of the day waiting. Waiting for news of Orie. Waiting for nightfall. Waiting for the pokers to come crashing through the door. Waiting for the fear to go away. The house seemed strangely dark with us all wearing gloves. Mama De-Grave and a few others sang soft carols by the propane stove. I sat with Granny and my parents, trying to pry open Grandpa's lock box. We had tried all the combinations I'd thought of earlier and several dozen more.

"This is so unlike him," Granny said, "to purchase something like this on his own. He didn't go near the shops if he could help it."

"It was probably last minute," I said. "He knew he had made a breakthrough. I'm glad he protected it before he told Gaspard."

"But I can't imagine him reading the instructions on how to set the silly thing, let alone—"

"That's it!" I said. "Try all zeros."

Mom had the box on her lap so she turned the six dials to zero and pulled.

The file opened.

The subsequent gasps and cries of excitement brought

everyone in the room over to examine the contents of Grandpa's papers.

Sitting on top was a life drawing of me as a six-year-old on Grandpa's shoulders. I seemed to be playing the drums on his head with a wooden kitchen utensil. Grandpa Zacharie looked supremely annoyed.

"Why would he commission a drawing like that?" Mom said with a laugh. She handed the file to Dad.

Granny shook her head and squeezed my hand. I tried not to look at the tears in her eyes. I was not going to get all weepy around Véronique.

Dad held the file out to Granny—but she waved him to go ahead. He carefully took each item out and set it on the table. There were diagrams of fires and pages of notes. Although his drawings seemed kind of middle-schoolish, I was struck by how neat his handwriting was.

Granny touched each page as if it was her husband's face.

"Here's something," Dad said. "You remember Grandpa reading you this story, Bruno?"

I looked at the page. It was written in Grandpa's hand and titled, "The Jealous Jellyfish."

"Grandpa mentioned this to me in the estate. He acted like it was important. I don't remember him reading it to me, though. Where did he get it?"

"His grandfather told him that story as a child," Granny said. "It is supposed to be some kind of religious fable, but for the life of me I can't figure out what it's trying to teach."

I took the page and was about to read when a sharp intake of breath made me look up.

Dad held an envelope at arms length as if it were made of gold.

"For rainbow's sake, Andre," Granny said. "Don't just sit there gasping—what is it?"

"It's addressed to Sabine Victorieux."

"Victorieux is Briette's maiden name," Mom said.

"Briette, Marin's mom?"

She nodded. "Maybe this Sabine is related."

"Who's it from?" I asked.

Dad removed the letter and handed me the envelope. "King Jean Pierre." He scanned the letter.

I felt my eyes bulge. "You mean the one who issued the King's Requirement that made me royalty?"

Dad scanned the letter, then swore softly.

Granny rolled her eyes and took the paper.

"That's it," Dad said. "That's the King's requirement."

Granny and Dad shared a look, then she said, "Well I don't suppose there's any point in protecting her secret now."

"Um… who's her?" Crêpes, did I really just say that? Next I'll be dangling modifiers.

"Sabine was Marin's great-grandmother and a close friend of Zacharie and mine. She was also Jean Pierre's only daughter."

A few nearby people inched closer.

"Marin never told me," I said. "I'm surprised he wasn't lording it over everyone."

"Marin doesn't know," Granny said. "Only those of us who remembered King Jean Pierre knew, but Sabine asked us and her children to keep it secret. She didn't want her grandchildren feeling as if they were better than others, or somehow more deserving."

My body went cold. "Did Gaspard know?"

"Yes, Gaspard grew up with Sabine's son. It was one of the reasons he had no trouble taking the position of the Commissaire after stealing Zacharie's fire."

A sudden realization came to me. "I'd bet money Gaspard didn't arrest Marin just because of me," I said. "I think his whole intention was to take out the direct descendant of the last King."

Granny looked startled. "Get rid of the Victorieux line...," she said as if to herself. "Perhaps Bruno gave him the excuse."

Mom smiled at me. "Good thing my heroic son got Marin out of there."

"Gaspard is not a fan of the Molyneux line either," I said. "He claimed he's gonna—going to—exterminate us."

Dad called Gaspard something I won't repeat.

After a few minutes of everyone bashing on the new emperor, Philippe said, "Read the letter from the King."

Mama DeGrave shot him a look.

"Please," he said.

"It's only fitting that the current king read it," Dad said. There were a few nods, and he handed me the thin yellowed paper.

I took a breath. This was the first time I'd done anything kingly in front of my friends and family and it made me feel like a complete dork. But other people were watching who didn't know me personally. It was easier to act like the king if I kept them in mind.

34th of March 1040

Chère Fille,

I trust this correspondence finds you safely. I would sooner have waited 'til you returned to speak of such sensitive subjects, however, of late my constitution has taken a turn for the worse and I do not trust an one of my advisers to see that you receive this missive. (I tempted my chauffeur with nine hundred cuivres to drop it off in a letter box in Hameau Vert.)

The Dominateur assure me that my signature was on the aforementioned document and that it must have slipped my mind. You know as well as I that my cognitive skills have not diminished and my memory continues as ever it was.

My corporal shell is a different matter entirely. Even since you left me, I have grown so weak as to require assistance in rising from my reading cushion. Sadly, my vision has also somewhat deteriorated. I feel as though I'm aging in reverse. Am I to be treated as a naive young prince, summarily placated while the weighty decisions are made elsewhere?

I believe us prudent in keeping our secret from them.

In such case as I do not survive the next fortnight, there are sundry important issues of which you must be privy. I trust you do not object to my intentional vagueness.

I have at last discovered the reason we have not been able to contact "the others" in recent years. A surprisingly clear "message" came through only two nights prior, which took me completely aback. I attempted to reply with marginal success. The message was from our Red "neighbors."

They had lost their version of The Guide and had only recently discovered how to use the "tool" to contact us. They concluded that our difficulty in making it function was due to the degeneration of our fires—which they claim has happened as a result of "shade incest." According to the woman relaying the message, the adults of her kind are White and growing more powerful with each passing century.

If Télesphore is to survive we must adapt. Although the woman did not make clear exactly how one was to gain a white fire, there was no doubt it is something we must accomplish soon.

Rather than take the issue to the Dominateur (who will certainly discount it as foolishness), I've decided to make a royal decree without their knowledge. I feel to trust the people in this—and to motivate them to discover the secret to white fire, I will offer the throne as a reward.

I know you have always thought to be Queen, but I hope you understand what I mean to accomplish. A dying Télesphore is more a burden than a prize. After I am departed, please see that this decree is made public and please help the Dominateur understand the importance of this directive.

I have spent the afternoon devising a pithy rhyme which may help our citizens remember the goal:

If the kingdom thou dost desire, temper white thy inner fire. Make the Crystal Scepter shine, then the kingdom will be thine.

You may edit it if you like, but I'm quite proud of myself for coming up with it on short notice.

In the following pages you'll find all the legal verbage to prevent the Dominateur from attempting to take over the country or elect their own ruler. The wording does allow for a Steward or Commissaire, but the throne of Télesphore is to remain vacant until a true white fire "makes the scepter shine." I am still not clear exactly what the woman meant by this, but I trust it is crucial to the future of our race.

Please return as quickly as you are able. If I hear again from our neighbors, I shall ask for clarification—but until such time, we must all do our duty to ensure the continued growth of our beloved nation and citizenry.

Adieu,

Votre Père,

Le Roi Jean Pierre Le Vingt-Deuxième

No one spoke for a minute after I finished. Finally Dad said, "Wow."

No kidding. There was so much there, already a hundred questions were screaming to be answered. I needed to look over it again, but first I wanted to read Grandpa's jellyfish bedtime story.

I handed the king's letter to La-la who was trying to dissect it over my shoulder. While the rest of the room debated what "neighbors" Jean Pierre might be referring to—and how they might be contacted—I slipped Grandpa's story into my pocket and went to find a quiet place alone.

I wanted this to be special. I also figured it might make me cry and I didn't want anyone to see.

I found my room empty. The light was dim enough that I considered removing my glove—but this room had a large window and I didn't know who might be passing by. White fires weren't exactly commonplace in the Taudis.

I held the pages close to my good eye and walked toward the bed.

There was once a mermaid witch who worked goodly magic, and the ocean animals made her their Queen.

At dawn on her third day as ruler, a young jellyfish approached the throne.

"Change my body so I can't feel the cold," he asked. "I wish to explore what lies beyond our tropical waters."

"Magic is valuable," the Mermaid Queen said. "What will you give me in return?"

"I'll bring you back something beautiful."

So the Mermaid Queen took a precious stone from her crown

and sang to it until the jewel glowed golden yellow.

The moment the young jellyfish touched it, each of his tentacles felt bathed in warm eyelight.

"Keep this with you always," the Queen told him.

```
Have to take care of something at the mines.
         Don't follow. Back soon.
                  Neek
```

The mines? What was she thinking? I examined the window. Sure enough, it was unlocked. She must have slipped out while we were looking through Grandpa's files.

What could Véronique possibly need to do at the mines on the eve of revolution? Probably saying goodbye to that dinofish. Didn't she know how reckless this was? She was putting the entire operation at risk.

I carefully refolded grandpa's story and slid it into my back pocket. Then I stood, intending to take Véronique's note to Eloi—but I hesitated. What was the point of telling the others? No way would they let anyone go out after her. That meant if I told the others, she'd be on her own. I couldn't abandon her.

The only way to ensure her safety was to catch her and make her come back. She couldn't have gone far. Just a few minutes ago I'd seen her getting food out of the fridge.

I took a pen from the dresser and wrote:

I went after her.

-Bruno

I should have brought a coat. Although the sky was still white, the eye had disappeared behind Mt. Tremper and it was only going to get colder. Once it got dark there was no chance I'd be able to find my way around with one mediocre eye.

So far I hadn't seen any patrols. In fact, the streets were empty. It's the only reason I was still chasing her. I hoped the others didn't freak out when they realized we were gone.

When I reached the rundown cinder-block buildings at the edge of Taudis Rouge I spotted her. Véronique was sprinting across the open field toward the mine entrance with a paper bag in her arms. She looked like a manic grocery attendant.

I almost called out to her but figured it wasn't worth drawing attention to us. I tried to pick up the pace, but I hadn't run in months and my body was stuck in first gear.

Véronique reached the metal slab, set down her bag and knocked. Almost immediately, the earth rumbled. If I didn't get to her before she went down the elevator I might be trapped up here alone.

But I was already exhausted. No way I'd be able to sprint down there in time. I picked up a rock and aimed it at the rising metal slab. It fell short less than halfway. I was glad Coach Fontaine wasn't there to witness my disgraceful performance. I picked up a handful of smaller rocks and chucked them with everything I had.

Still short of the elevator, but Véronique must have heard because her head snapped up. I waved and began hobbling toward her. She sprinted back to me in a few seconds.

"Are you crazy?" she said.

"I was about to ask you the same thing."

"Well, you can't stay up here." She threw me onto her back and carried me to the elevator.

Letty's eyes went wide upon seeing Véronique's passenger.

"Is that...?"

"Yes," Véronique said as she deposited me next to the elevator. "And we need to get him underground before the pokers see."

"You're late," Letty said to Véronique. "They're getting out of hand."

Late for what? I furrowed my eyebrows at my ex-girlfriend. Had she forgotten Letty was Claude's cousin—that she ran the single cruelest work area on Télesphore for Gaspard himself? "But this woman—"

"Is my friend," Véronique said. "Get in."

"What are we doing here?"

Véronique picked up her paper bag and pushed me into the elevator. "I'll explain when you're not in plain view of every soldier and guard for two miles."

Letty squeezed my forearm as I stepped in. She looked different somehow—and it wasn't only the lack of make-up or her gloved light hand—it was her eyes. Her fixed gaze reminded me of Granny Jade when she got angry. Cold and ruthless. Maybe this wasn't such a good idea.

"Hold onto something," Letty said.

I grabbed the handbar in time to avoid toppling over as the elevator plummeted downward.

Into chaos.

CHAPTER EIGHTEEN

HUNGER

T he elevator hadn't even hit the bottom before I heard the shouting and saw hundreds of Dark Orange fires moving in the distance like molten lava.

"Can't leave them alone for a second," Letty cried.

The elevator stopped and we tumbled out.

Véronique handed her bag to one of the gloved men working the gears. "What's going on?"

A single Orange light sprinted toward us. "Madame Letty! They're trying to kill Mére Blanche!"

Véronique peeled off her glove, held her white fire aloft and sprinted toward the mass of writhing figures. Letty did the same.

I was surprised to see Letty was Orange, although a much brighter shade than the others. I took off my own glove and managed to shuffle into the main chamber just as Véronique tackled a man thigh-deep in Mére Blanche's pond—a man holding a rusted, metal table leg.

Without thinking I jumped in after her. But instead of swimming out to rescue her from the crazed workers, I splashed a bit and sank to the bottom. Luckily, it wasn't deep yet and was able to half crawl back to dry earth where I lay gasping for breath.

How does someone lose the ability to swim? I couldn't

tell if it was my emaciated body, or my complete lack of energy.

I looked back. Véronique and the man struggled for control of the table leg near the center of the pond. I really hoped she'd learned to swim recently.

Although Orange lights swarmed the area, Mére Blanche was nowhere to be seen. Probably hiding at the bottom.

Letty stood in the water up to her waist and with the fury of an enraged snow lizard, threw one person after another toward the shore.

"Amazing isn't she?"

Quinlin stood above me, balancing on his good foot. "Too bad she's married," he said.

"Letty?"

"No, Vern."

Vern? Was this kid still enamored with Véronique? Why did he not seem concerned there was a riot going on?

"Where did all these people come from? There weren't half this many last time."

Quinlin gave me a look that made me want to smack him.

"Excuse me for being out of it. I've spent the last few months being tortured by Gaspard."

"We're not here to work—this is an army."

"To kill the dino-fish?"

"No, I think they're just hungry. We've been collecting down here for weeks to go against the Emperor."

Cries sounded around us as Mére Blanche surfaced. Véronique launched herself over the top of a woman and landed beside the white beast.

"This creature is not your enemy!" she shouted.

"It belongs to the enemy," an Orange woman screamed. "We're gonna hit the Emperor where it hurts."

"Step away, DeGrave."

A muscular coffee-skin man stepped forward holding a jagged piece of glass. "Maybe our revolution will work, maybe not—but I'm not coming back as a servant to the Emperor's pet. The mines are closed."

Enough people shouted their assent that I knew pulling the I'm-King-so-do-what-I-say card wouldn't go well. These people were through being told what to do.

The man took another slow step forward. Véronique didn't move. "You think because his prize fish is dead, Gaspard will let you choose your occupation?"

But no one was listening. Others approached from the sides.

I wanted to call Véronique back, but it felt like a betrayal. How could I keep her from getting hurt? She was all that I cared about. The fate of the white fish didn't matter.

Except, it would be a tragedy to have all that golden caviar gone forever. Maybe I could use these people's hunger to my advantage.

But first I had to draw their attention away from the big fish. If only I had the scepter. I could make a flash to bring everyone's eyes to me.

Wait, since when did I need a scepter to make a flash? I held out my hand to Quinlin. "Want to shake?"

He stared at me a moment, then slapped his hand into mine. I was surprised by the heat and intensity of his fire. For a second, we felt the hum of each other's life force, then the muscles in my arm locked up, as if I were being electrocuted.

Our fires flashed, then our muscles slowly relaxed. I pulled my hand away. Pins and needles moved up my forearm.

The flash hadn't been nearly as impressive as the tricks I'd done with the scepter—but the shouting did die down a bit, and few of those closest to us were watching us instead of the brawl in the pond.

Maybe a few more reactions. I motioned to one of the watching Oranges, and she bounded right up and took my hand.

This time the flash brought forward a stream of people wanting to react. After I'd mixed colors with four Oranges, even the ones trying to circumvent Véronique and Letty realized something was going on.

I took advantage of the lull in screaming to state my case. "Who here likes caviar? Raise your light. I'm sure you've plucked a few eggs from the salting tables. I won't tell anybody."

Quinlin made a face of disgust, but several of the ladies whom I recognized as salters timidly raised their fires.

"Has anyone tasted Golden Caviar?"

The fires lowered.

"No, because Gaspard kept that for himself. Why? Because Mére Blanche's roe is ten times better than the dark stuff. It's buttery and has a slight nutty aftertaste."

"All the more reason for us to—"

"Kill her?" I shouted over the top of the interrupter. "And always wonder what Golden Caviar tastes like? This revolution is going to succeed. I'm even more confident of this as I see this mighty Orange army. Gaspard will fall—and we will have our chance to take his treasures for our own, to share them with our families, or even to destroy everything that reminds us of him."

Since the line was only getting longer, I continued to react with the workers as I spoke.

"We attack the estate at dawn. If we work together and follow the plan, we will take control of Télesphore. If our army turns into a bunch of rioters we will destroy Télesphore and ourselves."

Letty raised her hand. I was about to call on her when she shouted, "Hail Bruno, Rightful King of Télesphore!"

Véronique followed, her eyes fixed on me as she spoke.

Letty looked around. "Orange Army! What do you have to say to your king?"

Several hundred fires rose. "Hail Bruno, Rightful King of Télesphore."

"Do you fight for yourselves or do you fight for Télesphore?" I shouted.

"Télesphore!"

"You can't fight on empty stomachs. Eat all the caviar you can find and any fish shorter than two feet. Then sleep. Letty will wake you an hour before eyerise and lead you to battle."

I'd expected the last part to be more of an informative post-speech addendum, but before I'd finished with "lead you to battle" the Oranges erupted once more into cheers and war cries that went on for a good two minutes. I was glad they were on our side.

After Véronique and I had reacted with most of the Oranges, they became downright pleasant. They built a tiny combustion—as far from the water as possible—to cook some of the smaller Poisson du Roi, and passed around the extra food Véronique brought. We also reacted with Letty for good measure and I learned she was the one who had turned the Reds Orange in the first place.

"I can't get over the change in her," I said as Véronique and I crept between the dilapidated buildings toward her house. "Letty is a completely different person. How did you convince her to come to our side?"

Véronique waited for a family to pass before she stepped onto the street. "I don't really know. Since we both loved Mére Blanche and became friends, I guess some of my ideas rubbed off on her."

"You do have very assertive ideas."

Véronique narrowed her eyes. I grinned. Then I remembered she was married to Luc and my grin faded.

"Why didn't you tell the others about your tin mine army, Vern?"

She gave me a look. "Quinlin is a sweet boy. I hope you weren't nasty to him."

"Have you ever seen me nasty?"

"Anyways, to answer your question—before you showed up, Philippe and Luc thought an uprising was a bad idea—so I kept it secret. Then after you arrived, I asked about gathering the tin workers and Philippe shot me down—said we can't trust them."

I realized I was falling behind and quickened my shuffle. "But you do trust them."

Véronique nodded. "No one would hole up in a lava tube for weeks on end with hardly any food unless they really believed we could overthrow Gaspard."

"Lava tube?" I said through heavy breaths.

Without asking, Véronique crouched under me and lifted me onto her back. I wanted to protest, but common sense said it would take us twice as long to get home with me huffing along on my own.

"The tubes are the only reason we were able to hide so many down there. Estate officials and even Gaspard came down periodically to check on caviar production, and they had no idea."

"Those must be the same tunnels the Feu Noir have been using. I didn't realize they were lava tubes. I'm assuming that means Mt. Tremper is a volcano. How did I not know that?"

"I imagine you didn't pay attention in school," she said. "It hasn't been active for hundreds of years. The lava can do some weird stuff as it cools—lavacicles. And some of those tunnels are miles long. Quinlin knows them better than anybody. He sometimes hangs out under the Crystal Cathedral to listen to the choir."

A cold wind hit the back of my neck and I automatically buried my face in Véronique's hair.

Black, it smelled good.

Married woman. Married woman.

"I'm surprised we didn't see him when Marin and I were sneaking around under there," I said to distract myself from how much I wanted to nuzzle into the back of her neck. I seriously needed to get over her. "I wonder why Mallory didn't think of—"

Paralyzing pain coursed through my body. Véronique gave way underneath me. Before I blacked out my mind managed to transmit three belated messages.

Quick footsteps from behind.

A brown-gloved hand.

Electricity entering my ankle.

CHAPTER NINETEEN

THE WHITE SERPENT

Véronique shook me awake.

"You okay?"

I nodded—then realized I couldn't move. We were still sprawled on the freezing cobblestones.

The royal soldier stood over us speaking frantically into his radio. "How long does it take to recharge?" he said.

"Can't move," I whispered. "You?"

Véronique scooted closer. "Well, I might be able to crawl away—but I certainly can't carry you. He hit you with the yellow shock. It was lucky I took some of the electricity, or you would probably still be unconscious."

Why hadn't I paid more attention? I could have warned Véronique or made a flying leap onto him. He wasn't much bigger than me, even as skinny as I was. Now we were blacked.

I managed to twitch a finger on my dark hand, but in general the feeling seemed to have gone out of my limbs.

"How long have I been out?"

"Maybe thirty seconds."

"What's your location," came a crackling voice over the radio.

The young soldier looked around. "This is my first time in the area... I don't see any street signs."

"Taudis doesn't have street names, Clarque. Give me directions. How far from the river? Eyerise, Eyefall?"

Clarque—it was the kid following Claude around with the procedural manual. Except back then he was a police officer.

"I... I don't know. There are some small buildings. And a wall thing. Can't you just come find me?"

"You sure it's them?"

"Yes, it's Nazaire and DeGrave for sure."

"Your glove should recharge in a minute or so. Meanwhile check them for weapons."

Clarque stared at us, then spoke into his radio. "Hurry."

The radio fell silent and Clarque extended his finger toward us. I could see the silver contact point that had delivered the high voltage.

I forced myself to smile at him. "A promotion? I didn't think they turned officers into soldiers."

Clarque swallowed. "Turn out your pockets."

"Nice to see you again, Clarque," Véronique said. "Thanks for not hitting us with the Red charge."

"Turn out your pockets."

With stiff fingers and jerky movements, Véronique clumsily managed to pull her wet pockets inside out.

Clarque pushed his index finger at me. "You too."

"My muscles seem to be temporarily out of order. Maybe you should have tried the green setting."

"Do it for him," he told Véronique.

She patted me down. "Nothing."

"I can see something in his back pocket right now."

My throat constricted to the size of a drinking straw. I had completely forgotten about Grandpa's story. Why hadn't I put it in a drawer?

With both hands, Véronique awkwardly extracted the paper from my pants. "Just a piece of paper. Although it's ruined now. The Jealous Jellyfish? What is this?"

I closed my eyes. I was probably going to be tortured next to the girl of my dreams in a few hours, but all I could think about was never hearing Grandpa's story.

"I know this," she said. "I tell it to Jeannette sometimes."

What? Impossible. "About the jellyfish who got a magic stone from the mermaid queen?"

"Yeah, except we called it The White Serpent. My grandpa said it was a legend of the Quintum. I always thought he'd made it up."

The poker's watch beeped. The oversized wrist jewelry was the battery pack for the shock glove. It was probably fully charged again. "Keep your hands where I can see them," Clarque said. He looked like he was considering poking me again. Despite my complete lack of movement he seemed to be getting more anxious by the minute. He clicked his watch and the light turned red.

I stopped breathing.

"Clarque," Véronique said slowly, "you don't need to use the glove. We can barely move as it is. We will behave ourselves."

He swallowed, stepped back a few paces and picked up his radio. "Detainees are unarmed—but I'd still appreciate if you'd hurry."

"So are we escaping?" I whispered. "This guy doesn't seem all that stable."

"I really can't move," Véronique said. "That shock did something to my legs. They're weak and keep cramping up. But anyways, wouldn't you rather be popped by this kid than tortured by Gaspard?"

"Fair enough. As long as we're not escaping can you please tell me the white serpent story as quickly as possible?"

"Why? It's just a stupid—"

"My grandpa thought it would help me somehow. Not that it matters now, but I'd really just like to hear it before..."

Véronique took a breath. "Basically a girl jellyfish is picked on by the other jellyfish and wants to get away from them, so she goes to the mermaid queen who gives her the eyestone which heats the water immediately around her. You sure that's the same one?"

"If not, it's very similar. Keep going, please."

"So the eyestone kept her warm all the way to the Winter-dark Sea where she caught a crystal ice fish and brought it back to... Oh, I forgot to say that she promised she'd bring something beautiful to the queen for her kindness."

I nodded. This was definitely the same story. Clarque was still talking into the radio trying to give some sort of landmark.

"And then?"

"She thought the Queen would like to keep the ice fish as a pet, but the Queen didn't want it—said she didn't find it beautiful."

"Rude."

"I know, right?"

"Nettie set off again—"

"Nettie?"

239

"Oh, my grandpa always called her Neek, so I started calling her Nettie when I told it to Jeannette. She set out again and this time came back with a feather star, which the Queen didn't accept either."

"Sounds like this should be called the Picky Queen."

"Or the Interrupting King."

"Sorry—continue."

"To make a long story short, Nettie spends years bringing back all kinds of plants and creatures, but the Queen always says she doesn't find any of them truly beautiful."

Clarque had finished with the radio and seemed to be listening to Véronique's story.

"The white sea snake noticed what was going on and told Nettie her problem was inefficiency. Basically, the more stuff you brought back, the more likely the Queen would be to find one of them beautiful."

I noticed I was starting to get feeling back in my limbs. Maybe we had a chance of recovering before Clarque received his back up.

"The white serpent went to the Queen and asked for a large cage. The Queen sang a song, and the bubbles drew together to form a glass sphere big enough to hold an entire school of fish. The serpent promised to help Nettie with her quest, and the Queen warned them never to let her two magical gifts touch or the magic would release."

"Wait," said Clarque, "what was the first gift?"

"A stone that kept her warm no matter how cold the water was," Véronique said with a smile in her voice.

Clarque cleared his throat and raised his Green fire so he could see us better. At least he wasn't pointing his shocky finger at us anymore.

"When the other jellyfish saw the glass bubble, which was actually a sort of submarine with a door and everything, they wanted to come too. Apparently, they'd been all jealous of Nettie's magical stone and ability to travel wherever she wanted."

"Maybe that's why my Grandpa called it The Jealous Jelly-fish."

"It's still a dumb title."

Clarque nodded.

"Nettie wasn't stupid. She remembered how the other jellyfish had treated her. She told them they couldn't come because there wouldn't be enough room to bring back beautiful things. But the vessel belonged to the white serpent and he said the others could help look. Different ideas of beauty or some nonsense."

I chuckled. "Ridiculous."

"Anyways... Sorry, I picked that up from Letty."

"Running out of time," I said through clenched teeth.

"So they pack up enough plankton to feed everyone and they all squeeze into the glass bubble ship thing. They drifted toward the Winterdark Sea with the eyestone keeping the water inside nice and toasty. They see a lot of cool stuff, but they can't agree on what's beautiful enough to bring into the ship with them so they end up passing everything by."

Véronique scratched her nose. It was a small gesture, but she glanced at me as she did it. She was telling me she was able to fully use her fingers and arms again. Did that mean her legs were better? If we took off now, she'd still have to carry me, but maybe in a few more minutes I will have recovered enough to hobble behind her. The problem was what to do about the kid in the brown uniform. I nodded to let Véronique know I was picking up on her signs.

"Anyways." She grimaced. "Ugh, that makes me sound like an imbécile, doesn't it?"

"Just keep—"

"Okay—so Nettie wanted to go back because the trip was a total bust, but the snake said, no, the boat was his—and in fact, he was going to be the sole judge of what was beautiful enough to be brought back in their bubble."

She tapped her foot against my arm. I looked at her, but she kept talking. What was she trying to tell me?

"The other jellyfish started treating Nettie worse than ever. They fought among themselves trying to get in good with the snake, who loved the attention."

The crackle of Claude on the radio startled me. Véronique waited, but Clarque didn't answer him, so she continued.

"They were in the coldest, darkest depths of the Winterdark Sea when the white serpent announced that snakes weren't meant to live on plankton. He attacked one of the younger jellyfish and ate it."

Clarque made a sound of disgust. I couldn't tell if it was the idea of eating a jellyfish or the moral implications.

"Rather than bonding together to protect their brothers, the jellyfish turned on each other, the largest cannibalizing the smaller ones."

I realized Clarque had stepped closer. If I had been my old rugby-star self I could have easily dropped him from where I was. Was Véronique feeling up to it?

"When one of the grandfather jellyfish came to eat Nettie, she pressed herself against the bubble, trying to escape. The eyestone touched the side and the glass sphere shattered in a burst of mermaid song. Freezing water rushed in and within seconds the white serpent and all the jellyfish except for Nettie had frozen solid."

"Did she still have the glowing rock?" Clarque asked. "I thought it was supposed to disappear or something."

"It shattered, but the single piece that she was able to—"

"What is this, story time?"

All three of us jumped as Claude appeared in an all brown uniform. He grabbed Clarque by the arm and pulled him back. "Black for brains—you want them to jump you and steal your glove?"

Claude grinned at me and shone his Green fire directly onto his black watch and glove. "That's right—desperate times. The Emperor thought we'd be more use as soldiers." He raised his radio. "Found 'em. Lower Eyefall Side. A block from..."

His face went slack.

I had to turn around to see what he was looking at.

Véronique was in a sitting position with a dart gun pointed at them.

"Don't say another word into that," Véronique said.

Claude looked at the radio, then back at the gun.

"This is not a tranq gun. This was given to me several months ago by a member of the Royal Guard. It's full of anoxium pentathol."

Clarque swore.

I looked at Véronique. "Eloi gave you plague darts?"

"Since my safety seemed so important to you, he wanted to make you happy."

"Oh, I'm happy."

Véronique slowly got to her feet.

I was really going to have to give Eloi some kind of

award. This was the umpteenth time he'd saved my life. But it bothered me that Véronique didn't think to mention the gun. Why hadn't she used it in the mines to protect Mére Blanche? "Why didn't you—"

"Bruno, could we have this conversation later?"

"Right." I managed to push myself into a sitting position. "Here's what you two are going to do. Turn your gloves on yellow, and shock each other at the exact same time."

Claude laughed and opened his mouth, but Véronique cut him off.

"Anyone who is still conscious in ten seconds will get a healthy does of ano-pent."

"We'll just go to the estate for dialysis," Claude said, raising his radio again.

"Have you ever actually seen anyone taken in for dialysis?" I asked. "They haven't been used in years—and even if it does work, you have no idea how many darts she has left. She can down you with one and put a few more directly into your fire. A shot to the fire and you'll be gone in minutes. You wanna take that chance? Or would you rather wake up with a head-ache in a few hours?"

"How do we know you won't shoot us when we're out?" Clarque said.

"If I wanted you dead, you'd already be writhing in pain," Véronique said. "Ten, nine, eight..."

Clarque and Claude looked at each other.

"Seven, six..."

"Get ready, Blackhead!" Claude said. "Let's sit down."

"Five, four..."

They sat down next to each other.

"Three..."

"Maybe we should lie down," Clarque said. They both threw themselves onto their backs and raised their index fingers.

"Two, one."

The pokers brought their fingers down on each other.

There was a loud pop, like a single firecracker, followed by the sickening smell of burning flesh.

Clarque lay still, but Claude sounded like he was choking. He raised his light hand and stared at the bloody crater that used to be his fire.

"That son of a Viol—"

His arm fell and he didn't move again.

The sound of distant shouts broke the silence.

Véronique had fallen against a wall. "What just happened?"

"Clarque forgot to change his watch from red. We can't leave him here or they'll execute him."

Véronique pushed herself from the wall and stared at me. "Who's going to carry him, you? I can barely walk."

Crêpes, where was Eloi when you needed him? I glanced up the street toward Luc's house, hoping to see him jogging toward us.

The shouting was getting closer.

"We'll have to hide," I said. "You know anybody around here?"

Véronique glanced along the street. "I know of people but not necessarily their names, you know?"

"As long as they recognize you and are willing to risk their lives for you, a stranger, and a poker."

"Well, there's this creepy old man that's always flirting with me." She shuddered. "I could probably convince him to hide us for a bit."

"Go go go!"

Véronique hobbled to one of the doors and knocked. She was too far away for me to hear her whispered conversation —but much sooner than I expected, I saw a short figure running toward me. The man smelled like urine and tobacco, but I breathed it in gratefully as he lifted me to my feet and half carried me to his door. Véronique helped me inside while the man went back for the poker.

Once we were all inside with the shutters closed, I recognized the man.

"You were selling catfish," I whispered.

He shook his head frantically. Did he not recognize me? I certainly wasn't going to turn him in—but there was no gracious way to say, "Remember me? I saved you." So I sat quietly while the pokers found Claude's body and grew more frantic in their search.

The old man sat close to Véronique, apparently trying to impress her with his single remaining tooth.

She smiled back at him. I could tell she was taking shallow breaths.

A half a baseball bat hung in a grocery bag next to the door. I smiled as I remembered my first visit to the Red slums. I glanced down at Clarque, who seemed even younger as he slept. He was going to hate himself when he learned what he'd done—but it wasn't his fault. It was an accident. I would have to convince him of that. He was only doing what he thought was right.

In that moment something strange happened. A weight

that I hadn't noticed before, fell from my shoulders and I felt tears on my face.

I'd been carrying that guilt for a long time. My mind had always known that Arnaud's death was an accident. I'd even convinced myself I was over it.

But it wasn't until I saw the boy's innocent face that I was able to truly let go of my shame.

Véronique squeezed my hand.

I grinned to let her know I was okay. In fact I was better than okay. I was holding hands with the girl I loved.

CHAPTER TWENTY

FEU DE LA MORT

W hile we waited, Véronique finished her story in a whisper.

The piece of the eyestone Nettie was able to hang onto kept her from freezing but only just. Her tentacles no longer felt bathed in a comfortable eyelight, but she could move and hunt to stay alive.

Despite the jellyfishes' treatment of her, Nettie mourned the loss of her kind. She determined to bring their bodies back to their homes for burial. Without the vessel, Nettie could only retrieve them one at a time.

First she chose a small jellyfish that had nearly been eaten, positioned him carefully in her tentacles, and set off for home.

To her surprise, only a few minutes into the journey, the jellyfish awoke. After that they swam together, both clutching the piece of the eyestone. It took many days to reach their warm waters, but they arrived as friends. On the journey they had spoken of the beauty they saw and slowly developed hearts of gratitude.

One by one, Nettie returned for them. Each jellyfish drew new breath at the beginning of the journey and learned a new way to live by the end. Only the white sea snake did Nettie leave frozen in the Winterdark Sea.

When she returned with the last jellyfish, the other creatures organized a formal celebration to thank Nettie for her service in bringing them home. It was a time of great joy. Even the Mermaid Queen attended the celebration—and near the end of the evening when all the jellyfish were joined together in a song of thanks, the queen caught Nettie's eye and nodded.

After several hours, the streets again grew silent.

"I don't care if the pokers are outside waiting for us," Véronique mouthed, "I gotta get out of here."

I smirked as the old Red finished braiding her hair.

"Very nice, Karl," I said.

My smile faded when I noticed Clarque. He'd awoken a while ago and had taken the news hard that he was now a fugitive. Véronique still held the gun on him—but so far he hadn't tried to run outside or call for help.

"Clarque, your options are to wait in here with Karl for a few days—tied up—or help us defeat Gaspard."

"Who's that?"

"The guy who calls himself Emperor."

Clarque covered his face for a moment, then nodded. "I'll come with you as long as you don't tell anyone what I did."

I nodded. We were going to work on that guilt.

Snow began to fall on our way back to Luc's house. We debated knocking on the front door when we arrived but decided we didn't want to get tackled by mistake. Instead, we entered through the window in my room.

"Thank the Créateur."

Luc sat in a chair against the wall. "Who's with you?"

Clarque peeled his glove from his light hand and illuminated his face with the green glow. "Clarque Durand. I used to be a royal soldier, now I guess I'm a rebel."

"You're still a royal soldier," Luc said. "You serve the true king."

Véronique rushed to embrace Luc and took most of my internal organs with her.

"I'm so sorry," Véronique said. "We would've been back much sooner, but—"

"I'm glad you weren't," Luc said. "A contingent of royal soldiers tore the house apart looking for you an hour ago. It was all we could do to convince them we knew nothing and that they were ruining our family reunion. Lucky they didn't make anyone remove their gloves. I'm sure they would've taken us all in for questioning."

"Where are the others?" I asked.

"Trying to sleep. They think you slipped out the window when the soldiers arrived and that you'd be back soon. I am the only one who saw the note. I thought you must be dead or dying." He touched Véronique's face and I felt an overwhelming urge to punch him again.

Mellow out, Bruno—this man did nothing except save the girl you love. If he hadn't married her she'd belong to Gaspard's harem.

"Thank you, Luc," I said, "for not telling them." And for everything else.

Véronique nodded. "Mama would've been sick with worry."

"And your husband?" he said, kissing her temple.

I couldn't watch this anymore. "Come here, Clarque. Let me show you around headquarters." I removed my glove so I could see the doorknob and froze. My fire was no longer pure white but tinged with yellow.

It looked like the celestial eye, warm and brilliant. Véronique gasped and removed her glove as well. Her golden fire bathed her face with such warm glow—she looked exactly like a queen.

If only.

I put my glove back on and took Clarque directly to the refrigerator.

It wasn't long before Eloi awoke and embraced me. "I'm glad you're safe. Let's wake the others."

"Is it time?" I was only half done with my sandwich. Okay, so it was my second one—but who knew when I'd get to eat again? I stuffed the rest of it into my mouth.

Clarque, on the other hand—who suddenly seemed very passionate about our cause—dropped his sandwich and immediately began to shake people awake.

We soon discovered that having an unfamiliar guy in a poker uniform wake people was a bad idea—but at least the screams got everyone else up quickly. Véronique introduced Clarque while Eloi handed out hunks of cheese by way of breakfast.

La-la raised an eyebrow. "So, the king gets a sandwich?"

"I got up early to make it." Actually, I'd never gone to bed —but I wasn't about to admit that to a group of people whom I was leading into battle.

"What if Aro's not waiting under the bridge?" Philippe asked.

"Then we go straight to the estate," Eloi said.

Oh, yeah—Eloi was the new leader now. I was half-blind

and walked like an eighty-year-old.

Dad distributed the weapons. He handed me a screwdriver. There were several kitchen knives, a few lengths of rebar brought from the construction site, even the amputated legs of chairs. It was a good thing we had the element of surprise, because we certainly didn't have much else going for us.

If it weren't for Letty's army, I probably would've lost my nerve. Since she had the key to the retractable bridge near the estate, the Oranges would cross the river downstream. Véronique had instructed Letty to hide behind the Green Barracks until they saw our approach. We'd have to warn the others in our group at some point so they didn't try to attack Letty's troops.

"I haven't seen a patrol for a while," Luc said from his perch by the window. "I think it's safe to leave."

One by one we stepped out into the frozen air. The night was still, made even quieter by the snowfall already a few inches thick.

Jeannette and Baptiste protested at being left in the house with Camille's children. But Mama DeGrave gave them a look that sent them running back inside.

Eloi led the way down the back alleys. Philippe and the other Feu Noir members followed. La-la carried Luc on his back, and Clarque, Véronique, Mama DeGrave, and Granny brought up the rear. I was somewhere in the middle with my parents on either side. Dad held a metal table leg, and Mom, an ice pick.

"Almost to the bank," Eloi whispered. His breath came out in a white plume. "Keep your eyes open for pokers—or in Bruno's case, eye."

"Very funny," I said.

It seemed an odd time to make a joke, but then I realized

what he was doing. He could sense the group's growing panic and was helping them stay calm.

"If I see any, I'll wink at you," I said.

Eloi took the bait. "You mean blink at me?"

Most of the group was smiling now. Mom was the only one who didn't seem to find it funny.

Eloi picked up speed. It took all my concentration to keep up. Depth perception is definitely one of those things you take for granted. I focused on stepping in Dad's footprints and tried not to let my exhaustion show. In total, I'd only walked a mile or two tonight, but my body seemed to think it was still on its deathbed.

Of course, I had recently been electrocuted. The thought of Claude lying dead in the street made me sad. It made no sense. He was a horrible human being. But like Nettie and the jellyfish, he was still my kind, and I mourned a wasted life.

Finally, the buildings ended and the street deposited us onto a snowy incline. We approached upriver from the bridge, using a cluster of sickly looking pine trees for cover. Luc hopped from La-la's back and climbed up the nearest tree using nothing but his arms.

Mom raised her eyebrows. I pretended not to notice since I was still embarrassed at having sucker punched a man with no legs.

I lowered my gaze and noticed a flash of color in the snow. A pink shell lay wedged among the pine needles—small but completely intact. What was it doing this far from the water?

I felt a strange urge to save it for Véronique, but I was already in enough trouble with her husband. Still, even if I didn't give it to her, it would be a shame to leave it here for someone to step on. I picked up the shell and slid it into my pocket. Maybe I'd keep it to remind me of what could have been.

"Luc," Eloi hissed up into the branches, "give us one short whistle as soon as you see a patrol. One long one if we should retreat."

"The river and park look clear," came Luc's voice from the darkness.

Eloi hesitated. "Something doesn't feel right. Maybe we should—"

"Look!" Monsieur Wedel pointed through the falling snow. "Is that Aro?"

Under the bridge, on the Taudis side of the river, a single white light traced random patterns in the air.

"The idiot," Philippe said. "Where are his gloves?"

"He's signaling us," Dad said. "Maybe he has the scepter."

"Listen up," Eloi said. "We're going to move in a straight line from the trees to the bridge. Move quickly—move quietly." He made a hand signal to those behind us and then jogged toward Aro's light.

That was the moment it became real to me. Fear and euphoria hit at the same time, lifting me into a sort of heightened reality. My exhaustion vanished. I heard the heavy breathing of the people around me, I felt snow creeping down my socks, but it was as if it were all happening in a dream.

Halfway to the bridge Mama DeGrave cried out. I spun to see the large woman running back the way we'd come.

"Jeannette," Véronique said, and switched direction to follow her mother.

Only then did I see the two small figures emerging from the trees. Jeannette and Baptiste had followed us.

At the same time, I realized Eloi hadn't heard Mama De-

Grave's cry and was still running toward the bridge with half the Reds on his heels. The few of us who had stopped didn't know whether to follow Mama DeGrave back to the trees or abandon the children and head for the bridge.

It was Dad who took charge. "Clarque, help Rosette get the kids home safely. Everyone else to the bridge."

Clarque ran toward the trees. Dad grabbed Mom's hand and they took off toward Eloi. After a second, the rest of us followed.

When I finally arrived, panting, at the riverbank, I found Eloi and the other men clustered under the bridge. My parents passed me going the other way—Mom was crying. "Awful... just awful."

My heart lodged in my throat. I stepped under the stone arch of the bridge and pushed my way into the center of the circle.

Aro sat on a large black box waving his fire in the air and grinning as if he were putting on a show for the men. A chain rustled at his leg and the front part of his head was shaved, revealing a long row of stitches. There was no scepter.

"Livius knows," Philippe said. " Aro betrayed us."

That's when I heard Mama DeGrave's voice. "...we get home you're grounded until school's out, little lady."

No.

I turned back the way I'd come. Jeannette couldn't see this. I pushed through the men and ran toward Mama DeGrave. Véronique and Baptiste were there too.

"Get back to the trees!" I called.

Véronique stared at me with wide eyes.

A long, shrill whistle pierced the cold air. Before my mind could register the significance of the noise, it was drowned out by an explosion.

A wall of heat slammed into me from behind, throwing me forward into Véronique's arms.

CHAPTER TWENTY-ONE

PONT EN PIERRE

L a-la. Philippe. Monsieur Wedel.

Eloi.

The names flashed in my mind as I fell into Véronique—names of the dead.

Véronique lifted me to my feet. I peered through the thick black cloud around me. Had my parents gotten clear of the blast? Véronique shouted something, but I heard only the ringing in my ears.

The smoke burned my lungs. We needed clean air, but the trees upriver were too far. I grabbed Véronique's hand and ran straight up the bank toward the Taudis. The position would be fully exposed, but at least we'd get a good view of both riverbanks.

Once clear of the smoke I could make out the shapes of my parents coughing and pushing their way toward us. Baptiste and Jeannette crawled uphill behind them.

Véronique put a hand over her mouth. I followed her gaze to the form of Mama DeGrave lying face down in the snow—at first I thought she was dead, but then her meaty fist pounded the ground. Was she trying to get up? No, she was sobbing.

"My brothers," Véronique said. Her voice was calm, but her expression lost, as if she'd forgotten what she were doing there.

I felt a surge of shame. I had promised myself to protect her from pain. Yet, not six hours ago I had punched her crippled husband. Before that I sent Aro directly to the only person he'd ever wanted to please. Of course he betrayed us.

I had killed her brothers.

"Look," Véronique said. "At the top of the bridge."

Through the smoke, a single white light appeared. It flickered, then burst into a thousand dancing colors. The thin rays of light pierced the black cloud in all directions, like the branches of a multicolored tree. After a few seconds the lights disappeared but not before I caught a glimpse of long white hair.

"It's Gaspard," I said. "He's got the scepter."

Now I understood why he had killed his grandson. Once Gaspard had learned the secret of White fire, Aro became expendable—no different than La-la, Eloi and the rest of the men who had been standing next to that black box. In a single stroke, Gaspard managed to wipe out two-thirds of our group.

A burning started in my fire and spread through my body, fueling me with energy. In the rush of clarity, I noticed something else through the fading smoke—the stone bridge still stood. The explosion hadn't destroyed it after all.

I took off down the hill.

"Bruno!" Véronique called.

I didn't answer—I ran. It was time to make good on my promise. It was time to fix Télesphore. My hand curled around the screwdriver in my coat pocket.

Halfway to the bridge, I realized I wasn't alone—my parents ran behind me, followed by Jeannette and Baptiste. Granny had joined in the charge as well, and from her angle she was going to reach the stone walkway first. I sped up.

Granny reached the foot of the bridge. I was only a few steps behind her when I noticed something strange. The cobblestones were clean. There was no snow on the bridge, not even on the guardrails. The explosion could have melted it, but there was also something wrong with the dimensions— they seemed oddly flat. At first I thought it was because of my bad eye, but as I got closer, the image flickered.

"The bridge is out!" I cried. "It's an illusion!"

But Granny had already stepped through the bridge and with a cry of surprise, disappeared through the walkway. I tried to stop but only managed to trip and twist my ankle. My momentum carried me headfirst through the illusion. I braced myself for a plunge into icy water but instead, landed on rocks.

Next to me, over the roar of the river, I heard Granny groan. I waited for others to fall down on top of us, but they must have stopped in time.

"Nasty trick," Granny said.

"Are you okay?"

"Apart from fourteen broken bones."

I rolled to a kneeling position. My back felt bruised, and something warm ran down my arm, but otherwise everything seemed in working order. Before I could crawl over to help Granny, the bridge above us vanished.

My mouth fell open. Nearly half of Pont en Pierre was missing. From the bank, all the way to the nearest supporting pillar, the stone arch had crumbled into the water, damming one whole side of the river and making a rocky pathway into the center of the rapids.

Next to me, a gaping hole lay open in the earth, and a good portion of the river flowed into it. It took a moment to make sense of what I was seeing. The bomb must have broken through to the caverns underneath. Hopefully Letty was already on her way across the lower bridge. If the army got trapped in the flooded mines...

"Bruno, my boy. I seem to remember blinding you." Fifty feet above the rubble, Gaspard stood on the bridge wearing an enormous white robe, the scepter shining in his hand. "I suppose that's what I get for cutting corners. Next time I'll use a hot poker."

My instinct was to ignore him and help Granny, but I was sure he wasn't alone. Guards or soldiers would be nearby.

My only comfort was that Aro hadn't known about the other army. The Oranges had to have heard the explosion. Would they come to help? Or maybe they'd go straight to the estate while Gaspard was occupied. Either way we needed to give them time.

I looked up at Gaspard with what I hoped was a defeated expression. "Why do you hate me so much? All I wanted was to help people."

"Child, I don't hate you. I admire your strength. If only you would've trusted my counsel—you could have helped me build this empire. People don't want equality and responsibility. They want someone to make their decisions for them—to show them their place in the world."

"Full of hot air as always, Gaspard," Granny said.

The smoke had cleared and the snow was letting up, so I was able to see Gaspard's smirk.

"Been a while hasn't it, Jade?"

"I'd offer my condolences on your late wife," Granny called from the rubble, "but I'm starting to suspect her death wasn't accidental."

Nice work Granny—keep him talking.

"Madeleine never shared my vision of a Utopian Téles-phore," Gaspard said. "And just think—it could have been you at the bottom of the Ocheanum."

"Is your memory going already, old man? I was never interested in your oily charms—although I have to say, you were the most tenacious of my admirers."

I stared at Granny. Why hadn't she mentioned this history before? At least now I understood why Gaspard had avoided my family at the estate. Thank the Créateur Granny had the foresight to refuse him.

"Tenacity is one of my best traits," Gaspard said. "As you can see, it has done great things for me thus far."

An image of a much younger Gaspard appeared in the air —a bigger-than-life-sized portrait with bright green eyes and long black hair.

What a show off. At least he was wasting time. Where was the Orange army? I hoped they hadn't lost their nerve when they heard the explosion.

"Well, your tenacity didn't get the girl," Granny said. "You weren't half the man Zacharie was."

"Yes, your husband made quite a mess on the steps of the cathedral."

The imaged changed to Grandpa's twisted form, lying in a pool of blood.

Granny gasped.

I tore my eyes from the image and screamed at Gaspard. "You sick son of a black."

A scraping sound startled me. Several boulders from the bridge tumbled into the gap beside me, widening the hole. The water rushing into the mines gained speed. If I didn't get back from the hole I might get sucked down too.

Gaspard released the illusion and Grandpa's corpse vanished.

"Your manners have gone downhill since you left the estate, Bruno."

"And you're just as blind as I remember," I called out. "You've probably killed your golden egg-maker with that bomb."

"Blanche is perfectly fine," Gaspard said. He made an illusion of Mére Blanche.

So far he'd made four static pictures but no projections—must be too difficult for him. There was no doubt he'd want to show that off as well.

"The fish ponds are quarter mile upstream," Gaspard said. "As long as we're discussing foresight, your battle strategy is certainly ambitious. You thought to march in waving garden tools and take over?"

With a jolt I remembered the plague darts. Where was Véronique? Was she close enough to hit him?

Gaspard tapped the staff on the cobblestones, creating a surprisingly loud crack. All along the bank on the Taudis side, dark-suited royal guards appeared, gloved and holding dart guns. Three held the leashes of horse-sized badger hounds.

Gaspard struck the cobblestones again and this time the Hameau Vert side filled with rows of brown uniformed soldiers.

"Well, well," Granny Jade said, "you certainly can put on a show, Gassy—should have been a clown."

"Take them."

Mama DeGrave shouted something. I couldn't see from my lower angle but got the idea the guards were gathering up the rest of our group.

Still no plague darts flying toward Gaspard. What was Véronique waiting for?

"I brought them to you," a young voice called. "I'm on your side."

"Ah," Gaspard said, "the missing soldier."

I closed my eyes. Clarque had promised me. I felt the betrayal like a weight, pressing me into the rocks. First Gaspard, then Aro, now this. When was I going to learn to stop trusting people?

"You killed one of our finest soldiers," Gaspard said. "Guards, please take care of him."

"No, it was the girl!" Clarque screamed. "She stole my glove and killed Claude. See, I have a dart gun!"

Wait—had he in fact switched weapons with Véronique? That explained why she hadn't fired. Obviously Clarque hadn't used it because he was a cowardly piece of trash.

"I have no use for a soldier who can't keep hold of his weapon," Gaspard said. "No, Marwig, don't waste your anopent on that insect—use a rock."

Although I didn't see the blow, the sound of stone on bone made me light headed. Someone whimpered—one of the kids, I think. It was hard to process anything. The water pouring through the hole next to me was definitely growing louder. My mind seemed to slow and pins and needles moved up my legs. Was I going into shock?

"That soldier was only a boy," Granny shouted. "Like you were once. What happened to twist your soul in knots?"

"Jade, I think you underestimate my attachment to you," Gaspard said. "Even now I would take you back. You could be the wife of an Emperor."

An image of the dark-haired Gaspard and a teenage Jade

appeared in the air. The illusion took my breath away. Even at my age, Granny had possessed that same intense fire in her eyes. For a moment I hoped she would accept his proposal—if only to survive.

"And join your high school slumber party? I can't believe it's taken me this long to realize you're irretrievably insane."

Gaspard made a motion with his hand and a guard climbed over the rocks to stand above the broken old woman.

"Remove her glove," Gaspard said.

The guard obeyed. He hesitated when he saw her white fire, but after a glance at Gaspard, pressed the muzzle of his dart gun directly into her light.

"You can live a surprisingly long time with ano-pent in your fire. The esca wears itself out trying to burn away the poison. Seems as if it should know when it's beaten. This is your last chance, Jade. You will be my equal. I swear it."

Where was Letty? Hundreds of people couldn't up and disappear. Had the soldiers taken care of the Orange army even before joining Gaspard at the river? The thought made me weak with despair.

"You want to prove your love?" Granny said. "Let my family go. Maybe then I'll think about not hating you for the rest of my life."

"You're not in the position to negotiate."

"Then shoot me and get it over with, drama queen."

No! I jumped up, but my dark ankle wouldn't hold my weight. I fell back to my knees.

Gaspard nodded and the guard fired two darts directly into her fire.

Granny cried out.

Never as a prisoner or a slave had I felt so wretched and helpless. I was no king. Granny had saved me countless times, but I couldn't help her when it mattered most.

I couldn't even watch her suffering. Instead I stared longingly at the ever-widening hole beside me. If I stayed here, it would swallow me up, and I would never have to think about anything again.

I wouldn't have to feel the ripping, clawing pain of my grandpa's death all over.

"Emperor," one of the guards shouted, "the estate!"

I looked up from the hole and smiled. Flames engulfed Gaspard's home.

At least one person hadn't betrayed us. Thank you, Letty. Maybe this revolution would succeed after all.

"Commander Whisnant," Gaspard shouted, "take your troops. Destroy those responsible. Do not leave any prisoners."

Whisnant saluted, but before he could issue any orders, his fire popped and he fell to the riverbank.

Sheri DuPont stood over the commander's body in her brown uniform, gloved index finger still extended. Four nearby soldiers quickly thrust their gloves at her—but not before she raised her Green fire and shouted, "Long live the White King!"

Her light exploded, and she fell on top of her commander.

The soldiers looked up at Gaspard.

"What are you waiting for? You heard my orders—kill everyone."

The pokers disappeared into the trees of Green Park, leaving the riverbank empty.

I hoped Letty was ready for them—but how could she be? The Oranges would be as unprepared as we had been to face trained soldiers.

"Bruno," Granny called.

I crawled over to where she had fallen. Black tendrils of poison wreathed her fire and spread up her arm. Her light flickered.

"Jump in the river," Granny said through a grimace of pain. "Get away from here."

"I'm not leaving my family."

"I should have protected you."

"You gave me something better," I said.

"Yes, you did get your looks from my side."

My throat seized up. "You opened my eyes."

Granny smiled. "I think maybe..."

Her expression melted and faded into shadow as her hand went dark.

CHAPTER TWENTY-TWO

LIES AND LIGHT

I ripped off my glove and pressed my Golden fire into Granny Jade's. Nothing happened—we had mixed light several years ago. Our fires knew each other and would not react again.

I couldn't take any of the poison. I couldn't bring her back.

I removed Granny's horn-rimmed glasses and tucked them into her front shirt pocket. I reached to close her eyes but hesitated. Somehow it seemed appropriate to leave them open. I pressed my fire to her cheek.

"The Créateur bring you into His light and be One."

The movement of the royal guards pulled me back to the present. A dozen of them tighten the circle around the other rebels. Véronique stood next to her mother—Jeannette and Baptiste huddled between them. Dad held Mom in a protective embrace while menacingly waving his table leg.

I had to do something. I couldn't watch them die. What could I offer Gaspard?

"I figured it out," I shouted. "I know how to make the scepter sing."

Gaspard pulled his gaze from the burning estate and stared down at me. "You can perform the Sacred Song? I find that difficult to believe."

"If you let the others go, I'll teach you—then you can do

whatever you want with me."

Gaspard held up a hand to stop his guards. "So, you suddenly 'figured out' this secret that has been lost for centuries. Please enlighten me."

"My grandpa told me—but I'm not giving you anything until they're all safe and far away from here."

"Shoot the fat one," Gaspard said.

A guard stepped toward Mama DeGrave. Véronique moved to defend her, but the man threw Véronique to the ground and pulled off Mama DeGrave's glove.

"You have to sing a song in your head," I shouted, trying to think back to the jellyfish story. Grandpa had acted like the two were related somehow. "And then make a projection."

The guard pointed his gun at Mama DeGrave's fire.

Gaspard leaned against the guardrail as if he were only humoring me. "And once the scepter is singing, how do you 'release' the song?"

I swallowed. What had Nettie done to defeat the white serpent? Dropped the stone? "You have to... break the diamond."

"Lies," Gaspard shouted back. "You think I haven't tried that? The diamond is indestructible. Infect her. Infect all his little friends—and not directly in the fire this time. The boy needs to watch them suffer."

Mama DeGrave fell to the ground, a dart protruding from her light arm. They shot the kids next. Baptiste stumbled forward clutching his shoulder, and Jeannette fell onto her back and lay still, as if she'd fallen asleep in the middle of a snow angel.

My father swung his table leg at the nearest guard, knocking the gun from the man's hands. Two other guards tackled

Dad and shot multiple darts into his neck.

"The revolution was my idea," I cried. "Once I'm dead they will follow you."

"No, Bruno," Mom said. "Granny taught me to do the right thing—it's just taken me thirty-five years to find the courage." She pulled off her glove and held her fire out to the nearest guard. He hesitated only a moment before shooting her wrist.

My strength left me completely and I fell against a boulder. I watched Camille and her eldest son take darts to their forearms and fall to the ground together, writhing in pain. Still, none of the guards had approached me. Were they saving me for last?

Finally only Véronique was left. Two guards stood over where she lay on the ground. One of them pulled off her glove.

A wave of nausea swept over me. I looked at the clouds. Not even a single patch of starlit sky shone through. Far away, the horizon glowed gray with the approach of dawn.

It seemed strange that so much horror could happen on such a peaceful night. Could anyone up there see what was going on down here? Did anybody care?

Then, from the trees upriver, came a shout. A single white light appeared, waving wildly among the topmost branches.

"Whoever that is, kill him," Gaspard said. "Mustn't leave any white fires around to start another rebellion."

The guards jumped at the chance to prove their marksmanship. They abandoned Véronique and fired toward the trees. A steady volley of poison assailed the branches until finally, the distant fire plummeted to the ground, flickered and faded completely.

"Luc!" Véronique was on her feet and running toward the trees. I thought the guards would release the dogs, but instead they aimed their dart guns and dropped her like a fleeing animal.

The whole world seemed to spin to a stop as Véronique landed in the snow. Every cell in my body went cold, then burning hot. Gaspard had done this. He had to die.

I felt in my pocket for the screwdriver—it had fallen out. Next to Granny's still form lay the polished hunting knife she'd gotten from Eloi.

My breath came in short stutters. Eloi had risked everything to get us to this point. I wasn't going to fail him now. I'd never thrown a knife, but it couldn't be that different from a rugby ball. I lunged for the weapon, clumsily pulled myself to my knees again and brought the blade to my shoulder.

"Stop him!" Gaspard cried.

Just before the knife left my fingers, a brilliant light exploded from the scepter. My hands flew to my eyes and I cried out.

Gaspard's chuckle confirmed my fears. I hadn't come close to hitting him. I opened my eyes, but my vision consisted of sparkling dots. Was it temporary, or had he re-damaged my good eye?

"Were you not some sort of sports hero?" came Gaspard's voice. "I didn't expect such a weak throw."

"I'd rather be weak than a murdering, toilet-pouched serum-sucker."

"Watch yourself. I promised to let you live, but that doesn't mean I have to leave all your limbs attached."

Had I heard him correctly? Promised whom? "You're not going to kill me?"

"Sadly, no—but there are conditions."

The pain in my eye was fading, but opening them only brought more flashing colors. I was quickly losing hope I'd ever see again. But that didn't mean I had to play along with Gaspard's sadistic games.

"Forget it. I'm through being your page boy."

"The first condition is that you leave Télesphore immediately."

I tilted my face toward Gaspard. To my surprise I could make out his fire. The rest of the world appeared as a big black nothing, but I could see where he was. A lot of good it did me. I was out of pointy objects to throw.

"You're wasting your time," I said. "I don't care what you —"

"The second condition is that you marry this young lady."

Next to the white light at the top of the bridge, a faint green dot appeared, followed by a blue. The Green was probably Sébastien. And since Emma was dead, the only other Blue girl it could be was...

"Orie?"

"You seem surprised," Gaspard said. "Had you thought it was my grandson who betrayed you? That little pest released his foxes in the estate as a distraction, then waltzed right in and stole my scepter. He might have succeed had I not been ready for him. You see, Mademoiselle Talbot arrived at my door a few hours earlier with a most compelling proposition."

"I did it to save you," Orie cried in an anguished voice. "I knew you were all going to your deaths and I couldn't bear it. At least this way some good can come of it."

I put my arms out. "Do you see anything good about this? We had a chance before you decided to help."

"Don't be too hard on the girl," Gaspard said. "I too, know the sweet misery of unrequited affection. Love makes us do crazy things."

"I never meant for this to happen," Orie said. "I thought we could just leave together and no one would get hurt."

I closed my eyes. "You were wrong. Everyone I care about is dead or dying."

"I know, I'm sorry—but you still have your whole life. You can still have a family of your own. Just come with me."

"Go, Bruno," came Mom's weak voice between convulsions. "There's nothing you can do for us."

"No—I'd rather die with my family."

"Please," Orie said. "I can't live without you."

"Shut up," I shouted. "So I don't love you back—big deal. I've been fire over heels for Véronique from the first moment I met her, but you don't see me trying to kidnap her from her husband or hold her family hostage. I moved on. I got over it."

Orie choked back a sob.

"So run away to the mainland if you want," I said, unable to keep the bitterness from my voice. "I'm not going with you."

"I guess that's your answer, child," Gaspard said. "Sébastien, take her away. I'm sure we will find some use for such a beautiful young woman."

I cringed as the blue and green lights disappeared down the far side of the bridge. Had I made a mistake?

"I was hoping you'd refuse her," Gaspard said. "I had so looked forward to watching you stop breathing."

"Emperor Livius!" Véronique called. "Take me with you."

In a sea of darkness, I saw her pale Golden light float down the hill. She moved slowly, clearly affected by the ano-pent, but at least she could walk—that meant she'd probably only gotten a single dart. Her coat must have protected her.

"Take you with me?" Gaspard said. "What good would you be?"

"I'll be twice as useful as that blond bimbo. I'm an athlete. I can run errands, I can work in the kitchens, or the bedroom—whatever Your Imperial Excellence requires."

What was she doing? There's no way Gaspard would fall for that.

"Do you take me for a fool?" Gaspard said. "You think I'd bring you into my home, heal and train you, only to have you take your revenge in the middle of the night?"

"My friends and family are already dead. I do mourn their loss, but I'm not stupid. I recognize who has the power, and I have no loyalty to an imaginary ideal like some people."

Okay, so Véronique was making a very convincing argument—but would Gaspard buy it?

"I want to live," she continued. "I don't care about anything else. The second you sense anything but devotion from me you can kill me."

I hadn't realized Véronique was such a good actor. She *was* acting—I refused to consider the alternative.

"Well," Gaspard said. "You do pose quite a tempting offer. Why don't you come up here so I can get a better look at you."

"But how do I—"

"If you're really as agile as you claim, a little rock climbing shouldn't be a problem."

He wanted her to climb up the support? Véronique was terrified of heights. Was he hoping she'd fall? I wanted to call out and warn her not to try, but I didn't know what she was planning. Maybe she still had Clarque's glove with her. I had to trust her.

Slowly, her golden light passed, moving carefully across

the rubble pathway until it came to a stop near the middle of the river. She'd have to jump to get to the base of the pillar. The gap was probably even wider now, with the water tearing at the rocks. The water sounded different for some reason. Louder, and more violent. The scraping of rock against rock accompanied the ever-growing roar of the river.

Véronique's light lurched forward and disappeared. She'd fallen in! I pushed myself to my feet, ready to fall in after her, but the light reappeared and made its way upward. How was she doing it? She was soaked through. Her hands had to be frozen.

It would all be worth it if she could only touch Gaspard with the red charge. Would he notice the glove before she could got close enough?

The golden light finally reached Gaspard and he moved to help her over the guardrail. I was desperate to see what was going on, but my vision wasn't getting any better.

"Let's get that wet coat off," came Gaspard's slimy voice. "Here, take mine."

"Thank you, Your Excellence."

"Better? My goodness you are a lovely one. I suppose we can give you a try. But the moment I sense any duplicity…"

"Of course," Véronique said. "Could I make one request?"

"And what would that be, my dear?"

"I need to say something to Bruno before you kill him."

"I suppose it wouldn't hurt."

There was a pause. I stood facing Véronique's light, trying to ignore the pain in my ankle.

"Bruno," she, "there was a time when I thought I liked you —but after what we did in the woods near the shelter, I only have one thing to say."

My mind raced. Had I done something outside the shelter to make her hate me? The only thing I could remember doing was catching the...

"Dark shoulder!" she yelled.

"You little whore!" Gaspard screamed.

Almost without thinking, I brought my light hand to my shoulder and plucked the crystal staff out of the air as it sailed past my ear.

My full sight returned in time to see Véronique lunge at Gaspard with the poker's glove. He knocked her hand sideways and kneed her in the stomach. She brought her head up hard into his chin. He stumbled backward—I thought he would fall, but he gripped the guardrail and kicked her in the chest. Véronique cried out and collapsed inches from the edge of the broken cobblestones, still wearing Gaspard's white coat.

The men in suits approached me and raised their weapons. Gaspard took a step toward Véronique.

She needed time to recover—something to distract both the guards and Gaspard. Could a golden fire still make the scepter fuction? It was certainly bright enough. I sent a pulse of energy into the scepter and summoned the memory of my first trip to the mines. It worked! Screams echoed across the water as Mére Blanche flew out of the river toward Gaspard. She was at least three times the size she should have been, and somehow my subconscious had replaced her wide mouth with the open jaws of a great white shark. The projection had a warm, natural quality to it, even more realistic than the ones I'd made as a White. A few of the guards shot at the beast, but most simply stared in horror as the teeth closed on the Emperor. Gaspard fell backward against the guardrail—but then the animal passed through the bridge and disappeared into the river.

That's when I noticed something was wrong with the river downstream—it was barely moving and the water level was only a fraction of where it had been.

Then I saw the hole. It had tripled in size. What would happen when the caverns filled up? The water was entering too quickly for it to soak into the ground.

Gaspard peered over the handrail where Mére Blanche had disappeared, then his eyes fell on me holding the scepter.

"Get the staff, you fools!"

Most of the guards stared at the water as if waiting for the albino beast to resurface—but at Gaspard's command, the men with the badger hounds crouched and detached the leashes. The three animals shot toward me, teeth bared.

I concentrated on creating an image of Gaspard and thrust the scepter toward the dogs.

They skidded to a stop ten feet in front of me and started begging for food.

The real Gaspard growled and turned his attention back to Véronique. "Sticks and stones will break your bones," he said in a manic voice, "but illusions will never hurt me."

Then he kicked Véronique over the edge.

The white coat flew off and fluttered toward the icy river, but Véronique hung suspended by her hair which had gotten tangled in the metal mesh holding the stones together.

The sight of her dangling over the fifty-foot drop sent new panic coursing through me. She was directly over the jagged rock pathway—but even if she somehow managed to swing and land in the water, she would drown. I had to get under her.

While holding the illusion to keep the dogs at bay, I hob-bled along the rock pathway that lead out into the river.

Gaspard stepped to the lip of the broken bridge and peered

down at Véronique. He took a moment to secure himself to the crumbling guardrail, then kicked once more at her head, trying to dislodge her hair. It seemed he couldn't reach far enough without toppling over himself.

Despite the pain shooting up my leg, I forced my body to move faster. Hold, on Neek—nearly there. The dogs had followed me onto the path. As soon as I released the image of Sébastien they'd come for me and I'd be trapped.

The other guards finally pulled their gazes from the river. One of them pointed his gun and commanded me to stop. He seemed unsure about whether to fire at the illusion. Was he worried he might kill Gaspard by mistake?

Through the scepter I spotted a shadow far back on the bridge. Had the real Sébastien come back? Gaspard pried a stone loose from the walkway and pushed it toward the edge of the drop. The rock was almost the size of Véronique.

Despite there being little hope, I continued to hobble toward her. A stone that size would kill Véronique as easily as the ground below. The most incredible girl in all of Port was a few strands of hair away from death and I limped along with my useless, broken body.

I needed to surprise Gaspard again—but this time shock him so badly that pushing that rock would be the last thing on his mind.

Something occurred to me. Did a projected memory have to be based in reality? Or was it enough that the memory be real to me?

I'd have to release the image of Sébastien. The dogs would come for me. But it would be worth it if it gave Véronique time to pull herself back up.

I reigned in my light and released the illusion. The scepter went dark. For a moment the dogs looked around for their master. As soon as they spotted me, they bristled and started picking their way across the uneven terrain. They'd reach me soon. I had only seconds.

Calling on all my remaining strength, I pushed a bolt of energy toward my fire.

On the bridge, Gaspard was straining against the boulder —but it had settled into a groove, preventing it from sliding any farther over the edge. He repositioned himself, but before he could throw his weight into the final shove, he looked into the air and screamed.

A massive black shape descended, its leathery wings silently beating at the air. As the dragon appeared, the ground beneath me groaned and shook. A distant explosion echoed through the trees—followed by another from downriver. A third groan and crash sounded from even farther away. What was going on? Had the Orange army found Gaspard's explosives?

The timing couldn't have been more perfect—the dogs yelped and scrambled up the bank, away from the flying reptile. The guards also scattered, making for the trees upriver. Gaspard crawled backward. His face looked much older somehow, as if the fear had twisted him into a withered old man.

The dragon held no terror for me now. It hovered protectively over Véronique. Its long slender head bobbed from side to side, tasting the air like a snake. Then, as it always had in my dreams, the writhing mass of teeth and scales opened its maw. Bright blue fire engulfed the tiny figure on the bridge.

The flames were imaginary—why, then did Gaspard twist and rock as if in pain?

Then I saw the shape on his back—a boy. With his dark hand he clutched Gaspard's white hair, and in his other, his orange fire illuminated a shard of glass.

"Stay away from my girlfriend," Quinlin screamed as he brought the glass down on Gaspard's shoulder.

Despite the blinding blue inferno and the blood pouring from his shoulder, Gaspard reach behind and grabbed Quinlin's wrist—then he seemed to fall forward.

Quinlin flew over the top of Gaspard and his back hit the guardrail with an audible snap. Was he dead? He lay on the railing, legs and feet dangling over the edge.

I released the projection and the dragon faded. Véronique still hung by her hair. Her body had gone rigid, as if she were trying to keep as still as possible.

"Quinlin?" I shouted.

Gaspard bent down and picked up the jagged shard of glass. Before he could use it, Quinlin sprang to life and launched himself into the river.

Gaspard yelled something to the dogs and pointed at the boy being swept away by the current.

The dogs jumped around as if excited but obviously didn't understand the instructions. Almost immediately, Quinlin was sucked into the gaping hole. It happened so quickly I didn't have time to consider jumping in after him. He'd never survive in the flooded caverns. He had given his life in an attempt to save Véronique.

But she would die anyway—just like Granny, and my parents, and the rest of my friends.

What more could I do? I had the scepter, but what good was light against the physical world? As impressive as the projections were, they were only delaying the inevitable.

It was clear now the Oranges weren't coming to save us. They were probably lying dead in the street.

Half the sky had already changed from gray to pearl. The

eye would be up any minute and complete my transition to blindness.

That gave me an idea—maybe I could blind Gaspard first. I shot another burst of energy into the scepter. This time I let it explode out the end in a flash. The light stabbed at my good eye, but I forced myself to look directly into the diamond.

Through the scepter I watched the surrounding countryside light up like a rugby stadium. The bodies littering the riverbank stood out in stark contrast to the brilliant white snow.

But almost immediately, the luster faded. In panic, I opened my eyes wider, trying to take in more of the scepter's light, trying to loop it back into my fire—but it was no use. My natural eyes were too damaged to hold the Celestial Burning loop.

Gaspard staggered toward Véronique. With his dark hand he held his wounded shoulder while the other clutched Quinlin's glass shard.

I tried to push more energy down my arm, but my body had reached its limit. There was nothing left to draw on.

Gaspard lay on his belly and wiggled toward the edge. With the broken shard he swiped at her hair.

"Swing for the river!" I shouted.

I was going to have to jump in as well. Maybe Véronique would notice and fall in after me. Somehow I'd have to hold on to the scepter so I could see where I was going. But how would I swim with the scepter in one hand and Véronique in the other?

I couldn't. Even if I had my sight and both arms, I was too weak now. In fact, just holding onto the staff was becoming difficult.

Gaspard connected with a chunk of hair and Véronique

fell a few inches. Her scream echoed across the riverbank. Gaspard wiggled farther over the edge and swung the jagged glass with renewed enthusiasm.

At that moment, I was sure of two things. First, that Véronique DeGrave was going to die. Second, that one person trying to do the right thing would never amount to anything in an evil world. Hatred was too strong. I had done everything I could, and it hadn't been enough.

The light from the scepter winked out. I let my exhausted arm fall. My fingers automatically relaxed—but before the staff fell from my hand, a patch of warmth touched my cheek.

The first rays of the eye peeked over the horizon, heralding a new day—Le Jour de La Naissance. Day of the Créateur's birth.

I tightened my grip on the scepter but didn't bother with a blindfold. What was the point? I only had moments to live. In a way it would be easier to let the eye blind me. Then I wouldn't have to watch her die like the rest of my family.

But as the eye pushed its way up from the earth, I found myself completely transfixed. Had it been overcast on the days Aro had practiced outside? Or maybe it had been too late in the afternoon for the courtyard to get direct eyelight. For whatever reason, this was the first time I'd seen the eye through the scepter.

It was breathtaking—like a ball of liquid crystal shooting tendrils of gold fire in all directions. Every color conceivable shimmered across its surface and I could sense the unimaginable power that stirred underneath.

It was our star—the ultimate source of light. If only there were a way to harness that energy and direct it into the scepter.

Wait.

I spun around and faced the horizon. Both my eyes exploded with pain and my eyelids spasmed in an effort to block out the light, but still I held them open, drawing the energy inside me. Even as it broke down the cells in my eyes with its fury, I could feel the raw power flowing into my body, replenishing my strength and racing toward my fire. The circuit completed. Light shot out the diamond in every direction. Within seconds it had doubled and then tripled, until the brightness rivaled the eye itself. The entire staff began to vibrate. My cold fingers prickled as the crystal grew hot.

Then it happened—a low hum issued from the diamond. It rose in pitch and volume until it became a ringing tone. The mere sound of it was so beautiful it made me lose my identity completely. I was the music. All that mattered was that it go on forever.

But something in the back of my mind whispered that I wasn't done yet. There was something I was forgetting.

A scream pierced the air. I turned my focus back to the bridge in time to see the shard of glass rip through Véronique's remaining hair. Glowing white from the light of the scepter, she fell.

Pain. Hatred. Injustice.

With a rush I realized I finally had the ability to stop it all. The only thing I had to do was release the song.

I took the scepter in both hands, lifted it into the air, and brought it down hard on the rocks. The diamond shattered. My vision went black. The song faded, and with it went the roar of the river.

For a moment I stood in perfect darkness. I knew the eye had finished off my retinas, but had I gone deaf too? No, I could still hear the sound of my own breathing. What had happened to the river? Maybe I was dead. If that was the case then why did my ankle still hurt? I could still feel the rocks beneath my feet.

"Véronique?" I called. My voice echoed in the silence.

Véronique didn't answer.

I discarded the useless crystal rod and scrambled across the rocks on all fours. It took a few minutes, but I finally found her. She was cold. Her stiff body lay splayed out in an unnatural position. She'd fallen on a pile of rocks only a few feet from the water.

I was too late.

"Take me with you," I whispered. "Wherever you've gone."

I found her face with my hands, bent over, and pressed my lips to her forehead. Her skin felt strangely hard, and her hair brushed my face like coarse little wires. It was almost as if she'd been frozen solid down to the roots of her hair. Had I passed out and lost track of time? Why wasn't I frozen too?

Something warm touched my leg. I reached down and felt Véronique's rigid hand—her fire was humming.

She was alive.

Yet, she wasn't breathing—there was no heartbeat. The only sign of life was the faint vibration coming from her fire.

I tried breathing into her mouth. I tried rubbing her cold limbs to get the blood circulating. After ten minutes without a response, I sat back, exhausted and nearly defeated.

There was only one more thing I could think of to try. I slid my light hand into hers and pressed our fires together.

Nothing happened. Why wasn't this working? Despite my multiple attempts, Véronique and I had never reacted. I could feel her fire burning next to mine. There had to be a way to bring her back.

I gripped her hand tighter in mine and this time, instead of simply holding it there, I shot a burst of energy down my arm and into my fire.

Her hand melted in my grip, becoming soft and warm——and then came a sound nearly as beautiful as the scepter's song.

A cough.

CHAPTER TWENTY-THREE

VÉRONIQUE

I opened my eyes. Staring down at me, with a sort of far-away look, was the most beautiful boy I'd ever seen.

"Neek?" he said.

The name triggered a memory. Véronique—that was me.

"Why does my back hurt?" I asked.

"Hopefully it's just the ano-pent."

I was about to ask him what ano-pent was but realized I already knew. Now I remembered running in the snow and feeling a prick in my back.

"Can you move your legs?" he asked.

"Yes."

The boy seemed relieved. His steady gaze made me shiver. It was as if his stone blue eyes were looking right through me.

"Who are you?" I asked.

His face registered surprise and then concern. "It's me, Bruno."

Before he'd even finished saying the name, I knew him. And with the force of a tidal wave, I remembered how much I loved him. But there was something else—guilt. Why did I feel so guilty about loving this person?

"Can you sit up?" Bruno asked. "We need to get you to the dialysis machines."

I nodded, but as soon as I tried to move, I realized something was wrong. The pain in my back doubled and spread down my arm. I looked at my light hand and nearly choked. Ugly, black tendrils shot through my fire.

"What is it?" Bruno asked.

"I think all that running and climbing made the black stuff spread faster."

Without a word, Bruno slid his arms under me and lifted me into the air. My entire body shook with pain and everything went dark.

When I came to, the first thing I noticed was Bruno's fire. Since he was still carrying me, I had a close-up view of the little, black lines converging at his palm. With each step, he winced with pain.

"Did you take some of the poison from me?"

"A while back," Bruno said. "It was the only way to unfreeze you."

"Unfreeze me?"

"Now that you're awake again, would you mind directing me toward the river? I thought I was headed toward it—I got lost."

"You can't see?"

"That's not important. What matters is that I find the river so I can swim you across before my ankle gives out."

I ignored the pain shooting through the upper half of my body and sat up as best I could. In the morning light, I could see the bridge—or what was left of it. Green Park lay directly in front of us. But that meant…

I looked at the ground. What in the rainbow? The surface Bruno was walking over was uneven and strangely translucent. Almost like ice—or water.

I clutched Bruno tighter and almost passed out from the pain. "The river must have frozen in the last ten minutes because you just crossed it."

"Really? Can you see Gaspard on the bridge?"

"Yeah, he's on his belly, not moving. There's another frozen guy straight ahead of us."

"I think I'm starting to figure out what's going on."

"That's good," I said with a grimace. "Because I think I'm going to pass out again."

The next time I awoke an older man with a cleft chin was

carrying me along the riverbank. We were moving much faster.

"Where's Bruno?" I asked. "Who are you?"

"My name is Sébastien, I am—was Le Capitaine of the Royal Guard."

I tried to wrestle free but only succeed in passing out again.

This time when I awoke he explained that the blond girl had run away from him in Green Park. He'd been looking for her when he heard Gaspard scream. He never made it back to the bridge. Bruno broke the scepter and it had somehow turned everyone into lifeless statues.

"You were the frozen guy I saw on the bank."

"When Bruno woke me, he explained a few things and made me promise to take you to the dialysis machines."

"He suddenly trusts you now?"

"Let's just say it's in my best interest to find the machines as well."

It dawned on me that the captain must have taken some of the poison when Bruno woke him. "But what about Bruno? He's infected too."

"At least one of the machines is equipped with a battery. After I heal you, I'm supposed to bring it back to cleanse the others."

The others. That's right, I wasn't the only one to take a plague dart. Could the others still be alive? Hopefully they had held on long enough for Bruno to freeze everything. The scepter seemed to have paused everything, including the spread of the ano-pent.

Sébastien slowed to a stop in front of an attractive blond guy that had obviously just climbed out of the river. With one body draped over his shoulder, he held another under the arms. The three of them stood unmoving, like some three-dimensional drawing.

Sébastien made a sound between a laugh and a sob. "The explosion must have knocked them into the river." He strode forward, his fire extended.

"What are you doing?" I said.

"It's Eloi. It's my son."

My memories of Eloi returned with a rush of emotion. I remembered the day of the flood, when he'd shown up like magic and helped us to safety.

Sébastien reached for Eloi's gloved light hand.

"No! If you wake him now, you're going to transfer the poison," Véronique said. "Not to mention he's probably half dead from the cold. He'll be safer like that until we can get blankets and the machines."

Sébastien nodded but continued to examine the frozen bodies. He put his ear to one gloved light hand, and then another. "Looks like this one didn't make it." He pointed to the bald one Eloi had under the arms. "But the other one's fire is still humming slightly. Hey, he looks just like you. Is this one your brother?"

With as little movement as possible, I glanced at the person slung over Eloi's arm. He looked vaguely familiar. Was he my brother?

La-la. That was what I called him.

"Yes! You have to unfreeze him. We have to get him help."

"No, you were right. We'll wake them when we're better prepared."

"But what if they die before we come back?"

"I don't think they will—but we'll hurry anyway."

Then he began sprinting. The jostling was too much and I happily succumbed to unconsciousness.

I awoke to Sébastien shattering a large window. I was sitting in a wicker chair on a porch that was definitely not part of the royal estate. From the enormous gabled houses on the street I figured we must be somewhere in Ville Bleu.

Next to me on the porch, sat a machine the size of a large suitcase with tubes and cords sitting on top in a tangled mess.

Sébastien stepped through the window and disappeared into the house. After what seemed like forever he returned with another blond man in pajamas.

"Sorry," Sébastien told me. "Bruno tried to explain that energy transfer thing, but doing it yourself is something else entirely—took me a while."

I glanced at the pajama man, then around at the snow-covered bushes. "What are we doing here?"

Sébastien untangled the cords of the machine. "This is Doctor Talbot. He's going to show us how to use this thing."

I didn't like needles. Especially anywhere near my fire. I explained this to the doctor and he was kind enough to fix me up with a morphine patch. This time my descent into darkness was almost peaceful.

I awoke in a soft bed feeling like a million cuivres. When I rubbed the sleep from my eyes, however, the peaceful feeling vanished. It was dark outside.

"Sébastien?"

The doctor entered, now dressed in a suit. "He's at Pont en Pierre, but you're supposed to stay—"

"Did he get to Bruno in time? What about my brother and Eloi?"

"All I know is that there is a meeting tomorrow at Green Park. They said they will answer all our questions." He paused. "Do you have blank spaces in your memory, too?"

I stepped out of bed. "Sorry, I can't wait until tomorrow."

Doctor Talbot raised a hand as if to protest, but I was already stumbling my way to the front door.

Once outside, I ran to the end of the street and was momentarily distracted by an enormous glass castle.

A cathedral. That's what it was. But it wasn't the see-through walls or the elegant crystal spires that caught my attention. It was the jagged pillar of ice stretching from the doors of the building all the way to the snowy street. I approached the translucent white pillar and laid a hand on it. Although it was cool to the touch, it was certainly not ice.

Closer to the cathedral, I could now see things floating inside it. Benches, books, and even people, suspended in the air or rather, in the same glass-like substance that was shooting out the main entrance.

I shook my head to clear it. Whatever had caused this strange phenomenon wasn't important. I needed to get to Lala—and Bruno.

After jogging a few feet, I stopped again. I'd never been in Ville Bleu before. I realized I didn't have the slightest clue how to get to the bridge and there didn't seem to be anybody to ask.

Noises and voices sounded in the distance, but it was impossible to tell what direction it was coming from.

And it didn't help that all the streetlights were out. The only light I could see was the reflection of orange light off a tower.

I squinted in the darkness. That wasn't a tower, it was another of those ice pillars, except this one rose twenty feet straight up in the air.

I jogged to the pillar. It was a wide column of what looked like petrified water shooting directly out of the street. Beautiful houses surrounded the strange pillar. There was no sign of where the orange light was coming from. I climbed up onto the roof of one of the fancy houses and peered out at the city.

I saw the river and bridge a ways off—and past that, another towering pillar of glass shooting out of the earth.

Downriver from the bridge, an enormous house glowed with that strange orange light I'd seen reflected on the pillar. Had the building combusted? Yes, I could see the smoke—but it didn't seem to be moving. It was as if someone had made a three-dimensional drawing of a burning house.

Orange and green fires dotted the grounds around the estate—dozens of frozens locked in battle. So few orange fires remained. I felt a vague sense of loss. Had I known them?

This high up, I could hear the voices more clearly and realized they were not coming from the estate but from stone bridge. Small campfires lay scattered on the bank, but the flames in these danced and changed.

I made a mental note of my direction, hopped onto the grass, which felt like concrete through my shoes, and sprinted summerward.

By the time I arrived, my hands and ears were completely numb.

"Véronique!"

La-la ran toward me with a huge grin.

"Where's your coat, crazy girl?" He took a blanket from his own shoulders and draped it around me.

"When the bridge exploded, I—"

La-la pointed to his ears and shook his head. "Can't hear anything. Guess I was a little too close to the blast. Burned my arm pretty good too, but at least my face is still as handsome as ever."

I put my fire to his cheek. My brother was deaf, but all I felt was joy at seeing him alive.

La-la kissed my fire, winked, then led me toward a small group of people on the bank. "Bruno zapped everybody that needed a doc," he said. "Well, except for the frozen mess at the estate and the cathedral. They're gonna have to plan first."

"What did happen at the cathedral?"

"Huh?"

I repeated my question with La-la watching my lips.

He smiled. "The water from the river filled the caverns with such force that it exploded into the air all over Téles-phore. Bruno froze time right afterward. One came up near Red High. The biggest jet came through the entrance to the mine. Another flooded Bruno's neighborhood, and the last one came up directly under the cathedral. Good thing the pressure was mostly diffused by that point or it might have thrown the whole thing into the air. Can you imagine? Watch out for the falling glass building."

"But the people with plague darts—they're okay?"

La-la nodded. "They've been cleaned out. The rest we are leaving petrified until after the meeting tomorrow. Mama's okay. So is Jeannette. They found Philippe under the rocks, though. He didn't make it."

Philippe? Then the memories came. It was as if I could feel a bristly chin on my cheek. I remembered the time I'd seen him cry all through breakfast. And most of all, I remembered the smile he saved only for Jeannette. The pain hit a moment later, like jagged stones working their way up my throat. I leaned on La-la and tried unsuccessfully to swallow.

"Mademoiselle DeGrave!" A cute little blond boy bounded up like a chubby golden retriever. "Sébastien said you were safe, but we were still worried."

"I've got to go," La-la said with a squeeze of my hand. "I'm supposed to be looting food from the supermarket shelves."

I nodded and began walking with the boy, still a bit numb.

"In case you don't remember, I'm Jean-Baptiste Wedel. It's hyphenated."

"Wedel. Your Dad was under the bridge, wasn't he?"

The boy's face clouded over, but his smile didn't fade. "Yes, I cried about that for a while, but it's impossible to stay sad with everything that's going on."

"What's going on?"

"Don't you see?" Baptiste said. "We're starting over. We can make the world however we want it. We can choose who to wake up and what to tell them."

"The world? You don't mean—"

"We've tried calling everyone we know in Ulfig and Estoria—no one's answering. When Bruno smashed the scepter it stopped time all over the world!"

I put my hands on my head. Stopped time? How could a little walking stick stop an entire world?

"The coolest thing is how the land and animals are frozen until you bring your fire close, then they just kind of thaw."

We were almost to the bridge. I could see Mama speaking with Eloi. My heart swelled with relief to see them both alive.

Baptiste kept jabbering away in the background. "Do you know how they unfroze the pond in Blue Garden? Bruno and another guy had to zap it at the same time before the water became liquid again. They're waiting on the river because it will probably bring down the water pillars and they don't want any of the people in the cathedral for Naissance to get hurt, you know?"

I nodded, but my attention was on the line of bodies laid out under the emergency beacon. At Philippe's feet, Jeannette sat wrapped in a blanket.

Even seeing him lying there, it didn't seem real. Philippe had been a father growing up. He couldn't be gone. I wanted to cry, but my eyes wouldn't cooperate. I needed to be held. I needed to collapse into somebody. Maybe then my tears would come.

Then I saw Bruno. He stood near the bodies, talking to a pretty woman with frazzled hair. I felt a flash of jealousy until I noticed she was older. Was it his mother?

"Oh and guess what," Baptiste said. "When Sébastien came with the portable dialysis machine, Bruno didn't even need it. They think he has a permanent immunity to plague darts because he spent those months building up anti-bodies. Isn't that chanmé?"

"Yes, chanmé." I walked faster. That's where I wanted to collapse. It was Bruno's shoulder I wanted to cry on.

"He almost got hypothermia, though," Baptiste called from behind her. "He spent the whole morning pulling frozen bodies from the rocks so they'd be ready when Sébastien—"

But I wasn't listening. Bruno stood only a few steps away. His mother noticed me and whispered something. He turned, and although his eyes remained staring off into space, his mouth split into a broad, beautiful grin.

Falling into him felt like coming home. I was just about to begin my uncontrollable sobbing into his neck when he spoke.

"I'm sorry about Luc."

Luc. My husband. Now I remembered where the guilt came from. Loving one person while being married to another. But that wasn't the worst of it. Luc had given his life for me. Yet when I saw him fall from that tree, the first thing I'd felt was relief. What kind of a person would be relieved to see her husband die? The shame overwhelmed me, plugging up the torrent of emotion I'd been about to loose.

I released Bruno's neck. "Thank you. I'm glad you're okay."

Bruno didn't let her go. "Only thanks to your throwing skills—but I can't figure out how you got the scepter away from Gaspard. Wasn't he using firelock?"

"He'd set it down to help me with my coat," I whispered.

Bruno pulled me tighter. "You're amazing," he said into my hair. "But you had me worried—for a second I thought you really wanted to go home with the old man."

"Eww." I pushed Bruno away. Despite my forced smile, when he released me it felt like my insides had been wrenched out.

He was perfect. That's why it hurt so much. I knew I'd never be good enough for him. He was brave and selfless. I was cold and self-serving. I couldn't even cry for my own brother.

Then Mama came up behind me. She scooped me into her arms and we stayed like that until my sobs finally ran out.

Letty didn't survive. They found her on the front steps of the estate with a crater in her hand. Quinlin's body was never recovered. Twenty-one Oranges in total made it through the poker assault with fires burning, the rest lay on the cobblestones, blood and serum pooling near their light hands.

Rather than trying to dig graves in the frozen earth, the bodies of the dead were cremated. The bonfire was still burning the next morning when we met at Green Park. There were sixteen "unlocked"—as we were calling ourselves. Bruno led an informal memorial service, and as the victim's names were spoken, their faces and lives returned to my memory. Most of them had been neighbors and friends growing up in Toi. Bruno spoke of Philippe's strength, Sheri's loyalty, and Luc's generous heart. He told of Granny Jade's wisdom, and the courage it had taken for Aro to change. I said a few words about Letty and my other friends from the Tin Mines. Sébastien then made a general remembrance of the soldiers and guards who were only following orders.

No one mentioned Clarque or Claude, which I thought was a kindness.

After everyone had warmed themselves by the pyre, Bruno brought out a huge book encased in metal.

"We are here because of this," he said. "Most of the world thought this was a book of fairy tales and nonsense—but not Gaspard. With all his faults, he at least had a broader understanding of our universe."

"Gaspard was a monster," Camille said. "I still think we should put him straight into the fire."

"Death is too good for him," one of her sons said. "We should keep him locked forever as an example to others."

I was about to offer my agreement when I noticed Bruno's face—he looked like he might cry.

"At this moment," he said, "we represent the entire population of the world. We have the power to remake it however we choose. If there is hatred in the world, it is because we brought it with us."

"Are you saying we should wake up the old psychopath and let him ruin our lives again?" Camille said. "My husband's dead because of him."

"He deserves another chance," Sébastien said. "When the King woke me, I too, was reminded of the mistakes of my past. I could see them clearly, as if all my self-delusions had fallen away."

"So you think everyone's just going to magically want to be good when they wake up?" Camille asked.

"No," Bruno said. "Sébastien was a good man to begin with—he just needed the chance to rethink the path he was on."

"So everyone will be awakened," Mama said. "But that doesn't mean we can't be smart about it."

"That's right," Bruno said. "A few of us have come up with a plan. Once we've reestablished ourselves, each of us can choose one person to awaken. We should try to start with those we know will be partial to our cause."

A cold wind whipped at my coat and I stepped closer to the fire. A musical tinkling filled the air coming from up river. I would be sad when the trees were thawed—the breeze through the frozen pine needles sounded like a thousand tiny birds.

"What is our cause?" Dr. Talbot asked.

Everyone looked at Bruno.

"Our cause is to create a peaceful society of cooperation, freedom and equality. If we first wake up those with the same goal, we'll be more likely to succeed."

"In other words," Monsieur Nazaire said, "the Reds come first."

"You have the right idea, Dad—but we aren't going to tell anyone whom they should awaken—and we certainly won't do it based on shade. We only need to remember that it will be much easier to deal with the imperialists if our society of equals is already set up and running smoothly."

"Creating a government isn't easy," Sébastien said. "It will take years simply to debate and write all the statutes."

"To begin, we will have only three laws," Bruno said, "and they're already written."

Sébastien furrowed his eyebrows but remained silent.

Bruno touched Mama's arm. "Rosette, would you like to explain our plan?"

She beamed and took a step forward. "Each of us can awaken one person per month. We are to spend that month with them, helping them transition into their new lives, and teaching them the three rules."

She looked at Eloi, who began passing out strips of leather with tassels on the end.

"I thought we could all wear these as bracelets," Eloi said, "to remind ourselves of our purpose."

"On the inside," continued Mama, "we've engraved the three rules."

I reached to take mine from Eloi, but he smiled, took my hand, and tied the bracelet around my wrist.

"Thank you."

Jeannette raised her hand as if waiting to be called on.

"The king is blind," Monsieur Nazaire said with a laugh, "so it might be a while before he notices your hand, sweetie."

Jeannette grinned. "I was going to say we should hurry and build the castle so he has a nice place to live."

"The castle will be built," Bruno said. "But it will be a multi-shade school. I've appointed Rosette and my mother to be joint directors of the Académie de la Lumière. I've also decided that the sixteen of us will act as a sort of council. We'll meet often to discuss the best way to serve our world."

"You mean Télesphore," Baptiste said. "Everyone else is locked."

"Not for long," Bruno said. "In a few days I will be traveling to the mainland."

"Absolutely not," Madame Nazaire said. "You're sixteen."

"I'll be seventeen in a few weeks. And anyway, Eloi will be with me. We have a duty to awaken those in other lands."

"He's right," Sébastien said. "If disease or a tidal wave wiped out our island, it would mean the end of our race."

"Let someone else go," Madame Nazaire said. "You're the king. We need you here."

Bruno set down the metal book and retrieved a leather pouch from his pocket. "Sébastien found these for me." He poured a few shiny rocks into his palm. "The diamond broke into four identical pieces. From what I've read in the Guide, I believe I need to find a way to turn them into four light manipulators."

"Chanmé!" Baptiste said. "Can you imagine how powerful Télesphore would be with four scepters?"

Bruno smiled but shook his head.

"What?" Baptiste asked, "We have to share them with other countries?"

Bruno nodded and Baptiste sighed.

"I will return as soon as I can," Bruno said. "Meanwhile, you fourteen will be in charge of the island."

Camille cleared her throat. "Your Grace…"

Bruno nodded. "And if she'll agree to come, I'd also like Véronique to accompany us."

Mama began to cry.

What was going on? Had they discussed this behind my back?

"Well?" Bruno asked.

I realized he was talking to me. Did I want to go? Honestly, I'd rather stay with my family. But my King was asking me to join him in saving the world.

I nodded. Then realized he couldn't see. "I'll come—if you're sure you want me."

"Let's just say," Madame Nazaire said, "that the parents involved will be silly enough to let teenagers take a road trip across the world. Who would lead the council in your absence?"

"I don't think we should call it a council," Camille interrupted. "None of us have very fond memories of the Dominateur."

"What about the circle?" I said. "It's simple and suggests equality."

"And it discourages titles," Bruno said. "I love it. We all belong to the circle, but we are not above anyone else. Thank you, Neek."

I nodded but didn't look in his direction. I knew he would be looking at me with that smile that made my heart splinter. I focused on the memory of Luc's ano-pent riddled body. I remembered the weight of it as I carried it onto the pyre.

He was a good husband. He didn't deserve disloyalty.

A few of Camille's kids began to complain of hunger, but she ignored them. "I would like to know who'll be the final say in the circle? I mean, a government of equals is sugar-dandy until we can't agree on something. We need a tie-breaker— Someone who's opinion carries more weight."

"The other guards are used to following me," Sébastien said. "I could help them understand why I switched sides."

"Like black you will," Camille said. "I wouldn't trust you to lead my horse. What about Mama DeGrave for leader?"

Dr. Talbot cleared his throat. "I don't have anything against this woman, but I worry that when Blues and Greens wake up, they might find it hard to follow a Red."

This was met by cries of "She's White!" and "Shade shouldn't even be considered."

Talbot nodded. "It's not her fire as much as what she stands for. She represents one side of the conflict. To some, Sébastien may represent the other side. If we really claim to be peaceful and equal, shouldn't we choose someone who is unbiased and yet still intelligent and fair?"

"I hope you're not speaking of yourself, Émile," Monsieur Nazaire said. "Since you're the one who removed my son's fire."

Talbot reddened and denied any notion of self-election. This prompted more shouts paired with name-calling.

Bruno sighed and stared blankly into the pyre. He looked so desperately sad that I nearly strode over and embraced him.

Instead, I picked up a stump and threw it into the flames. Orange exploded upward in a swirl of embers.

The shouting stopped.

"Dr. Talbot is not my favorite person," I said. "But he's on to something. If we're looking to make our temporary leader as impartial as possible, why not Officer Juenes? Bruno told me she was feisty and fair."

"One of Gravois' police officers?" La-la said. "How is that impartial?"

"Juenes didn't fight alongside the other pokers," I said. "I was looking for her—hoping she would help us."

Dr. Talbot nodded. "I would feel more assurance that those previously on the emperor's side wouldn't be discriminated against if this Green police officer led the circle in the King's absence."

Camille stared at Talbot a moment, then sighed. "Better

than a royal guard—but don't come crying to me, when the old woman turns out to be an Imperialist."

It took several days to find Officer Juenes. She lay in bed, in a duplex just winterdark of Baptiste's apartment. Her eyes were open and she stared at the ceiling with frightened, unblinking eyes.

The King was sent for and Bruno asked that I act as his eyes when he woke Juenes up. Everyone else waited outside.

The old woman screamed when she saw us next to her bed.

"Sorry to frighten you, Yvette," Bruno said. "You were asleep and we woke you."

She pulled her hand away from his and stared at it. "Did you just paint me?"

Bruno scratched the back of his head.

"It was necessary," I said. "And the heat reaction, as they're calling it, is a little different than the kind we're used to."

Juenes pulled her blankets to her chin. "Heat reaction?"

"It still mixes your shade," Bruno said, but it also transfers some of the giver's energy. That's how it restarted your body.

Sort of the difference between liking someone and loving them—similar feeling, but you put a lot more energy into the latter."

Bruno's face tilted toward me slightly at this. I closed my eyes. I'd put massive amounts of energy into trying to love Luc but don't think I ever managed it.

"I remember a loud noise," Juenes said.

Bruno crouched next to the bed. "The river decided it was tired of dividing the haves from the have-nots. What you heard was the formation of three new rivers. Well, four, but two joined and—sorry, I'm getting off subject."

"How long was I out?"

"Five days."

Juenes sat bolt upright. "It's Sunday. I'm going to be late for church."

I smiled. "Yvette, there have been some big changes since you've slept and before we go into all that, there are a couple of questions we'd like to ask you—is that okay?"

Juenes narrowed her eyes, then sniffed. "Go ahead."

"Why didn't you join the other troops when Gaspard called them to battle?"

Juenes' eyes bulged. "Battle? Why would I know about a battle?"

"You're a law enforcement officer."

Juenes stared at Bruno a moment. "That's, right. I am—or was."

"You quit?"

"More or less. Someone spread the rumor I was retiring. When they stopped sending me paychecks I stopped coming in."

Bruno wore a stricken expression, but I had to hold in a laugh.

"How do you feel about Gaspard?" I asked, still smiling.

"Who?"

"The Emperor."

"My brain seems to be a little fuzzy right now."

"That's normal," Bruno said. "Here's an easier question— How do you feel about cooperation, freedom, and equality?"

"I'd say sign me up."

This time I didn't hide my laugh and Bruno joined in.

"We just did," Bruno said. "By the way, you're going to be in charge of the circle of leaders until I get back from the mainland."

Juenes seemed to think about this for a moment, then waved her hand. "Well, I'm going to need you to leave my room so I can get dressed. I'm not leading anybody in my nightdress. The girl can stay and help me with the buttons."

"The king is blind," I said, "he can't see you changing."

"And I ain't got much to display, but that doesn't mean I want him in here."

Juenes took the news that the government had been over-thrown and the planet turned into a frozen forest of living statues remarkably well. Probably because on the force she'd grown accustomed to rolling with the punches.

It took a few days to bring her up to speed. Eloi, Bruno and I used this time to pack and convince Bruno's parents that our trip across the Ocheanum was a good idea. It helped that Eloi had proven himself a responsible adult. We were all careful not to mention that he was actually only twenty.

But no matter how many times I asked, neither Bruno, Mama, nor Camille would explain to me why I was singled out to join the boys on their trip. Were they hoping Bruno and I would get back together? If so, they were in for a big disap-pointment.

Eloi removed Gaspard from the bridge and hid him away in the cave once prepared for Bruno's grandpa.

The estate ruins were cleared away and the lot turned into farmland.

The cathedral was useless as a place of worship since it now had a giant lake inside it. A few days after the river had been thawed, the workers had found Mére Blanche, alive and well, soaking in the eye-rays coming through the cathedral's glass ceiling.

Sébastien refused to let the badger hounds be slaughtered and had taken charge of their care and re-training as domesticated pets.

Finally, the morning of our voyage arrived. Bruno, Eloi and I set off in Monsieur Nazaire's enormous utility vehicle. Eloi had never driven before, but Bruno's dad gave him a crash course and insisted he wouldn't have anything to worry about since he'd be the only one on the road.

We made it to the coast in one piece, only to be presented with a new problem. The Ocheanum seemed to be missing. In its place was a big blue concrete slab. The water from the river flowed right out over the top, creating a sub-zero wading pool.

We discussed trying to drive to the mainland, but since the road would've been more than a little bumpy and we probably didn't have enough gas, Bruno thought our best bet was to unlock the water and use the boat. That way, even if we ran out of fuel, at least we could use the oars.

Thawing the ocean was easier than I expected. It took me a few times to figure out the heat reaction, but when the three of us tried it together, the surface of the ocean rippled outward and came alive with a deafening roar.

I was so startled, I almost fell in. Thankfully, Eloi was close by.

We were moving our equipment into Bruno's fishing boat when I discovered the stowaway behind the back seat.

"Baptiste! You can't just run off without telling—"

"My parents?" Baptiste held his tiny suitcase to his chest. "Why do you think I'm coming with you? I have to find my mother."

Bruno came up beside me, his arm nearly touching mine. I felt a sudden urge to take his hand or move his hair back from his face, but a wall of guilt prevented me from even looking at him. Luc had died only a few days ago, and I was already anxious to start flirting again?

"Mama DeGrave will be looking for you everywhere," Bruno said. "We need to take you back."

Baptiste's eyes filled with tears. "I wrote a note. I didn't ask because I knew they wouldn't let me come. I have to come. My mom's all I have left now."

Bruno sighed and rubbed at his sightless eyes. "Well, I hadn't decided exactly where to start. I guess Deatherage is as good a place as any."

"At least he thought to bring his own food," Eloi said, glancing at the boy's chubby arms. "Although you might have brought a bigger suitcase."

Baptiste's cheeks colored. "Actually this is full of books."

I laughed and gave Baptiste a hug. "Welcome to the team. You can be our historian."

Once everything was packed into the boat, and Bruno and Eloi had deciphered most of the maps and compasses, we set off.

I was watching the island shrink into the ocean when I realized someone was standing next to me.

"What does it look like?" Bruno said.

"Like a big ugly rock," I answered, both pleased and terrified to have him so close.

Bruno laughed. "Yup, that's the Télesphore I remember."

"I'm sorry about your grandmother. I know you were close."

"It's for the best. My Grandpa Zacharie was never a patient man. He'd been without her long enough."

Once again I nodded, and then remembered he couldn't see. His father had tried various drugs and salves, but nothing had worked. Bruno would never see again without a scepter.

"I've been meaning to give you something," he said. "Hold out your hand."

I lifted my light palm and he took me by the wrist. His touch sent a flood of warmth up my arm and into my chest. With his other hand he placed something small onto my golden fire.

A single, perfect shell.

I couldn't speak as a flood of memories came back to me. I was glad Bruno couldn't see the tears in my eyes. For a moment I allowed myself to wonder what Papi would say if he were there. Would he be proud of me for helping to better the world? Would it make up for all my mistakes?

"So is this like a belated Naissance present?"

Bruno grinned and scratched his arm as if suddenly embarrassed.

"Thanks," I said. Then, because I hated to see him uncomfortable, I changed the subject. "So will I ruin my reputation if

I tell you I already miss my mom?"

Bruno seemed happy for the distraction. "She's an incredible lady. You know she came up with the three rules by herself."

"I forgot about those." I pulled my bracelet off. "I guess I should read them since it's what we're going to be sharing with the world."

Bruno smiled again and it sent waves of pain through me. I quickly looked down at the tiny scratches on the leather.

Love the one who awakened you as a parent.

Love those you awaken as your children.

*Treat each person as family. For
the King is the father of us all.*

"Not bad," I said. "Maybe a bit optimistic. I mean, you think people will actually live by these rules?"

Bruno looked back at Télesphore as if he could see it receding into the horizon. "I'm not worried," he said. "If I can manage to live them myself, I'll call it good."

Long after Bruno had gone below deck, I continued to watch darkness swallow the only home I'd ever known.

When only the light from the stars remained, I kissed Bruno's perfect shell and dropped it into the ocean.

END OF BOOK TWO

ABOUT THE AUTHOR

RC (Revived Corpse) Hancock is slightly older than portrayed in this photo. (But twice as cute.) It's a well known fact that one does not have to have hair to be ultra cool. (Proof: Vin Diesel, President Eyring, Mahatma Gandhi.) RC is slightly less attractive that most of these people.